what was meant to be

Age is Just a Number ~ Collection One

karla doyle

Print ISBN 978-1-990500-46-6

age is just a number

Collection One

This collection of age-gap romances includes these
three previously published novellas:

WEDDED MISS
THE DEAL WITH LOVE
GINGERBREAD MAN

Each novella is a standalone book,
and the three stories are not connected.

These romances include profanity and
sexually explicit content,
and are intended for adult readers only.

contents

wedded miss

the deal with love

gingerbread man

wedded miss

Wedded Miss

KARLA DOYLE

wedded miss

An age gap, marriage of convenience romance

troy

A thirty-nine-year-old man has no business getting involved with a twenty-three-year-old woman. Especially if that woman is his daughter's best friend. But that's exactly what I'm doing.

I tell myself I'm marrying Cricket because she needs my help. That I'll keep her at arm's length while she's wearing my ring, then set her free when she doesn't need my last name and health insurance anymore. My intentions are good. My self-control isn't.

I want her from the first kiss. I need her from the first touch. I'm going to love her forever, but that's my problem, because I know I can't keep her. Too bad letting her go is the hardest thing I've ever done.

cricket

I fell for Troy Mannington the day I met him. I've done everything within reason to tempt my best friend's dad, but he's never crossed the line. He wants to, though. I see the desire in his eyes—and in his shorts.

When he offers to marry me, I jump at the chance. Because I need his health insurance, yes. But I need him, too.

Every minute we're together, we get closer, until there's no space between us. My five years of fantasies are nothing compared to reality. Our connection is more than physical, it always has been.

Our wedding vows may have been for show, but I meant every word. So did Troy. I just need him to forget about our ages, and focus on our forever.

one

. . .

troy

MOWING the grass in the sweltering July heat was a sweaty job. Had to be done, though. My neighbors are decent enough—until my lawn is too long for their liking. Then the nitpicking starts. Comments about the damaged piece of siding I haven't had time to fix. The faded mulch. And so on.

If it were just me, I wouldn't give a shit. But the neighbors aren't above criticizing my daughter to get to me. The last time I got busy at work and neglected the lawn for a few extra days, I came home to find Gina in tears, vowing never to go in the backyard again, because Mrs. Sanderson stood at the chain-link fence and suggested that a young lady of Gina's proportions ought to choose less-revealing swimwear.

I called in half a dozen favors and dropped a boatload of dough to get a six-foot board fence erected that weekend. I also made sure I got the lawn cut on schedule from then on, even if I had to do it when the moon was out. Or in the blistering fucking heat.

"Gina," I call, closing the kitchen's patio door behind me. "I'm hot as hell from cutting the grass. Going to hit the shower, then we'll go grab dinner, okay?" I don't wait for her to answer before stripping off my sleeveless tee.

Odds are, she's flaked on the couch, on her phone and only half-absorbing what I hollered. Twenty-two years old and still enjoying mindless oblivion when she's at home. The way it should be.

By the time I was twenty-two, I had an ex-wife and full-time custody of a kid in kindergarten. Hard times I wouldn't trade a day of, yet I'm equally glad my daughter will never personally understand what I went through.

My thumbs are hooked under the waistband of my Adidas shorts when I pass the entrance to the living room. One glance is all it takes to understand why Gina didn't answer. My daughter's not there—but her best friend is.

This is where a normal father would apologize for walking around half-dressed, or hustle out of view. But I've never been a typical dad, and Cricket's not just any friend of my daughter.

Hands on my hips, I stand my ground, my dick getting thicker as her gaze runs all over my body. I keep *my* eyes on her face. Not an easy job, because she's stretched out on my couch, wearing the world's smallest pair of denim shorts and a cropped t-shirt that hugs her full, perky tits.

I try not to notice how hot she is, I really do. But it's impossible. I'm a man, for fuck's sake. A healthy, single, thirty-nine-year-old man, and she's a twenty-three-year-old bombshell who spends the majority of her free time in my house, wearing an assortment of extremely tiny clothing. I'd have to be blind not to notice.

"Gina's in her room, on the phone with her boyfriend. Sorry I didn't answer when you called to her about dinner. I didn't know what to say." Cricket's eyes drop to my dick—again. Her lips part slightly, and God fucking help me, the tip of her tongue peeks out.

Now I'm fully hard, and there's no way she doesn't see the hefty bulge through the clingy, light-gray material.

When she meets my gaze again, her big, blue eyes are glassy, her pupils dilated. I'm so close to asking if she likes what she sees, I have to literally bite my tongue. Doesn't matter how hot she is, how hard she makes me. She's my daughter's best friend. I'm a pig for even thinking about her in any way other than that.

"You can come if you want to," I say. It's a dinner invitation on the surface, but a hell of a lot more in my mind.

Pink floods her cheeks as she hugs herself, a motion that squeezes her tits together, thrusting them higher.

There's no way I can look anywhere else. I've always been a boob man, and Cricket's tits are mouthwatering. I'd give up food for a week for a chance to have them in my mouth.

"I'm buying." I force my eyes upward, and my mind back to dinner. "I want you to save your summer-job money for school."

The words are barely out of my mouth before moisture wells in her eyes and she pulls herself into a scrunched-up ball on the end of my couch.

I'm beside her in a blink. Sweaty or not, horny or not, there's no way I'm keeping my distance when she's upset. "What's wrong? Is it school?" I know it's not a matter of grades, she's been an academic achiever since she transferred to Gina's high school in senior year. "If you need money for tuition and stuff, I'll help."

Fat tears roll down her cheeks as she shakes her head. "It's not for school. It's for—personal stuff."

If she tells me she's knocked up and the bastard who did it won't man up... I'll hunt the little prick down and crush him. Happily.

"Tell me." I dare touching her to slide my fingers beneath her chin and tip her face up. "I'll never judge you. I'll understand. I'm not some ancient old fart."

A small laugh escapes between gentle, hiccupping sobs. "You're definitely not."

My ego swells, so does my dick. But neither matter right now. "You can tell me anything," I say, stroking her cheek. "Come on, sweetheart."

"I like hearing you call me that." Her voice is as soft as her skin, as she leans into the touch and rests her face against my palm. "Please don't tell Gina."

I nod. I hate keeping things from my daughter, but this moment, whatever it is, can stay between Cricket and me. "Whatever you need, I'll help you." Fuck, I'd give her the goddamn world on a silver platter if she asked me to.

"She has a lump."

At the sound of Gina's voice, Cricket and I separate like a pair of adolescents caught making out. I should turn, face my daughter—and the music—but my focus remains on Cricket. "What kind of lump?"

"In my breast." Her long eyelashes flutter as she pointedly avoids meeting my gaze. If she's embarrassed by a soft term like breast, she'd turn crimson at the words I'd like to say to her.

"What did the doctor say?"

"She hasn't been to the doctor," Gina says when

another sob robs Cricket of speech. "Her parents have the crappiest insurance you can get. They told her she'd have to pay the annual deductible if she goes, and it's huge. Even if she did that, their policy has garbage coverage."

"Is there a clinic at the college?" I ask, trying to lock down my rage at her parents.

"Student services are closed until the fall semester, and then there'll be a waiting list." Cricket lifts her head, meeting my eyes. "I know I'm young, and it might be nothing, but my aunt and grandmother both had cancer at an early age. I'm scared."

Angry heat roars in my chest. At her family, for being pieces of shit who don't care enough for their daughter. At the world, for inflicting this pain on someone undeserving of bullshit. Someone I care about.

"Too bad she's too old for you to adopt," Gina says, dropping into an armchair across from us. "Then she could use our insurance."

I clear my throat to mask the choking sensation *that* scenario causes. "Yeah, it would be great if Cricket could use our insurance." My brain's already in gear, composing an email to human resources. If Cricket takes time off school, we can hire her at my company. Then she'd have her own insurance. It wouldn't cover everything, but I'd top it up, on the sly.

My mouth's opening, ready to make my proposal, when Gina jumps up from her chair, snapping her fingers.

"I've got it," she says, clapping, then pointing at me. "You could marry her."

This time, I choke for real. "What?"

"You could marry Cricket." She laughs at my stunned silence. "I know what you're thinking, Dad."

No, she doesn't. And thank fuck for that.

"It's a great idea. You're both single, consenting adults, so that part's ready to go. You've known each other for five years, so nobody could say it's sudden, or out of the blue. Just think about it, okay?"

I grunt, rather than speak. I'm already thinking about it. Cricket would have to move in here to make it seem legit. I'd see her every day. In public, she'd have to behave like my wife, not my daughter's plus-one. At night, she'd be across the hall while I jerk off to thoughts of her misbehaving in all manner of wifely, consenting-adult ways. It's a terrible idea.

"What do you think, Cricket?" Gina asks. "Would you marry my dad if he agrees to it?"

My full attention is on Cricket now, as she blinks those beautiful, expressive eyes at me. And nods. "I would marry you."

Every dirty thing I've thought about doing with her rushes into my head. My dick is crowding the space between my legs—there's no way I'm going to be able to stand up anytime soon. I should laugh this whole insane idea off, then tell them my plan.

"I'll start getting stuff lined up," are the words that exit my mouth instead. "Because I want you to see a doctor as soon as possible."

Cricket's lips part and her eyes are wide as saucers.

In my peripheral vision, Gina jumps up and down, clapping. "Oh, my God, you're going to do it? You're going to marry her?"

"That's up to Cricket," I say, holding her gaze. "Do you want to marry me?"

Her blonde hair shimmers as she nods. "Yes."

"Looks like we're having a July wedding." And a July

honeymoon. But that's a hard-on and blue balls for another day.

cricket

My phone lights up on the nightstand, breaking the darkness I've been staring into for the last two hours. I reach over and grab my cell, opening the newest text from Gina.

GINA:

> OMG! I can't believe you're marrying my dad!

I laugh because it's the same text she's sent me six times since I got home. So, I send back the same reply.

ME:

> I know! It's so crazy!

She sends a string of laughing face emojis, followed by a new text.

GINA:

> I absolutely cannot wait. You're going to be a gorgeous bride, and I'm going to be the sexiest maid of honor ever. I've been looking at dresses online. Soooo pretty. Can I choose my own dress, or are you going to be a bridezilla?

ME:

Well, duh. Bridezilla, of course! LOL.
Seriously, though. Do you think he'll want
an actual wedding?

GINA:

Yep. He said it has to look real.

That he did. After agreeing we'd get married, Troy left to get cleaned up. He reappeared looking handsome and sexy, as always, grabbed the keys to his SUV, and motioned us to get going. All normal enough. Until the three of us got to the driveway, and he insisted I sit up front, instead of Gina.

"We're about to commit insurance fraud," he said. "Nobody can know what we're doing, only the three of us. Everyone else needs to believe the marriage is about love. Starting now, the world needs to see Cricket as my fiancée."

In the restaurant, Troy pulled out my chair. Scooted his seat closer to mine and put his arm across the back, letting his fingertips graze the back of my neck. He held my hand on the tabletop. After paying the check, he guided me out with his hand on the small of my back.

A lot of people stared at us tonight. They weren't the reason for my pounding pulse. Troy caused my heart to race. He always has.

ME:

Can you find out what he wants us to do
for the actual wedding? I feel weird
asking, because he's paying for
everything, and I'm mooching all his
money.

I send the message and exhale. I'm lucky to have a

friend I can be honest with. Well, mostly honest. I haven't told her I'm secretly in love with her dad.

> GINA:
>
> Don't worry, he has plenty of money. Unless you're planning on going for the royal wedding package, I'm sure it's all good. But I'll talk to him and get back to you.

> ME:
>
> You're the bestest bestie! XOXO

> GINA:
>
> Bestie? You're almost my sister now!

> ME:
>
> Sister? Think again. I'm going to be your stepmother. In fact, I should go ahead and ground you now, because I know all the naughty things you've been up to, behind your father's back!

My soon-to-be husband's back. His broad, strong, nicely muscled back. A back I plan to put my hands all over, the first opportunity I get.

> GINA:
>
> Whatever, stepmonster dearest. LOL. See you tomorrow.

I smile at the text, tap and send a row of kissy faces, then place the phone back on the nightstand. We're joking about what's going to happen, but it's serious business.

So is the lump I found. I cup my left breast, my fingers finding the marble-sized bump instantly. Now that I know it's there, I can't stop checking it. Hoping that one of these times, it'll simply be gone.

The lump is the single worst thing ever to happen to

me, and if I could wake up tomorrow and discover it was part of an elaborate nightmare, I would drop to my knees and thank God. But the lump is reality, and now, it's making an otherwise impossible dream come true.

I'm marrying Troy Mannington.

Yes, it's because I need good medical insurance, and he's the kindest, most generous man I've ever known. That doesn't mean I'm not going to enjoy every fake minute of it. Or that I'm not going to try making it real.

There's something between us, and it's not father-daughterly. Troy has made me tingle since the first day I met him. He might never admit it, but he feels the same. There's raw desire in his eyes when he looks at me, which he does a lot. His eyes aren't the only telltale sign. I've watched his nostrils flare when I get really close to him. I've heard him growl when I mention boys while talking to Gina.

That's all they are, those names I drop. Boys. They could never measure up to the man Troy is. I can say that quite literally after seeing Troy in his gray shorts today. Well-formed muscles glistening from exertion, he'd stood there and let me look my fill, as his sweat-dampened shorts showed off every ridge of his long, hard cock.

He wouldn't have had a hard-on if he wasn't attracted to me. He wouldn't rush to my side, stroke my face, and call me *sweetheart* if he didn't care about me.

I know he won't act on his feelings right now. But once we're married, I'm going to make it impossible for him to do anything else.

two

· · ·

troy

THE CEREMONY WAS SUPPOSED to start nearly ten minutes ago. The officiant hasn't said anything yet, but we both know he's watching the clock. City hall ceremonies are efficient. Get in, get hitched, get out. I snagged the only available slot this week, so I know another couple is waiting in the wings. No room to overflow once the minute hand hits the six. If my bride-to-be doesn't arrive in the next few minutes, we'll be out of luck.

Unless she's not running late. Maybe she changed her mind.

"Fuck," I mutter, after turning my back on the handful of people waiting to witness our big day.

The officiant shoots me a sympathetic look. He's probably seen it all. Enough to know better than to offer false hope.

I shove my hands into my pockets. "How often do you see the groom get stood up?"

"We average a fifteen percent last-minute cancellation rate. Bearing in mind, it's not always a runaway bride situation."

I grunt. "Doesn't help me much, but thanks."

"I don't think you have anything to worry about," the man says, nodding toward the entrance.

I turn—and lose the ability to breathe. Cricket stands in the doorway, looking like the perfect combination of a fairytale princess and my filthiest fantasy. My soon-to-be wife. In name only, but I'm still the luckiest bastard on Earth. I'm going to enjoy every minute I get to play the role of happy husband.

Cricket reaches me in the time it takes to resume breathing. She told me she didn't care if we had a city-hall ceremony or a church wedding. I opted for city hall because it was easier and faster. I should've waited. She deserves a church. One with an aisle long enough to do her beauty justice.

"You're absolutely fucking stunning," I say, taking her hand, once she passes her bouquet to Gina.

"Thank you." Somehow, she manages to glow even brighter. As if my opinion means something. She has no idea how much I'd love to worship at her altar. Her lips are painted bubble-gum-pink, and her cheeks take on the same tint as she says, "You look pretty fucking hot."

My laugh is too loud for the hushed space. Too rough for the moment. It's who I am. You can put a monkey in a monkey suit, but underneath, he's still an animal.

The clerk clears his throat, dragging our attention in his direction. "Are we ready to get started?"

"Definitely," she says, smiling at me.

The rest of the ceremony breezes by. The standard vows are exchanged, then it's time for the kiss. The clerk says the magic words, cuing the moment I've been waiting for since Cricket walked into my house for the first time. We discussed the obligatory kiss during our prep and planning. I promised her it'd be the only time she had to do it, but it needs to look legit. She gave permission for the real deal.

That's exactly what she's going to get.

"Mrs. Mannington," I say, cupping her delicate face in my hands. My dick went to half-mast as soon as she walked in, showing off her hourglass curves and luscious tits in that white, strapless dress. As I dip down and seal my lips over hers, I'm pretty sure I couldn't get any harder.

Until her hands find my waist and she tugs me closer. Then opens for me, teasing her tongue into my mouth.

Jesus fuck. I slide one hand to her nape, the other to the small of her back, and pull her tight against me while I plunder her pretty mouth. I don't care who's watching, who's judging. Right now, she's my wife. My beautiful, sexy wife.

troy

Gina rode with us in the limo I hired, robbing me of an opportunity to talk to Cricket about the kiss. Our stop at a park for photos was too public. Dinner at the steakhouse wasn't the place for that conversation, either, despite being in a private room. Too quiet a setting, since our only "guests" were Gina and her boyfriend, and my business partner and his wife.

Cricket's parents didn't show for the ceremony or the

dinner. Not surprising, they've always been useless pieces of shit. She said it didn't bother her, but it had to have hurt.

She fell asleep as soon as we headed for the airport. She's under a lot of stress, she needed the rest more than a conversation about our kiss. Then came the bustling airport, more sleep during our overnight flight to Jamaica, and a crowded shuttle-bus ride to the resort.

But we're finally here. Together. Alone.

"Fuck," I say, opening our suite door. "I specifically asked for a room with two beds."

"You did?"

My eyes meet Cricket's. "Of course. We're married so you can see a doctor and get whatever care you need. I know it's not more than that."

There's so much unvoiced emotion in her expression, in her eyes, it takes everything in me to stand there and silently wait for the answer that never materializes.

I jerk my head in the direction we came from. "Let's head back to the lobby so they can fix their mistake."

"This room is fine."

I glance inside and grunt. "Says the woman who'll be sleeping like a queen, sprawled in the king-sized bed. I'd rather not spend the next five days camped out on that loveseat."

"You won't have to." Her face turns the prettiest pink. "We can share the bed, it's really big."

"If I share the bed with you, it won't be the only thing that's really big." The words are out of my mouth before my big brain kicks in. Since I can't take them back, I own them with a grin and gruff laugh. "Don't want to traumatize you when you come into contact with my morning wood."

"That's a real thing?"

"Hell, yeah." So is afternoon, evening, and all-night-long wood, when I'm around her. "You've never spent the night with a guy, and woken up to a hard dick pressed against your ass?" *My* dick grows fully hard as my adorable bride shakes her head furiously. I set our suitcases on the tile floor and lean closer to her, with one arm braced on the doorframe. I shouldn't be talking to her this way. Definitely shouldn't be this close to her. "Does that mean you've never spent the night with a guy, or that he wasn't man enough to wake you up the way a woman deserves?"

"The second one," she says softly. "I'm not a virgin, Troy."

Fuck, I shouldn't have pushed her into sharing that information. Knowing she's not saving her V-card for some decent, appropriately aged guy down the road isn't going to help my control this week.

I push off the wall and grab the suitcases. Gotta keep my hands occupied before I do something stupid. "And I'm not a saint. Sharing a bed is a bad idea." I tick my head toward the front of the resort again. "Let's go get a different room."

three

...

cricket

A COUPLE YEARS AGO, I saw Troy slice his finger open while sharpening lawn mower blades. Earlier this summer, I watched him scrape the crap out of his forearm and shin when Gina's kitten darted out the door, and he full-on nosedived to the concrete to catch it before it reached the road. So, I know what pain looks like on his handsome face.

He made a similar expression the moment the resort's concierge informed us they have no available rooms for us to swap. I've never been so happy to see Troy in discomfort.

I got super lucky. I should've taken the opportunity to tell him what I wanted when he opened our suite door the first time. I chickened out. That won't happen a second time.

He's waiting for me on the opposite side of the bathroom door, I can hear him out there. He hasn't knocked, hasn't asked me what's taking so long, but I'm sure both things have crossed his mind. He's not a do-nothing kind of guy. He's always got something going on, whether it's his business, stuff around the house, or working out.

Oh, the working out. Troy has a home gym, and boy, he knows how to use it. I never understood the hype when my fellow cheerleaders would giggle and swoon over the guys in the high school fitness room. Not that they weren't built. Most were. They just didn't do it for me.

Nobody did. Not the athletic guys on the football team. Not the preppy guys captaining all the intellectual clubs. Not the tough guys getting into fights and smoking on school property. Not the girls, either. I was honestly starting to wonder if I even *had* a sex drive...until I met Troy Mannington.

My flaky parents moved us around a lot, as they flip-flopped between jobs, or simply ran out of money for rent. Central Collegiate was my third high school. I met Gina my first day there, in biology, which I only took because mid-semester enrollment meant my options were limited. It was the best class I've ever hated because Gina became my best friend. Then, by default, her dad became the only man I've ever loved.

Yes, love. A crush would have fizzled over the past five years. My feelings for Troy have grown. Grown so big, I've barely contained them. Especially the night of my twenty-first birthday, when Gina and Troy threw me a surprise party.

Troy tended bar for us that night. He stood behind the pool-house bar, serving free drinks to a patio full of twenty-somethings, his watchful gaze never straying too far from Gina, or from me.

"Better slow down with this one." His fingers had lingered on the third cocktail he passed across the bar.

"Don't want you getting too wobbly, and falling into the pool in your pretty dress."

In hindsight, I know he was complimenting how I looked in the soft-pink, body-hugging tank dress I'd bought. At the time, I took it as a hint to get more of his attention. A lot more.

I drank the entire rum and cola right there, in front of his twinkling eyes. Then I fake-wobbled to the pool and "fell in."

The splash drew every reaction imaginable—shrieks, gasps, hoots, and laughter. Troy did rush to my rescue, as expected. Unfortunately, he wasn't the first person to do so, or the closest. He had to come out from behind the bar, then weave through the partygoers and patio furniture, before reaching the pool. Gina's boyfriend happened to be poolside and dove in immediately. Not at all the scenario I'd concocted in my lovesick mind.

I spent the rest of that evening nursing a cup of coffee and a lot of soggy disappointment. Throughout the party, Troy's attention had lingered on my corner of the patio. Because he cared about me, obviously. He always has. As the party wound down, he left his post to join me. I'll never forget the intensity in his gaze, or the sensation of his warm, strong palms splayed just above my knees, as he crouched before me.

"I know what you did, what you wanted," he'd said, his thumbs making sweeping passes over my skin.

"And?" Between embarrassment and excitement, it was all I was able to say.

"And, I see you, sweetheart." It was the closest thing to an acknowledgment of our connection, to his attraction, and the first time he ever called me that. The only time, until the night on his couch.

I'm going to make him say it again. I want him too much to settle for less than everything. He wants me, too. His kiss at our wedding was more than for show. A lot more.

Troy may be determined to keep this trip platonic, but I'm determined, too. We're sharing that king-sized bed in the other room. Our marriage is moving from a sheet of paper, to between the sheets. Tonight.

I issue a confident nod at my reflection, then open the bathroom door. He's not waiting on the other side anymore. He's on the balcony, arms spread and braced on the railing, his heather-gray t-shirt pulled taut across his broad back and shoulders.

At the sound of my sandals clicking on the tile floor, he turns. His gaze travels over every inch of me as he enters our suite and closes the slider behind him. "New bathing suit?"

My pulse races as I nod, and do a slow turn so he can see the whole thing—not that there's much of it. "I bought it for this trip."

His Adam's apple slides up and down, then he clears his throat and grabs two towels from a chair. "Ready to go?"

"You're not going to tell me I can't wear this in public?" I ask, doing another half turn, just in case he missed the fact that my entire ass is on display in the thong bottom of the world's tiniest string bikini.

"You're a grown woman, you can wear whatever you want."

"And you won't mind if some men check me out?"

"There's no *if* about it. No *some*, either. Every man out there will be tongue-on-the-ground staring at you. There'll be enough male drool on the concrete to make the pool seem like a desert. But you know that, and it's obviously what you want since you bought that bikini."

Is he that oblivious? Maybe he truly isn't interested in taking our relationship further, and wishful thinking has allowed me to read too much into things, even the world's hottest kiss. "Never mind. I'll change." I stomp to the bed like a sulky child—exactly how I *don't* want him to see me. Not a great way to start our trip.

"Hey." He crowds my personal space as I straighten, another swimsuit wadded in my fist. "Don't change because of me. You look gorgeous in this bikini. You're a fucking wet-dream goddess."

"So, you like it?" I ask, turning to meet his eyes.

A gruff, grunted laugh tickles my cheek because we're that close. "Yeah, I like it." His gaze drops to my breasts, and his nostrils flare. "Too much, but that's my problem, not yours."

"I don't think it's a problem. I like looking at your body, too. I don't get to ogle you the way I want when Gina's around, so I plan to take full advantage of this time alone with you. I think you should do the same," I say, tapping the center of his chest.

In a snap, his hand flattens mine on his chest. He holds my gaze while sliding my palm downward, all the way to the front of his swim trunks—and his thoroughly hard cock beneath. He raises an eyebrow at my gasp. "Our ideas of 'taking full advantage' are very different."

"I don't think so."

He groans when I squeeze his thick shaft, then plucks my hand from his body, and steps away to pick up the towels he abandoned. "I know so." He nods toward the door. "Come on, let's go make you the highlight of every man's day."

troy

The wet-dream comment was bad enough. Putting her hand on my dick... What the fuck was I thinking? I wasn't. Couldn't. My brain was scrambled the moment she appeared in those scraps of fabric she calls a bathing suit.

Will I mind if other men check her out? *Will I fucking mind?* Guess I've done a decent job of hiding my true feelings for her, because not only will I mind, I'm going to lose my fucking mind. Maybe it'll rain. Then I won't have to sit at that pool and silently play it cool while every asshole in the place gawks at Cricket's sinfully hot body.

Even now, as we walk through the resort, it takes every ounce of my willpower to leave a buffer between us. She has no idea how much I'd like to "take advantage" of this time with her.

"Full sun, or shade?" she asks when we reach the pool.

"Shade." My gaze drops to her ass. "Don't want you getting a sunburn on skin that's not used to being exposed."

She's clearly in the mood to push my buttons, because she turns that perfect peach toward me and arches her back. "You could rub sunscreen all over it, make sure every inch is thoroughly taken care of."

I grunt while dragging a pair of lounge chairs to a location that will limit everyone else's view of my hot, young bride. "Keep it up and you'll learn there are other ways to get a red ass. You're not too old for a spanking, you know."

Her full lips part, but there's no shock or disgust in her

expression. I focus on spreading out towels, but she's in my peripheral, staring as I peel off my t-shirt. The intensity of her attention sends more blood to my already fat dick. And when she stretches out, stomach down, on one of the loungers, I know I'm royally fucked.

"Troy."

"Yeah?" I have no choice but to look at her directly when she says my name.

"Spank it or lotion it." The sassy little brat wiggles until *it* jiggles, smiling at me over her shoulder. "I'll enjoy whichever you choose."

"Then, you're out of luck, because I'm not doing either." I park myself on the chair beside her, cross my arms behind my head, and close my eyes. Self-preservation. I need some.

She huffs, and I can't help laughing. Also, letting a victory smile take its rightful place on my face, at the sound of the sunscreen bottle lip snapping open beside me.

"Troy."

"Cricket." My eyes stay closed. Fool me once.

Another adorable huff comes from her direction. "I'll give you another choice. You can rub lotion on my body, or I can get another guy to do it."

Now, I have to look. I crack one eye open and find her waving the bottle at me. This is the perfect opportunity to set her free. Encourage her to enjoy this trip to its fullest by choosing an age-appropriate guy to make memories with. Even if I do that by calling her bluff, it'd be the right thing.

"Give it to me." I'll do the right thing later. Right now, it's self-induced torture time.

"I didn't think you'd really do it," she says, passing me the sunscreen.

"There's still time to withdraw your ultimatum." I shift to the edge of her chair, shake a generous glob of sunscreen into my palm, then give her one more chance. "Last call for takebacks."

She shakes her head. "I want you to do it."

"Move your hair to the side." There's no mistaking the huskiness in my voice. Good thing I'm sitting, or there'd be no mistaking the huge bulge I'm sporting.

"It's cold," she says when I flatten my palms on her shoulder blades. "But your hands feel good. I've always liked your hands."

Answering is a mistake. Like every other one, I go ahead and make it anyway. "My hands, huh?" I ask, sliding mine downward, spreading the lotion over every inch of her nearly bare back. *Bare back.* Not a good word combo to think of while I'm touching her. Now all I can think of is bareback, and how it'd feel to sink inside her pussy with nothing between us.

"Among other things."

Not taking that invitation. I keep my mouth shut, focus on her gorgeous body that I'm touching this one time only. I skate my hands over the dip of her lower back, right above the edge of her thong bikini bottom. I add more lotion to my hands, rub them together to warm it up better this time, then make the move that might actually kill me.

Thank fuck her eyes are closed when I set my palms on her sweet, round, sexy ass. She can't see how much I'm enjoying this. How much I want her.

Cover her soft skin with lotion, then get the hell away from her—that's what I should do. But when she parts her thighs beneath my touch, I'm not going anywhere.

I knead her firm, full cheeks. This isn't sunscreen application, it's a massage. One I don't stop. I slide my hands lower, sweep my thumbs along the smiley curves where her ass meets her legs, all the way to the fabric covering her pussy.

"I shouldn't be touching you." I press the pad of my thumb against her entrance, groaning when the tiny strip of material dips inside, revealing a hint of her soft, pink pussy lips. "Yell at me. Hit me. Tell me to get my filthy fucking hands off you."

"Never," she whispers, opening her legs wider. "I've been thinking about this since forever. I still do, every day."

I plant one arm on the other side of the lounge chair, caging her in place and sheltering her upper body from view. "Every day?"

She pulls her bottom lip between her teeth. "Constantly."

Fuck. *Fuck.* I'm in so much trouble. "Do you touch yourself when you think of me?" I ask, stroking her through the fabric.

"Yes."

"Do you make yourself come?"

Her eyelids flutter when I roll firm circles over her clit. "Always."

"Tell me how you do it." I'm a glutton for punishment, making this demand.

"Mostly like this, on my stomach."

Fuck, I can picture it. Vividly, as if she's doing it right now. Something else for me to think about when I'm jerking off, grunting her name as I blow yet another Cricket-inspired load.

"It's my turn now," I say, slipping my fingers beneath the fabric. I slide them up and down through her slick, soft heat. Teasing. Rolling. Pressing. "You want me to make you come, sweetheart?"

"Yes." Her breath catches, coming in soft, panted gasps as she matches my rhythm. "God, so much."

"Fuck, you're beautiful." My dick is so hard, it's aching. I'd do just about anything to be buried inside her. I flex my fingers, giving her more pressure. "So fucking sexy."

She doesn't speak. Just rides my hand. Her lips are parted, her eyes pinched closed, her ass rising and tightening as she grinds against my fingers. Fucking perfection.

"That's right. Rub that hot little pussy all over my fingers. Show me how pretty you look when you come."

"I don't want anyone to see."

"Just me, I'm the only one who gets to see you." I lean over her back, groaning at the pressure it puts on my throbbing dick. "I'm so fucking hard for you. Always so hard for you. I need to feel you come."

The softest, sexiest moan leaves her mouth as she tips over, rhythm dissolving into frantic jerking against my hand. *"Troy...God, Troy..."*

Thank fuck we're in public, because there's no way I'd keep my dick out of her if we weren't. I hold myself in place after she goes limp beneath me, kissing her back while she catches her breath.

"Tickle?" I ask when a shiver ripples through her.

"No, I'm just..." Her blonde hair moves like lapping waves when she shakes her head against the lounge chair. "Embarrassed."

"Nobody saw."

"You did," she whispers, pinching her eyes tighter. "I can't believe I did that."

Is that regret? Probably. *Fuck.* I should've known better. I did know better. But I went ahead and took what I wanted anyway.

"You don't need to be embarrassed around me." I withdraw my hand from the heaven I'll never touch again and straighten her skimpy bikini bottoms. "We'll act like it never happened," I say, rising to a stand. "Going to have a swim. See you in a bit."

My focus is on the pool as I walk away. I doubt she looks at me, but I'll never know. I already feel like a douchebag, I don't need to see it written all over Cricket's face.

It's still relatively early since we grabbed an overnight flight. The poolside area isn't busy, and I honestly don't give half a fuck if anybody notices the tentpole at the front of my trunks. I deserve any ridicule that comes my way.

My body slices the water when I dive into the deep end. I've got the pool to myself and I carve it up, doing three quick lengths. I make the turn for the fourth lap, and spot Cricket bobbing in the pool, directly ahead. Fuck. I power out the rest of the lap, stopping at the wall where she's obviously waiting for me.

"You're such a strong swimmer. I can barely tread water." Seems she's accepted my suggestion to act as if I didn't just make her come. That'll make the rest of the trip smoother.

"I've seen you swim, you're not bad." My back against the pool's tiled wall, I stretch my arms along the edge. Casual. The opposite of how I'm feeling inside. "I can help you level up your skills when we get home. Teach you some strokes and techniques. You're going to be living at the house for a couple months, minimum. Might as well make the most of the time."

"That's what I'm hoping to do," she says, plastering herself to my chest, with her arms twined behind my neck. "I want you to teach me *all* the strokes and techniques."

"Cricket." I grind her name out between clenched teeth.

The concrete might actually crumble under my grip, I'm holding on that hard. Have to, otherwise, I'm going to touch her again. "This isn't how we pretend nothing happened on that lounge chair."

"That was your idea, not mine." Below the surface of the water, she wiggles until her legs are wrapped around my hips, a move that has her pussy cradling my steel-hard dick. "And for the record, it was a bad idea."

I laugh because she's cute, but there's nothing funny about my predicament. Or the blue balls I'm going to have. "You said you were embarrassed."

"Because I thought we'd be naked together, in a bed, in a dark room, the first time you made me come. I didn't expect to be so…front and center."

If she thinks she could be anything other than front and center around me, I did a decent job of hiding how I feel. Until today.

"Take me back to our room, I want to be naked with you," she says, nuzzling my neck with her cotton-candy-pink lips. "I know you want me, too."

No point in denying it, since there's a battering ram between my legs. "I can't fuck you, Cricket."

She pulls her head back, blinking at me with those big, blue eyes. "Do you—" Her eyelashes flutter as she whispers, "Do you have a disease?"

Bam, there it is. A one-way ticket out of her panties, forever. All I have to do is take it.

"No, I'm clean. I've never had anything." It's official, I'm a selfish bastard. I can tell myself I just didn't want her thinking less of me, and that's true, but not the whole truth. I want her more than I've ever wanted another woman. But I can't.

"Then why?" She frowns when I disentangle her from my body and swim out to a distance she can't reach.

Unlike my new bride, treading water is as easy as breathing for me. "You're Gina's best friend."

"Gina won't care. I think she'll be happy for us."

Fuck. I hadn't even considered the two of them discussing intimate, personal shit involving me. "Did you talk to Gina about—" My stomach rolls just thinking about the next words. "About the possibility of us getting together on this trip?"

"No..." She pulls her bottom lip between her teeth. "But, she shopped with me and watched me pack. She saw the bathing suits and dresses I brought."

"You're on vacation at an adults-only, Caribbean resort. Nothing wrong with wanting to attract the attention of some men your age while you're here. I'm sure that's all she thought."

"We're married, Troy. I would never cheat on you. Gina knows that."

"Gina knows we're married so you can get whatever medical attention you need. She wouldn't expect you to be faithful to me, and neither do I."

"But I don't want to be with anybody else." Her mouth curves into a frown, her eyelashes fluttering faster than butterfly wings. "Are you going to sleep with other women while we're married?"

Take the ticket, man. All I have to do is say yes, then she won't want to be with me. She'll probably hate me, but that doesn't matter. It might even be for the best. So, why is my head shaking? Fuck, I'm a stupid bastard.

"I won't be with anyone else while we're married." There. Committing to celibacy isn't the same as agreeing to fuck her. I'm good. This'll work.

"Okay."

The agreement's a little too easy, but this time, I manage to keep my mouth closed. "I'm going to swim a few more laps."

"I'll be right here, admiring the view," she says, assuming my previous position with her arms stretched along the pool's edge. The water lifts her tits, as if putting them on display especially for me.

Talk about a view. I've always been a boob man, and Cricket's are spectacular. For now. If that lump turns out to be something serious... I shake my head to clear the negative thought. Whatever it is, we'll get through it. Whatever she needs, I'll make sure she gets it. I don't care what it costs or how long it takes.

"Come on, then," she says, letting her legs float up, smiling as she playfully kicks water in my direction. "Give *me* something to stare at."

Busted. And I can't help smiling right back at her. The urge to join her at the wall, pin her with my body and kiss her is so fucking strong. I can't give in again.

I wink instead, then fill my lungs and plunge beneath the water. To stay fit. To blow off some pent-up tension. But most of all, to give my gorgeous, temporary wife something to stare at.

four

. . .

cricket

IF THIS TRIP is a contest of wills, I'm going to win. But Troy's not making it easy.

After the single hottest moment of my life happened on that lounge chair yesterday, he spent the rest of the day—and night—putting us in public settings and safe situations. We ate lunch in the open-air buffet dining room, surrounded by dozens of other guests. The afternoon included a group sightseeing excursion. Dinner was in one of the smaller restaurants within the resort, but at a table in the middle of the room.

Behind the closed door of our room, he offered me first crack at the bathroom, then proceeded to fall asleep on the loveseat before I finished prepping for bed.

I stood beside him for a full two minutes, saying his name. I even poked him. He didn't budge. Didn't crack an eyelid. Didn't see me in the lingerie I'd chosen especially for this night. I silently conceded. Grudgingly swapped my negligee for boy shorts and a camisole, then spent my second night as a married woman *not* having sex with my hot husband.

This morning, I woke up to the *ping* of his incoming text, telling me to meet him in the lobby, and to wear comfortable pants. I'm not into working out, but I'd give it a fresh try for him, so I showed up in my best ass-highlighting yoga pants and a sporty, cropped tank. My outfit had the desired effect. Troy didn't even try to keep his eyes off me. Unfortunately, he *did* keep his hands off me. All through our brief breakfast, and subsequent group activity —horseback riding. He didn't even boost me onto the saddle.

Wallowing and disappointment aside, it's actually a nice outing. The guide at the front of the line is entertaining, the other guests are friendly, and the jungle on either side of the path is pretty. The only negative is the distance from Troy. I can't even look back at him, because every time I ease up on the reins, my horse veers off course.

"You okay up there?" Troy calls when my horse makes another attempt to go left instead of forward.

I don't get the chance to answer. My horse does it for me—by ignoring my jerks and kicks, and walking into the greenery. To lie down.

"Oh my God, what are you doing?" Full panic mode engaged, I lean forward on the beast. "Please get up. *Please.*"

Troy's horse stops alongside, the model of good behavior. Holding the reins in one hand, Troy uses the other to give one of those loud, two-finger whistles. The rest of our group is far ahead, but the sound brings them to a stop, and the guide trots back to join us within seconds.

When nothing I try results in cooperation from the horse, I follow the guide's instructions and dismount. He does the same, then moves to my horse. He strokes its head, speaks to it gently, in a language I don't understand, finally coaxing it to stand.

"I'm not getting back on that horse."

"No, she is too tired to carry a rider, even one as small as you. We are close to the end, I'll lead her back." The guide nods at his horse. "You can ride with me."

"She'll ride with me," Troy says before I can respond. There's a no-tolerance edge to his deep voice, matched by the hard set of his handsome, strong jaw as he dismounts. "I'm an experienced rider and my horse is big enough to carry us both. Our combined weight won't put too much strain on him for a short distance."

The guide doesn't argue, just watches closely while Troy boosts me onto the saddle. "Take it slow. I'm leading the rest of the group back to the ranch. Stay on the trail, and we'll meet you there."

"We're good." Troy dismisses the guide with those two words. Within a minute, the guide, my horse, and the rest of our group are all out of sight.

We're alone. Crammed into a saddle, my back to his chest. My ass to his cock, growing thick and hard against my lower back. We couldn't get physically closer without being sexually interlocked.

"You know, I was kind of bummed about this horseback riding thing, but it's, um, growing on me."

"Yeah, it is." His gruff laugh against my ear sends a ripple of awareness straight to my clit. "Sorry about that."

"You have nothing to be sorry about," I say, wiggling against him. "Honestly, I couldn't have planned today any better."

"It's the opposite of what I planned." His muscular legs

squeeze briefly, then, like magic, we're moving. No kicking or rein snapping required.

"If you didn't want to be this close to me, you should have let me ride with the guide."

"You're right, I probably should have."

"Then why didn't you?" I know the answer, but I want to hear him say it.

"I don't want anyone else touching you. I tell myself I'll be okay with it, that it's what's best for you. But the thought of it makes me fucking crazy. Having self-control around you is getting harder by the minute."

"I can feel that. And I like it."

Another deep rumble slides into my ear. "The island is bringing out the bad girl in you."

"*Woman.* You need to stop thinking of me as a girl."

"I never have. Even when I met you. Felt like a dirty old man, but I couldn't stop myself. Still can't."

Finally, everything I've ever wanted to hear. Well, almost everything. "You've never been a dirty old man. You were thirty-four when we met, and I was eighteen. We've always been consenting adults." When all I get is silence, I move my hands from the saddle horn to his quadriceps. "We're *married* consenting adults now. You don't need self-control with me. I want you, Troy. Just as much as you want me."

"Not possible."

The admission fuels my confidence. My boldness. "Then fuck me tonight."

"Can't."

Not the answer I want. Or need. Now that I'm not holding the saddle, each stride of our rhythmic ride pushes my clit against the horn. Again and again, like a vibrator on the slowest, most agonizingly teasing setting. I pretend to shift for comfort, but it's to get more pressure. Not enough. I need more, and I need it from him.

"Please," I say, taking one of his hands from the reins, and placing it between my legs.

"Fuck. How am I supposed to resist you?" He slides his hand inside my pants. A tortured groan vibrates against me when his fingers reach my pussy. "You're so fucking wet."

"Because of you." I moan as he works my clit, barely breathing as he pushes me closer and closer to the edge.

"I wish I was eating your sweet little pussy right now."

The words, the thought of his face between my legs, tips me over. "Yes, God, *Troy...*"

He curses a string of perfect, filthy endearments as I come against his hand for what feels like forever, and also like a blink that ends too soon.

"I have to know." The spandex snaps against my waist, then he sucks his fingers into his mouth. "Fuck, so good." He nuzzles his face against my hair, until his mouth is against my ear. "Hold your pants open so I can have another taste."

I don't have to ask if he's serious, I know he is. And I love it. I pull the stretchy fabric forward as far as the saddle allows.

"You don't know what you do to me," he says, slipping his fingers between my legs, sliding and rolling them across my sensitive flesh, then sucking them into his mouth again. "I'm fucking addicted."

"Good thing I've got an endless supply of what you need."

"Good thing." His deep, rumbling chuckle fills my head as the trail opens into the ranch. He smooths my pants into place, then takes proper hold of the reins.

"Thanks for the ride," I say, tipping my head to smile up at him.

"My pleasure." He doesn't say any of the other words I'd like to hear. Just presses a kiss to my temple and steers us toward the barn.

But the day's not over. And neither are we.

troy

On short notice, I could only swing a week off from work. I took what I could get, because giving Cricket this vacation was important. Not only to keep up the appearance that our marriage is legit. Because she's going to have a lot of heavy shit to deal with once we're back home.

I wanted her to have a chance to let loose. Hook up with someone who'd appreciate her and show her a good time, in and out of bed, before her world—and gorgeous body—might change forever. I thought I could step aside, hide out for a few days. Distance myself while she got wild with someone.

I didn't plan to *be* the someone. I tried not to be. But now that I've kissed her, touched her... Now that I've tasted her...

I throw back the remaining rum in my glass, then set the empty on the balcony table. That's my second since we got back from our day's activities. The booze isn't helping me forget my favorite activity of all—making Cricket come. I want to do it again. To bury my face between her legs and eat that sweet pussy all night long. To sink my perpetually rock-hard dick into her hot body.

I can't do either of those things. I know that. Just not sure where I'm going to find the restraint.

"Troy?" Her voice drifts through the screen, from inside the suite.

"Out here." It's not really *safe* on the balcony—no place is safe when I'm with her. I proved that at the pool yesterday, and on the back of a horse today. But the first-floor balcony, with its glass railing and courtyard view, is the safest I can get right now. Somehow, I have to stay clear of that bed. For two more nights.

"I'm ready," she says, sliding the door open, and stepping out in a red dress that hugs her curves, shows off her tits, and screams sex. "Are you ready?"

So fucking ready. "Yeah." No point suggesting she go without me. Tried it during dinner and got shut down. If I don't take her to the resort's nightclub, we're spending the evening in our room together. We'll be safer on the dancefloor.

I push up from the chair, making no attempt to hide the fact that I'm checking her out. "You look incredible."

"Good enough to eat?" she asks, batting her eyelashes at me. "And fuck?"

"Definitely." I move in closer, grinning when I hear her suck in a breath. "But it's not going to happen. Not unless you changed your mind about picking someone up."

Her angry kitten noise makes me laugh—until she adds some verbal claws. "And if I decide to bring some random guy back here and bang him, where will you sleep?"

I know she's taunting me. Waving a hypothetical red flag in hopes that I'll charge. Nope. Not throwing fuel on the fire. Things are hot enough between us already.

"On a lounge chair." I nod toward the courtyard below.

"Close enough to come to your rescue if you call me. Far enough away to give you privacy."

"You've really thought about this." Her pretty lips form a frown. "You actually *want* me to hook up with somebody else."

Yet another opportunity to extract myself from the mess I've made so far. But I'm still too selfish to pull the trigger. "I want this to be an amazing vacation for you. One with no regrets, and lots of exciting, positive memories to look back on."

"Good." She loops her arm beneath mine and tugs me toward the door. "Let's go make some."

I laugh and let her pull me into the suite, then out to the hall, and through the perfect, Caribbean night, to the resort's nightclub. It's not exactly booming at nine thirty, but there are enough people to make it natural.

She stops near the bar, meets my gaze without looking up, because the heels she's wearing put us nearly eye to eye. "I just realized, I've never seen you dance."

If I do the math, it's been close to a decade. I quit clubbing around the time Cricket hit puberty. She would've been realizing she liked boys, while I was winding down my party profile. Hell of a difference. More proof that I'm too old for her.

"It's been a while."

"Are you going to step on my feet?" she asks, placing a palm against my chest.

"Only if you want me to."

"If only you were that agreeable to my other suggestions." She gives me a playful nudge, then grabs my hand and squeezes as the music changes. "Oh, I love this song."

"Then, let's go carve up the dance floor."

By the time we reach the growing group of bouncing bodies, she's beaming brighter than the kaleidoscope of spotlights. She's happy. Excited. Making those positive memories I want her to have. With me.

I'd be lying if I said I only care that she's happy, not how she gets there. Truth is, I love being the man she's happy with. Making her smile is everything. I don't want it to end when we leave the dance floor. I don't want it to end at the bedroom door.

For better or worse, I'm going to give her whatever she wants tonight.

We reach a pocket of free space, and I twirl her under my arm, smiling like a monkey when she laughs as if she's having the time of her life. I fucking love that sound.

My hands find her waist, and I tug her against me. "Time to show me your moves, Mrs. Mannington."

Her eyes light up and she wraps her arms around my neck. Calling her that is a mistake. The first of many I'll make tonight, no doubt. And I'm going to enjoy every damn one.

troy

"Well, how'd the old man stack up?" I ask, as we roll out of the club, energized and sweaty from two solid hours of bumping and grinding. I'm not fishing for compliments. I'm reminding her that I'm thirty-nine, not twenty-three. A last-ditch effort to push her away. A lame one, but it's all I've got left.

She practically throws herself at me, plastering her

wicked-hot body against my chest, as she has at least a dozen times tonight. "Oh my God, you were amazing. I had so much fun with you." No acknowledgment of the *old* comment. Maybe she didn't hear it. Maybe she truly doesn't care.

At the moment, neither do I. "You want to come back tomorrow night?"

"Yes!" she squeals, literally, while bouncing up and down. "I wish we had more time here."

"Me too." I wish time would stand still, and we could live in this window forever. Together, without judgment. Without health concerns looming in the wings. Those are next week's problems. "Want to grab a moonlight swim before going back to the room?"

"Before?" Little wrinkles form when she scrunches her nose. How she's adorable and sexy at the same time is a mystery, but she is. "What about swimsuits?"

"What about them?"

Her eyes open wide as it hits her, then narrow, just as fast. "Wait a minute. Are you going in with me, or is this another tease?" She gasps as I palm her ass, and pull her tight against the never-ending hard-on she inspires.

"No more teasing. The swim, and afterward. Whatever you want from me, you'll get."

"Even if I want everything?"

"Yeah, sweetheart." I slide my hand to her nape. Thread my fingers through her hair, and look into her beautiful eyes. "I can't say no to you anymore. I don't want to." I seal my mouth against hers, groaning at the taste of her lips, at her tongue dancing with mine. Even better than the first time, at our wedding. I was fucking crazy avoiding this. Two days I could've been kissing her, wasted. No more. Not one more wasted minute.

"Wow," she whispers when we break to catch our breath. "That was...wow."

"That was the beginning, sweetheart. When you close your eyes for sleep tonight, you're going to have a new definition of 'wow.'"

"Maybe we should skip the swim, and go straight to our room."

My lips brush hers as I shake my head. "We have two more days in paradise, and I want to fill them with as many memories as possible."

"God, finally," she says, smiling against my mouth. She shrieks when I scoop her off her feet, into my arms. Her head falls back as I move, her joyous laughter rising into the warm night air like the sweetest music I've ever heard.

I want to hear it all night long. Every night, every day. For the rest of my life.

Fuck me, I'm in love with her.

five

. . .

cricket

WHEN TROY SUGGESTED A SWIM, I thought he meant in the pool. Then he carried me past it. The beach is empty, except for us and whatever creatures are awake beneath the ocean's dark surface. I'd be scared if I were alone. If I were doing this with anybody other than Troy. I know he'll take care of me. He has since I met him, in little ways that would fill a book if I listed them all, and enormous ways, like marrying me. I trust him more than anyone.

Seeing the moonlight bounce off the Caribbean, hearing the waves lightly lapping the shore as he crouches before me, unbuckling my strappy heels...the beach is so much better than the pool. Even though it's late, the sand is still warm beneath my bare feet as he sets each on the ground.

"We don't have towels," I say, as he unties the laces of his Oxfords.

"You can use my shirt."

I try not to drool as he stands, unbuttons the

aforementioned white dress shirt, then shrugs it off his muscular torso. "I might not give it back, you know."

He moves behind me, his chuckle raising goosebumps on my skin as he lowers the zipper of my dress. "That's okay." His fingers loop under the spaghetti straps, then draw them over my shoulders, and down my arms. "You're going to give me stuff I'm definitely keeping."

Please, let him mean my heart.

"Fuck, you're beautiful," he says, circling back to face me, his hand never disconnecting from my skin for a moment.

Every part of me heats beneath his gaze, his touch. When he steps closer and cups my face in his warm, strong hands, my heartbeat is louder than the ocean's waves.

"The most beautiful woman I've ever seen."

My hands find his buckle as he kisses me. I fight the urge to pull him against me, working his belt and zipper open instead, then pushing his khakis down.

He groans into my mouth as I palm his cock through the underwear. Steps back when I try to peel them off. His white boxer briefs practically glow in the dark, and there's no mistaking the sizeable bulge he's packing up front. "Not here."

"But...I thought we were going skinny-dipping," I say when he takes my hand and leads me toward the ocean.

"Must've been wishful thinking, because all I said was 'moonlight swim.'"

"You also said 'no more teasing.'" I sound like a pouting child, not the woman I want him to see me as.

"And I meant it." He draws me into the water, pulling me against him when we get waist-deep. "I'm going to make you come tonight, as many times and ways as you want. You want my fingers in your pussy? I'll give you that here and now. You want me to eat your sweet little pussy, fill you with my dick? Those things are going to wait until we're in our room. I've ached for you for five long years, Cricket. I tried to fight it, deny it, resist you. It's the only goal I've ever set and failed to achieve. I want you too fucking much. Now that I get to have you, I'm taking my time. In private. I'm going to lay you out properly. Worship every inch of you."

"God, yes." I twine my arms behind his neck, wrap my legs around his waist. "You're not the only one who's been waiting forever for this night."

He takes us into deeper water, groaning as I rock and rub myself against his hard length. "There's one more thing you should know before you let me into your sexy body." His hand tangles in my hair, tipping my head back to meet his heated, hungry gaze. "I'm not just making you come all night. I'm kissing, touching, licking, and fucking you until I *ruin* you. I'm going to make sure your body sings my name every time you come, for the rest of your life. No matter who's inside you, you're going to think of me."

"Only you." Water slaps at our backs as I grind on him, harder and faster, until I'm so close to the edge, my vision blurs. "There's only ever going to be you."

His growl fills my mouth as he kisses me hard. His fingertips curl into my butt, and he drives me up and down against his cock, the meaty tip hitting my clit exactly right until I come. He holds me tight as the ripples subside, stroking my back and kissing my shoulder.

"Take me to our room and ruin me," I say, once I can breathe again.

His deep, sexy chuckle slides into my ear, the promise of more coming to come.

troy

I might burn in hell for what I'm about to do. For the stuff I've already done. Too damn bad. Let the chips fall, because I sure have. I know I'll have to let her go once we're back home. Not tonight. Tonight's about getting as close as she'll let me.

She protested when I sent her to shower alone. There's no way I could have been naked with her and not fucked her. And I will fuck her in the shower. Definitely. That's not how the first time's going down, though. Because I need a lot more space for *going down*.

Feels like my dick has been perpetually hard for days. Not for lack of beating off, I've done that five fucking times since we got to the resort. The last time was only a few hours ago, before we went dancing. It barely took the edge off. Only one thing will satisfy the hunger I've been fighting. Tonight, I'm going to feast.

My dick's at full mast when I open the bathroom door. I don't bother to cover up. Nuance unrequired. I don't need one more thing to take off.

Or so I thought.

"Jesus fuck," I say, at the sight of Cricket on the bed, looking like a goddess in a pink bra that pushes her perfect tits to the overflow level, and panties that are barely more than a collection of strings. Taking those off is going to be a pleasure.

A couple of strides and I'm on the bed, caging her beneath me. "You're so beautiful."

"I know you like me in pink."

"Right now, I'll like you *out of* pink." I dip down for a taste of her shiny lips, unhooking the front clasp of her bra and palming one glorious tit. I pull back when she gasps into my mouth. "Did I hurt you? Fuck, I didn't think about the lump."

Her golden hair shimmers against the duvet as she shakes her head. "The lump is in the other one."

"I'll try to be gentle."

"I don't need you to be gentle, touching it doesn't hurt."

"I'll try anyway."

"*Don't.* Please, Troy." She cups my face, strokes my brow line, currently bunched and tense. "I don't know what's going to happen to my body when we get home. I need you to just...be real with me. Rough, hard, or gentle. I want it all with you. While I'm still normal."

"You could never be normal. You're amazing."

"For now," she whispers, her hands sliding from my face.

It's time for me to show up. Really show up. I shift to my knees, bracketing her hips between my legs, and look down at her. "For always. Your body is hot as fuck, but you're so much more than your sexy tits and curves. You're determined and smart, but you're also calm and kind, and fun to be around, no matter what we're doing. You're an incredible woman, Cricket. The inside as much as outside."

"Thank you."

"It's all true." So are the things I didn't say. Like, how I'm not just impressed by her, I'm fucking in love with her.

She reaches for my dick, still standing at the ready. "Then, how about you use *this* damn impressive thing to get better acquainted with my *inside*."

I groan at the sight of her holding my cock. Deciding to fuck Cricket definitely makes me a selfish son of a bitch, but

I'm not selfish enough to do it without making her come first. Or, maybe that makes me *more* selfish. Either way, putting my dick in her sweet body isn't happening yet. Not until I put my tongue there.

I drop to my forearms and plunder her mouth. She tastes like fresh, sweet heaven, and fuck me, I can't get enough. My dick is hard as steel, and I press it against its future home, rocking my hips as if I'm fucking her. Soon. It has to be soon.

She wraps her legs around me, her heels spurring me close with each thrust. "God, when are you going to stop teasing and fuck me?"

"Not teasing you. Getting you ready for me."

"I've been ready for you for five years," she says, dragging her nails down my back, to my naked butt. "Don't make me wait anymore. I want you inside me."

"I want that too. But I'm a greedy bastard, and I want to taste you first." I nip her bottom lip, then soothe it with my tongue before moving downward. Her neck gets the same treatment, each nip eliciting a gasp that's a sexy mixture of surprise, pain, and pleasure.

"Are you going to leave a mark?" she asks after my soothing lick becomes a suck.

"No, I don't want you to be embarrassed."

"I wouldn't be. Actually, I'd like it if people looked at me and saw your hickeys and bitemarks on me." She pulls her bottom lip between her teeth while sliding her fingers through my hair. "Will you give me some? Please?"

Thirty-nine-year-old men don't give hickeys. Sure as fuck not intentionally. But that's exactly what I'm going to do, because I'm way past saying no to her.

"Anywhere I want?" I ask, tracing her collarbone with my tongue.

"Yes." Her whisper becomes a gasp when I nip the spot where her shoulder curves into the column of her neck.

I suck her soft skin between my lips, between my teeth, long and hard. I release the pressure and ease back to survey my work. "That's one."

Her beautiful eyes open wide. "Really? You gave me a hickey?"

"Oh, yeah." Now that I see it, I like it. Every man in the resort is going to know she belongs to someone. And since I don't plan to leave her side for the rest of the trip, they'll know that someone is me. "You have more skimpy bikinis to taunt me with?"

"A few." She giggles. "Why?"

"You'll see," I say, moving lower. The upper swell of her full tits is my next target. I choose a spot and get to work, then place a gentle kiss on the mark I've left. "That's two."

She lifts her head, her face beaming with a wide smile when she looks down at the coin-sized strawberry. "Oh my God, it's so dark."

"It's a bruise."

"A love bruise." A deep-pink blush floods her cheeks. "I'm not saying you love me. You know what I mean, right?"

The perfect opportunity to tell her exactly how I feel is right here, on a silver platter. But I don't. "I do," I say, instead.

"Give me more." Her eyes shine, and her tits jiggle as she wiggles her sexy body. "I want everyone to know where you've been."

"Dirty girl."

"When I'm with you," she says, holding my gaze.

Fuck, I want that to be always. I'll settle for a couple of fantastic days. I pepper her beautiful body with more *love bruises*. A couple more on her tits, one above the swell of her pussy. People are going to look at her, then look at me, and think I'm a dirty old bastard. And I can't fucking wait.

"Time for these to go." I slide the minuscule panties down and off, then reposition, pushing her legs apart and kneeling between them. A man at the altar of perfect fucking pussy. I could worship here for the rest of my life.

I run my hands all over her skin. Soft touches, firm squeezes. Every inch gets kisses, licks, and nips while I watch her expressions and actions, listen to her sounds. Learning her secrets, everything she likes, what makes her arch closer, desperate for more.

She moans when I suck her nipple into my mouth, laving, nibbling, sucking. "Oh, God, bite me harder."

I growl and pull her nipple between my teeth. Harder than before, hard enough to make a sharp gasp rise from her parted lips. I slide one hand between her legs, groaning at the slick heat that welcomes my fingers.

"Troy..." She breathes my name like a plea, as I roll circles around her clit. "I need to come."

"I'll take care of you, sweetheart. Going to make you come all night long." I shift to the other tit, giving it the same attention while I rub her clit the way I know she likes. I move back and forth, filling my mouth with one perfect tit, then the other. Sucking and biting, until both nipples are bullet-hard peaks.

Her breath hitches, her hips rising to meet my hand in jerky, desperate thrusts. The sexiest moan fills the air as she rides the orgasm until there's nothing left but shaking thighs and an irresistible, breathy giggle.

"Fuck, you're beautiful when you come. Need to taste it this time."

Her eyes open wide. So do her legs, as I kiss my way down her body and settle in for the feast I've been craving since I met her. "How many times are you going to make me come?"

"As many as I can wring out of your sexy body." I hold her gaze while placing a kiss on the silky skin above the hood of her clit. My plan to watch her disappears the instant my tongue connects with her pussy. Can't keep my eyes open while I'm in fucking heaven.

I band my arms around her thighs and lick her, top to bottom, growling against her skin. I'm already addicted to her fresh, tangy essence. I burrow in, eating her hot little pussy like a starving man. I need her sweet cream all over my face. Need her to come undone. To beg me for more. To tell me she can't take more, all at the same time.

"Troy," she says, pushing her fingers through my hair, those pretty, painted nails of hers raking the scalp beneath. She's close. Ready. Needy.

Part of me wants to back off. Keep her on the edge so I can stay right where I am. Because, fuck, I don't want this to end. I also want inside her. I want it all.

I slip one hand between her legs, groan as I slide a single finger into her pussy. Fuck, so hot. So tight. I give her two fingers, growling when her hips come off the bed and her legs open wider.

"More," she says, her breathy voice becoming a moan as I add a third. "Troy..."

My body's on autopilot, humping the mattress as I finger-fuck her tight little pussy. No more drawing it out, I need her to come. I suck her clit, circle, and flick it with my tongue, until she's bucking against my mouth, her sexy moans filling the room.

I ease back when her moans turn to giggles. "So fucking sexy." I place a kiss on either side of her pussy, then crawl up her body and claim her beautiful mouth.

She moans and folds her arms and legs around me, pulling me onto her. "Fuck me now," she says, as we kiss. "No more waiting."

"Condom." I get the word out, but the head of my dick is already cradled between her slick pussy lips.

"I'm on the Pill, and I'm clean, I promise."

Fuck, *she's* promising *me*? I don't deserve her. But I'm sure as fuck going to take her. "I'm clean too," I say, pushing deeper. Just the tip, but fuck, she feels so good. "I swear I'd never do anything that'd hurt you."

"I know, I trust you."

Fuck, she's everything. *Every. Fucking. Thing.* I crush my lips against hers before I tell her that, in three short words. I rock my hips, groaning at the sensation. The slick heat. I'm barely inside her, just a couple of inches, and I'm already on fire with the need to come.

Her heels spur my butt, urging me closer.

"Tell me if it's too much," I say when she gasps as I push deeper.

"It'll never be too much with you. Give me everything."

"You have every part of me, sweetheart. Everything I have is only for you." It's as close as I let myself get to telling her. I slide all the way home, groaning at the squeeze around my dick. "You're so fucking beautiful. So perfect."

Her breath catches as I bury myself completely, balls-deep in her pussy. "You're so big."

"You made me this way. Now I'm going to fuck you deep and hard, and you're going to come all over this big dick."

She moans when I thrust inside again. Digs her nails into my shoulders when I roll my hips to grind against her clit. "Don't stop," she says, as I slide back.

I chuckle and nip her neck, then lick the spot while

filling her pussy again. "You know I'm going to make you come. But you're so fucking tight, I won't last once you're squeezing me with your sweet pussy, and I need to fuck you hard before that happens."

"God, yes. Fuck me hard. Fuck me any way you want."

Fire rages in my balls at the thought of doing *everything* I want. "Careful what you offer, or I just might fuck every part of you."

"Do it," she says, licking her lips as my next hard thrust pushes her higher up the bed. "Make all of me yours."

The beast in me roars. I pull out, roll her over, and position the head of my dick against her tight little pucker. "Ever had a dick in this sexy ass?"

"No," she whispers. "But I want yours there."

"Fuck." I press against her rim, just the tiniest bit. So fucking tempting, but she's not ready for this. I reposition my cock, grab her hips, and thrust into her pussy, fast and hard.

She moans as I seat myself deep. Her breath hitches as I spread her cheeks and press the tip of my spit-moistened finger against her pucker.

"You like that?" I ask, rolling it until the smallest bit slips inside.

"Yes." She's almost breathless, and I've barely breached her.

"Easy, baby." I add a healthy dose of saliva and push deeper, banding my arm around her and holding her in place when her body instinctively jerks forward. "This is just the tip of one finger. You're going to need to take a lot more before I can fuck you. One finger, then two, then three."

"Three?" Her voice is a whispered squeak.

"Oh, yeah. My dick's thicker than three fingers." I pull

back and thrust into her pussy again, making her moan. "Feel how big it is?"

"Yes."

"You sure you want that big, hard dick fucking your ass?"

"Yes," she says, panting as I work my finger to the middle knuckle while fucking her pussy. "I want everything with you."

I get my finger good and slick, then ease it into her ass again, all the way this time. "You're fucking perfect," I say, finger-fucking her ass and pumping her pussy until stars roll up behind my eyes. "Need to feel you come." I slide my other hand between her legs, rubbing her clit hard and fast. "You own this dick. Come all over it, milk me dry." I grit my teeth, I'm holding on by a thread, but I will hold on, as long as it takes for her to—

"Troy..." Her body jerks beneath mine. Her ragged moans fill the room, my head, my fucking heart, as she rides my hand. Squeezes my dick, my finger.

I unload like a geyser, rutting on my sexy-as-fuck wife like a wild beast in mating season.

My wife. Mating season. I never gave having more kids a single thought until this moment, but with Cricket, it's crystal clear. I'd give her a baby if she wanted. I'd give her anything. All she'd have to do is ask.

Which she won't, because she's twenty-three. She's studying her ass off to start a career, not be the stay-home-and-raise-babies wife of a man old enough to be *her* father. No matter how interested she is right now, how hot our physical connection is, this time we're sharing is temporary. Our marriage is a stopover in her life, not the final destination.

I need to remember that. Enjoy the moment and keep

my feelings locked down, so we can be friends, once her medical stuff—and our marriage—is in her rearview.

"Wow," she says, as I slide free of her body and roll us onto our sides.

"Exactly what I was thinking." It's a lie as fat as my dick was a few minutes ago. I bury my face in her hair and breathe her in. "More 'wow' coming your way soon."

"More?"

I chuckle and press a kiss to her head, then slide my hand to her tit and strum her nipple. "Oh yeah. Did you forget what I promised to do to you tonight?"

"You said you're going to worship me."

"That's right, and I've only started with that." I pull her closer, so my dick is nestled between our bodies. "What else did I say I'm going to do?"

"Ruin me," she whispers.

"That's right." Goosebumps rise beneath my fingertips as I trail them downward, to the pussy I know I'll never get enough of. "And I'm a man of my word."

"That's one of the things I love about you."

I freeze, mid-stroke, at her words. I can't see her face, but beneath my arm, her heart is beating like one of the dance anthems from the club tonight.

"I didn't mean to freak you out," she says.

"Not freaked out at all."

"Okay." A nervous laugh rises from lips I can't see. "You just went all stiff on me when I said the L-word. Not the good kind of stiff."

It's the perfect segue, and I'm smart enough to take it. "You ready for more of the good kind of stiff?"

"Already?" She twists to look over her shoulder, her eyes opening wide when I slide my thickening cock between her thighs. "Did you take a Viagra?"

I shake my head while rolling her clit between my fingers. "It's you. It's always you, Cricket."

She wriggles, turning to face me. Our gazes lock as she wraps her arms around my neck, and drapes one leg over my hip. "And it's always only you for me."

There's a shift. Something big, almost tangible. As if everything I want is right there, in front of me, and all I have to do is stake a claim, and it'll be mine. I'm tempted. So fucking tempted.

When I open my mouth, I choke. Chicken out, and kiss her instead. Then cup her ass and slide into her hot, welcoming body. Nice and deep, but slow, this time. Long thrusts with lots of lingering grinding against her clit. I kiss her as if this is the only chance I'll ever get, making love to her mouth while I fuck her the same way. I won't say the words, but I'm going to make damn sure she *feels* how much I love her.

Her breath hitches mid-kiss. She's right there, on the edge, and I'm going to give her everything she needs.

I cup her ass and pull her as close as two bodies can get. I mold my hand to her nape, holding her to our kiss while I rock my pelvis against her clit.

Her soft moan fills my mouth as her body jerks and trembles against mine. Her sweet pussy clenches around my dick, and I push deeper, groaning as I follow her over, again.

When she goes pliant in my arms, I keep kissing her. Softer kisses, but still deep. Even when she giggles against my lips, I don't stop. I don't let her escape. I'm not ready to let go. Who the fuck am I kidding—I never will be.

six

. . .

cricket

THE ROOM IS FULLY LIT with sunshine when I open my eyes. I'm alone in bed, but this morning is different from its predecessors because I didn't sleep solo last night. Troy's pillow is empty now, but his handsome head was there all night long. Well, after he finished putting it in more interesting places, like between my legs. Which he did four times.

That's more oral than I've received in the past year—in one night. Four glorious, body-shaking orgasms delivered by the man who's inspired me to masturbate more times than I can count. I may have missed the odd day here and there—because, lady reasons—but other than that, he's been the only man in my head. Even when I've had boyfriends. I tried thinking of them, but my mind always strayed back to Troy.

Yes, it was only mental cheating, but I broke up with those guys. Not only because of imaginary indiscretions. Being with anyone other than Troy, in or out of the bedroom, in or out of reality, never felt right. I was meant for one man only. Holy crap, was he worth the wait.

I roll toward the empty pillow, my pulse rising when I spot a note. I reach for it, my engagement ring sparkling in the sunlight, and I have to stop and admire it for the hundredth time.

Troy didn't have to buy me a ring. He *absolutely* didn't have to buy me a beautiful, full-carat, princess-cut diamond that cost more than I make in two months. He has worked hard to forge a successful career, and he's financially comfortable, but he's not filthy rich. He can shrug the ring off as no big deal all he wants, but I know otherwise. This ring is more than a showpiece to make people believe we're in love. It's the silent, shiny truth.

Last night was more than hours of intensely hot sex. It was the not-so-silent, sweaty truth. Everything he does shows me how he feels about me. If only he would say the words, too.

I pluck the note from his pillow. Troy's strong printing commands the interior of the folded paper, and I can't help smiling at the first word I see—sweetheart.

Sweetheart, you are so fucking gorgeous, lying there with your hair messed up from all our fucking, and your pretty lips puffy from all our kissing. I'm so tempted to skip the gym and crawl back into bed with you. To carefully pull the sheet back and wake you by kissing every inch of your sexy body before I slide inside you. I'm addicted to you, Mrs. Mannington. Sleep well, beauty. You're going to need it.

My happy squeal breaks the silence in our honeymoon suite. I'll never be able to stop loving this man. I'll never want to.

cricket

The resort's gym isn't busy when I walk in. No big shock to me, vacations and heavy lifting don't go together in my book. But Troy never misses a day. Since that dedication has given him the wicked body I enjoy ogling, I'm not about to suggest he change his routine. Even if it did deprive me of wake-up sex.

I'm not dressed for exercise, and I feel out of place weaving around the array of machines, benches, and racks. That feeling amplifies when I spot Troy sitting on an incline bench, smiling and chatting with an attractive, fit woman.

His gaze shifts to meet mine, his eyebrows pulling

together as I force myself to smile. He can tell I'm faking. He knows me inside and out, now more than ever.

I know Troy pretty damn well, too. And I plan to make sure no other woman gets the same opportunity.

Spandex-chick follows Troy's gaze, her expression dropping at the sight of me headed their way.

"Hi, honey," I say, stepping between Troy's legs, and pressing my body against his chest. "I missed you in bed this morning."

He chuckles and palms my ass. "Did you see my note?"

"I did." I flick my hair over my shoulder, a move that makes two of last night's hickeys visible. The weight of the woman's stare raises my temperature several degrees. Just in case there's any doubt in her mind, I run my fingers through Troy's hair and leave my hand at the base of his neck. "Don't be so considerate tomorrow. I'd rather you wake me up the way you said than get another hour's sleep."

"Noted. I'm almost done in here. A couple more sets, then I'll meet you back in the room, and grab a shower."

"I'll wash your back...and your front." It's brazen talk in front of a complete stranger, but I can't seem to stop. It also does the trick, because the woman lifts one hand in a surrendering wave, then disappears. "That's right," I say, under my breath. "Get away from my man."

His eyebrows rise as a laugh slides through his smiling lips. "You're jealous."

"Of course, I am. She was pretty, with a nice body, and—"

"And she's not you," he says, tugging me closer. "I promised there'd only be you, and I won't break that promise."

"Even if you want to," I whisper.

"I don't." He cups my jaw in one strong hand, his gaze searing me with its intensity. "You're the woman I want to be with. Did I not make that clear last night?"

Every cell in my body is awake and on fire now. "Yes, but...maybe you should remind me anyway."

"Not maybe. Definitely." The smack he delivers to my butt rings in the mostly empty room, then he rises from the bench. "I'm done here."

"I thought you had more sets to do?"

"I'll finish my workout in our room." His wink sends my pulse racing. The muscles in his broad back, chest, and strong arms flex as he wipes down the equipment he used. "Be right back," he says, before striding to the locker room.

I glance around the gym, fleetingly meeting the attentive—and disapproving—gazes of several patrons. I fluff my hair into place over the front of my shoulder to cover the hickeys, then stare at my feet until Troy returns.

"What's wrong?" he asks, tilting my chin upward.

"People were..." I shake my head.

"People were what?"

"It's nothing. I'm being oversensitive."

His jaw clenches, his gaze darting around the room before returning to my face. "If anyone did or said something to you, I need to know." Protecting me, as always, in whatever way is necessary.

"There's nothing to tell. Nobody has come near me. They were just...looking. And that's my fault because I marched in here and made a spectacle because I was jealous of a woman talking to you. It was immature and uncalled for, and I'm sorry if I embarrassed you."

"I don't embarrass easily."

My cheeks heat at the memory of Troy standing in the doorway of his living room, wearing nothing more than a pair of snug-fitting, crowded boxer briefs, knowing fully well I was gawking at every hard inch of him. He definitely doesn't embarrass easily.

He strokes my jawline, cradling my face in one strong palm. "I understand how you felt when you saw us talking. Watching an endless stream of guys talk to you over the last five years has almost killed me." It's not the full admission I'm desperate for him to finally make, but it's close enough for now.

"I think we should go back to the room and make up for all that lost time."

His laugh booms in the open space, drawing judgmental stares from everyone in the place, once again. He doesn't spare a glance for any of them. All of his attention remains on me. "There aren't enough hours in the day, or days in the year for us to catch up. But we can make damn sure we don't lose another minute."

"I love that idea." And him. God, I love him. The un-take-backable words hang in the back of my throat, threatening to leap from my lips if I open them again. I smile instead, sending up a little prayer when he takes my hand and squeezes it.

"For the record," he says, leading me out, still oblivious —or simply unconcerned—about the gawking stares tracking our departure. "Even though you'll never have a reason to be jealous, I like that you were. Guess that's my arrogant caveman coming out."

"Can we get him an animal-print loincloth? Because he'd look super-hot in one."

"Whatever you want," he says, laughing and dropping one hand to the small of my back while guiding me through the doorway. "But if you get to dress me up, I get a turn with you."

"Deal."

"You're boldly agreeable for a woman who doesn't know the inner-workings of my filthy mind and all its fantasies about you." Not just fantasies, fantasies about *me*.

"It sounds as if you're trying to spook me, but maybe it's you who should be scared."

"Yeah?" He puts an arm around my shoulders and grins down at me, as we make our way across the resort grounds. "Hit me with your dirtiest fantasy. I guarantee it won't be too much for me to handle."

"You sound boldly confident for a man who doesn't know the inner-workings of *my* filthy mind, and all the late-night, masturbatory fantasies I've had about *you*."

A deep groan rumbles its way up from his chest. "Fuck. Just added a new fantasy to my list."

"What is it?" I know what the answer will be, but I want to hear him say it. I am his dirty girl, after all.

"Going to need to watch you getting yourself off to one of your fantasies." He slides his hand up my shoulder, then into the front of my sundress, to my breast. "Yeah, that's going to be your first orgasm when we get back to the room."

A shiver ripples through me, and it's not solely from Troy's fingers toying with my nipple. He has no idea how closely his wish intersects with my fantasy. "Okay. And what do I get?"

"Anything you want."

"Be careful what you offer," I say, mimicking his words from last night. "I might ask for everything."

He tugs me closer as we walk, pressing a kiss to my temple. "Ask away, sweetheart."

If I don't lose my nerve, I just might.

troy

The suite is cloaked in semi-darkness when I step out of the bathroom. Cricket has drawn the curtains, but there's enough light to see her lying on the bed. By the time I reach it, my eyes have fully adjusted, and I can make out every sexy detail.

Her white camisole is pushed up above her tits. She's playing with one, tugging at the nipple. A pair of white panties lay beside her hip, and her hand is between her legs, stroking that pretty pussy of mine.

And it is mine. For now.

I get my wish about watching, but it's on her terms. Because, apparently, having me catch her masturbating is *her* fantasy. She laid it out for me before I hopped into the shower, and it took all my restraint not to jack-off in there. My dick couldn't get any harder than it is right now.

There's no doubt she heard the shower shut off, heard my footsteps across the tiled floor, but her eyes remain closed. Mine are wide-fucking-open. Standing near the foot of the bed, my gaze is glued to her rocking body, my hearing finely tuned to every wispy breath.

I know how she likes to be touched. How to make her come. Watching her get herself there is still an education.

The soft strokes—a literal petting of that pretty pussy—end as she curls two fingers into her body. It's too dark to see, but I know she's wet. Hot. Tight. Her hips rise to meet the penetration, and the new angle allows her to finger herself deeper. In and out, then she brings those fingers to her mouth and licks between the V they make.

I bite back a groan, but there's no way I can leave my dick alone. I wrap my fist around it, gritting my teeth to resist tugging.

She nestles her fingers between her pussy lips, gasping as she squeezes her clit between them. Another dip into her sweet center, then she rolls the first circle over her clit. A soft touch, but not for long. Each pass is harder, faster, until the circles become a frantic back-and-forth. Her hips tilt upward, her ragged breaths filling the room.

I'm fucking jealous of her fingers, but there's no way I'm *catching* her yet. I need to see more. I need to see her come.

"Troy..." My name is a soft plea, but I know she's not talking to me. She's talking to the version of me in her fantasy. A wordless, sexy-as-fuck moan leaves her lips, her hips jerking wildly beneath her touch as she comes.

Fuck, I need to be in that fantasy. Now. For real.

She pulls her hand away when my weight dips the mattress, her eyes popping open, as if I've truly just caught her. As if we didn't plan this little show. "Did you—" Her eyelids flutter rapidly as she pulls her bottom lip between her teeth. "Were you watching me?"

Looks like we're staying in fantasy mode.

"I saw every sexy second." I slide my palms up the insides of her legs, then spread them, and wedge myself between her toned thighs. "Tell me what you were thinking about while you were rubbing this pretty little pussy."

Her eyes open wider. "I can't." Either she's legitimately embarrassed, or one hell of an actress.

"You said my name. You imagined me doing something to you. Tell me, and I'll make it a reality."

"It's embarrassing." Her voice is as soft as the skin I'm stroking. "You'll laugh."

This had better be part of the act, because if she believes I'd ever laugh at her private thoughts, I've really fucked things up with her. "I'd never laugh at you. You're too important to me."

"I am?"

Fuck, I wish I knew if she's playing or serious. Going to cover the bases, either way. "You have no idea how much you mean to me." I stroke her cheek, comb my fingers through her hair, where it's fanned on the pillow. Then lean in and brush my lips across hers in a teasing, too-short kiss. "Tell me your fantasy. What was I doing to you that made you come? I want to make it real."

"You were fucking me," she whispers. "Fucking me so deep, telling me all the ways you're going to claim me, and..."

"And what, sweetheart? Don't get shy on me now, I want to hear everything."

"It'll be too much."

"There's no such thing with you." I'm fucking putty in her soft little hands. How hasn't she realized this by now? Guess I'm going to have to show her. Keep showing her. One hand curled over her hip, I slide inside, groaning as her pussy hugs me tight. "Fuck, you feel so good. Made just for me." I rock my hips, eliciting a gasp when I hit her G-spot. "That's right. Your body sings for me, only for me. I'm the only man who gets to make you come."

"Forever," she says, digging her nails into my butt as I grind against her clit. "Tell me it's forever."

"It's forever." I pull out, then fill her up again, burying my dick deep. "Never going to let another man have you." No holding back now. I'm all in, in every way. Shooting my heart out of my mouth as I fuck her deep and hard. "Going to fill every part of you with my dick. Watch you swallow every drop when I blow down your throat."

"God, yes," she pants, between thrusts.

My balls are already high and tight, ready to unload. I shift to my knees, tilt her hips upward, so I can rub her clit, get her where I need her. "This sweet pussy is mine. Your virgin ass is mine. Your heart is mine. Every part of you is mine."

"All of me, forever." She breathes the word, tits heaving and thighs shaking. *"Troy..."* My name rides the world's sexiest moan. Then she's bucking against me, her pussy squeezing me tight as she comes.

"Fuck, baby, fuuuck..." Crushing my lips against hers is the only thing that stops me from telling her I love her. But I want to. I really fucking want to.

seven

. . .

cricket

"WHAT ABOUT THIS ONE?" I tilt my head, holding the red sunhat in place while giving him a cover-girl pose.

"You look beautiful, baby." Some guys might say that because they're tired of shopping with their wife or girlfriend. Not Troy. The smile on his face and his laidback-yet-attentive presence tells me he's happy to watch me try on a dozen more hats, or anything else that catches my eye in the town's open-air market.

As I've done for the last hour. I return the hat to the vendor, thanking the woman for her time before joining Troy, where he's leaning against a tree. "Okay, I've subjected you to enough hats and dresses. What would you like to look at?"

"You." His hungry gaze drifts down my body, as if he's mentally undressing me.

Beneath the thin cotton sundress, my nipples are hard enough to cut glass. I assume a posture that pushes my breasts up and out. I know he loves my boobs, and I'll take every bit of that attention. Especially since I don't know what will happen once the lump is diagnosed. But that's not a today thought, so back in the box it goes.

"I'm serious," I say when his gaze works its way back to my face. "There must be something you'd like to shop for."

"There is. More things for you." He pushes off the tree, banding an arm around my waist and pulling me in tight. "Why didn't you get a hat?"

"I don't need one."

He's smart enough to read between the lines, and based on the stern set of his eyebrows, he's not a fan of the subtext. His arm slides from my waist and he clasps my hand, then leads me back to the market stall. "We'll take the red hat she just had on. And the white one she tried on first, too."

"Troy, that's—"

"Careful, beautiful," he says, taking cash from his wallet. "If you say 'too much,' I'm going to walk back through the market and buy every single thing you touched."

"Why?"

"Because he *loves* you, girl." The vendor beats him to an answer, beaming as she places the red hat on my head. "Anyone with eyes can see this man in deep with you, and that's right where he wants to be."

Troy chuckles while handing her several folded bills. "Thanks."

My heart is racing in my chest, beating so hard, I wouldn't be surprised if they can see it. After the things Troy said to me a couple hours ago, while he was inside me, I can't help hoping the market vendor is right. Because while he didn't confirm that he loves me, he didn't deny it, either. And, God, it feels like he loves me.

"Let's go back to the resort," I say, once we're out of the vendor's earshot. "I'll model the hat for you in our room."

Once again, he's smart enough to get my gist. This time, his eyebrows rise, rather than draw together. "Just the hat?"

I turn my head and smile up at him. "Well...I think it'd look good with my red shoes from last night, don't you?"

"I think if you're standing in front of me wearing nothing but a hat and heels, we're not going to make it to the nightclub tonight."

"What if I'm not standing? What if I'm kneeling, or bent over the edge of the bed?" I gasp as he jerks me off the path, leads me behind the row of merchant stalls, then presses me against a tree.

"I can't get enough of you." He wedges his quadriceps between my legs. Cups my nape as roughly as the bark at my back. "I'm never going to get enough."

"Good," I whisper, before his lips seal to mine. Then I'm lost to his kiss, sucking his tongue when it strokes into my mouth, moaning as he kneads my ass through the thin cotton. I never liked public displays of anything with the guys I dated. Troy could hike up my dress and fuck me right here, where anyone could see, and I wouldn't just let him, I'd love every minute.

That doesn't happen though. He breaks the contact as quickly as he initiated it. His eyes are dark with arousal, his nostrils flared, but his brow line is tightly furrowed as he gently smooths my rumpled dress.

"You didn't have to stop."

"I shouldn't have started," he says, crossing his arms over his chest. "You deserve better than some manhandling and groping behind a shack."

"I happen to love it when you manhandle and grope me, whether it's behind a shack, on horseback, poolside, or anywhere else." I commandeer one of his hands and mold it to my breast. "Grope me, hunky husband. I want you to."

His laugh attracts the attention of the nearest vendor, who peers at us from around the side of their stall. Troy clasps my hand, weaving our fingers together. "Let's go back to our room, where I can give you a thorough groping."

"And a manhandling?"

"Whatever you want, beautiful wife."

"Really?"

He nods while lifting our joined hands, then points at my pinky finger. "See this right here? I'm wrapped around it. And like the hat-lady back there said, I'm right where I want to be."

cricket

Every minute at the resort with Troy was amazing, but the last couple of days...God, they were the best of my life. Two days packed with nonstop attention from the man I love.

He promised to worship me, and he kept his promise. Endless kissing, holding hands, hugging, dancing, and sex. God, the sex. I lost track of how many times he made me come. I'm not even sure I could accurately count the number of times we had sex, because one time melded into another and another, every hour we were naked together. He kept his promise to ruin me, too, but not in the way he thinks.

I'll only think of him while I'm getting fucked, because

I'll never be with another man. I didn't want to be before, and there's no way I could be now.

He's been quiet since we checked out of the resort this morning. The walls that finally crashed and turned to dust a couple days ago have reappeared, getting higher as we head toward home. By the time we exit the highway, his relaxed expression is completely gone, replaced by a clenched jaw and shuttered eyes.

I've already asked if he's okay. Twice. He claims fatigue. Totally reasonable, given we've barely slept for two days. Nonstop sex has to take a toll, even on a man as virile as Troy.

But there's more to his mood shift than fatigue. If that's all it was, he'd still be holding my hand. Kissing me every chance he gets. Smiling at me.

He hasn't touched me since we got in the car. Hasn't glanced at me during the drive from the airport. He's sitting in the seat beside me, but he might as well be a million miles away.

Exhaling, I let my head fall back against the backrest.

"Everything okay?" Troy asks, breaking his apparent vow of silence. The weight of his stare compels me to turn my head. He's still sporting the serious expression he chose for the return trip, but his eyes swirl with concern. It's a start.

"Just lamenting our return to reality."

"I feel the same way."

I grab the kernel and pour a bucket of hope on it. "I had the best time with you," I say, settling my hand on his muscular leg. "Every minute of it, even the ones you were being a pussy-tease."

His deep, manly laugh fills the car, a smile finally

breaking the strain that's been cemented on his face all day. "Pussy-tease. That's a new one."

"Yes, well, don't even *think* about going back to reclaim the title. I mean, you can tease—I do enjoy it when you tease—as long as you don't leave me hanging too long. Mrs. Mannington has needs and expectations only her husband can meet."

Darkness descends on his expression. "Yeah, I guess we should've talked about this already."

Doom swirls in my abdomen, tries climbing upward, into my chest. Not so long ago, I would have let it. Everything is different now, and I have no intention of backsliding. Time is precious. Our relationship is too amazing to give up.

"I could ask 'talk about what?' but I'm not dense. You've been giving me the chilly treatment since we left the resort. Are you breaking up with me?"

"We'll still be married," he says, focusing on the road ahead. "For as long as you need to be."

"And if I say that's forever?"

Still watching the road, he grunts. "You won't need me forever. Once we get your medical stuff taken care of, you'll be good to get on with your life."

"If that's your nice-guy way of telling me to get out of *your* life, please say it directly. Tell me our trip was a fun fuckfest, but you don't want me as your wife, and you want to end the marriage the first chance you get."

He glances over, long enough to meet my gaze with storm-filled eyes. "I'm not saying that."

"Because you don't want to hurt my feelings?" I huff when he looks away without answering. "Is it because I won't be pretty and sexy if I lose my hair, and maybe my breast?"

That makes him look at me again. Makes him glare. "Are you fucking kidding? You think I'm that much of a superficial asshole?"

The piercing force of his stare steals my tongue, so I answer by shaking my head.

He blows out a long breath, his knuckles turning white as he grips the steering wheel and returns to looking at the road. "It's complicated."

"Only for you."

The tension between us is palpable—and entirely new. I hate it. Enough to make tears blur my vision. I control them by tilting my chin up. Hide them by looking out the passenger window, though I see nothing as Troy makes the final handful of turns that ultimately end in his driveway. We're home. Only I don't know what that means.

He gets out, moving around quickly to open my door, but escapes having to touch me by loading himself with all the luggage. "You can go in the house," he says, closing the SUV's rear hatch.

Not-so-subtle hint taken, I semi-stomp up the pavement, probably looking more like a petulant child than a honeymoon bride. I stop on the stoop, turning to confront him, but don't get a word out before the front door whips open.

"Welcome home!" Gina bursts through the opening to tackle-hug me. "Wow, look at you... Did you even go in the sun? You barely got a tan."

"I used lots of sunscreen." I take a chance and shoot a smile over my shoulder at Troy. "Didn't I?"

"Yeah," he says, edging around us. "Excuse me, ladies. Going to take these bags in, then mow the lawn."

Seconds later, I'm inside the house with my best friend.

The lawnmower fires up in the backyard, and it takes everything in me not to cry.

"Okay, what's going on?" Gina asks, because I couldn't fool her if I tried. "I thought you guys would have a good trip. I knew it might be a bit weird, with it being just the two of you, but you've always gotten along really well, and you're both fun, laidback people. What happened?"

There's no point trying to hide it from her. She's my best friend. For the next however long I'm here, she's going to be my housemate. She'll either figure it out, or hound it out of me. I might as well tell her straight-up.

"I, um, we, uh..." So much for being direct. I can't tell her. "Everything went great. But we kind of had an argument on the way home."

"Aw, shitty way to wind down your vacation. Whatever it was about, I'm sure it'll pass. I can't imagine it was anything important, right?"

"Right," I say, nodding. Lying. Something I hate doing, especially with Gina.

"Why don't you grab a hot shower to get rid of the travel grime, and I'll order a pizza. We can pig out and have a couple drinks while you tell me all the dirty details of the hottest guy you saw at the resort."

I cough, practically choking on my own tongue. "I will grab a shower, but I'm going to bail on the rest. I could use a good night's sleep."

"Okay." Gina wags a finger at me. "But I get a raincheck on the dirty details."

That conversation is *never* going to happen.

"Oh, hey," she says, as I pick up the suitcase that has my toiletries. "You'll have to use the shower in my dad's en suite. The one in the main bathroom is broken."

I narrow my gaze when she bites the inside of her

cheek, totally failing to hide her smile. "Broken how, and since when?"

"Since Martin spent last week here, and I accidentally pulled the showerhead thingy out of the wall while we were having crazy-hot shower sex."

"Oh my God, you seriously did?" I cover my mouth to mute my snorted laughter.

"I did! And it was ah-mazing. The sex, I mean. Not cleaning the half-flooded bathroom afterward." Her eyes open wide as saucers before she cranks her head toward the rear of the house. "I'm not telling my dad the truth, obviously. He likes Martin, and my dad's no prude, but I doubt he'd want to hear about *that*. If he mentions that I slipped in the shower and grabbed the showerhead cord to save myself, you just nod and look appropriately concerned, okay?"

"Of course." Though, at this point, I doubt he'll mention anything about anything to me.

"What's that for?" she asks when I set my suitcase on the floor and give her a squeezy hug.

"For being my best friend."

"Easiest job in the world," she says, releasing me.

"I hope you always feel that way."

"Why wouldn't I?" The question is barely out of her mouth before she sucks in a shocked breath, grabs my shoulders, and holds me at arms' length. "Oh. My. God." She gives me a head-to-toe once-over, narrowing her gaze when I squirm on the spot. "You didn't get a tan while you were away, you got *laid*. And laid well, based on the color of your cheeks right now."

"A lady never tells?" It's weak, and I know it.

As does Gina, whose burst of laughter probably would've infiltrated the neighbors' kitchen, if not for the lawnmower noise beyond the nearby, open window. "Then we're not ladies, because we *always* tell. Spill it, you. Quickly, before my dad comes in." Her eyes open wide again. "Wait, is that what you argued about on the way home? Is he pissed off because you had sex with someone?"

"Um…"

She makes a stop gesture with one hand. "I'll talk to him."

"Please don't."

"Don't worry, I'll be nice about it. But he needs to remember he's not *your* dad, and he shouldn't act like he is."

"He doesn't act like he's my dad," I say, inching backward and snapping up my suitcase. "Please don't talk to him about this. Or about me, in general. Okay?"

"But I could help smooth things over."

I shake my head. "We need to work through our issues, personally."

"Okay," she says, shrugging. "But I'm around if you need backup. My dad's a great guy, but he can be a stubborn ass sometimes."

Don't I know it.

cricket

Troy added the en suite three years ago. He did most of the renovation himself, walking around shirtless for hours at a time, his fine physique glistening with the sheen of hardworking muscles. Good thing Gina never minded me hanging around her house, because I spent every possible minute here that summer.

Who am I kidding? I've spent every possible moment here since day one. For the friendship. The tightknit sense of belonging. To be as close as possible to the object of my infatuation-turned-lust-turned-love.

I've never done more than take a quick peek at the finished en suite until today. Troy did an amazing job. He turned a tiny, adjoining bedroom into his private sanctuary. The huge, walk-in shower has more jets than the whirlpool tub at the resort. It's glorious. And entirely open concept. There's no door, just an archway where his old closet used to be, then a righthand turn into the bathroom.

Vice-versa on the way out, which is where I run into Troy—literally—in all his naked glory.

"Fuck," he says, closing his hands around my bare upper arms. "What're you doing in here?"

"Having a shower. The other one is broken." I don't move.

Neither does Troy. He could step away from me, could grab something, anything, to cover himself with...but he doesn't. Instead, his palms skate downward, until his fingertips meet the edge of my towel, wrapped snugly around my chest. His cock thickens where it's wedged between us, and his nostrils flare. He wants me.

I shift my palms from his chest—where they landed when we collided—to the tucked-in edge of my towel. A gentle tug and it opens, the soft terry fabric sliding as low as our close clinch permits.

"Cricket." My name in his deep voice is a warning. To me. To himself.

Not good enough.

"If you have something to say to me, say it."

His lips form a razor-straight line. "I'm grabbing a shower."

"That's it? That's all you're going to say?"

His nod is as tight as his clenched jaw. He releases me, eating me up with his gaze when my towel drops to the floor. Then he turns and walks away, leaving me alone in his room. Near a bed he's clearly determined not to share with me.

Well, screw that. Until he says the words I don't want to hear—really says them, to my face—we aren't done.

I follow him into the bathroom. Into the shower, where thousands of drops of water are lucky enough to run over his hard, toned body.

"Cricket, what the fuck." There's an edge in his voice that could be anger.

I'll take my chances. I relieve him of the soap, lather it between my palms. Revel in the groan that vibrates from him when I slick my hands over his shoulders, chest, arms... then lower.

"Fuck, your touch is amazing." He widens his stance as I follow the V of his lower abs to the crease where his thigh meets his groin. Another groan rises from his mouth when I caress his balls, slide my fingers over his perineum while stroking the base of his cock with my other hand. "You shouldn't be in here, sweetheart. We shouldn't be doing this."

Sweetheart.

My heart races as I step back. "Then tell me to leave." Our gazes lock as water rinses the soap from his body. "If you truly don't want me here, tell me to leave."

"I can't."

"Because you're afraid I might turn into a crazy stalker if you end things?"

He grunts a laugh. "No."

"Then why, Troy?" I close the gap between us, twining my arms behind his neck while pressing my body tight to his. "Either give me a good reason to leave, or a better one to stay."

Hand tangled in my hair, he tugs me closer, angles my head, and takes possession of my mouth. Each sweep of his tongue is more insistent than the one before. He bands an arm around my leg and raises it, opening me for him.

The air rushes from my lungs when he fills me in one swift stroke. He holds me tight, his groan rumbling against my lips. Then my feet leave the floor as he picks me up. Pinning me between his body and the smooth, tile wall, he pushes deeper. Never withdrawing, he rocks his hips in rhythmic, upward thrusts that set my nerve endings on fire. But it's not enough to take me over, and Troy knows that. He knows all my secrets now. Well...almost all.

"Don't want to give up your mouth, but I need you to come," he says, sliding from my body and returning my feet to the ground. He bands my waist and turns me around. Circling my wrists, he plants my palms against the tile. "Hands stay up here."

"Yes, sir."

A husky rumble fills my ear. "I like the sound of that." His cock presses against the small of my back as he nudges me closer to the wall. "Going to like the sound of you coming more, though." He reaches in front of me to reposition the adjustable jets, then guides his cock home again. "I fucking love being inside you."

"I love it, too." I love *him*. God, he must know I love him.

His hands slide over my body. One settles between my legs, parting my lips so the spray does its rhythmic magic against my clit. "You like that?"

"Yes," I say, rocking against the invisible, watery tongue flicking my sensitive bud. I gasp when Troy cups my breasts, pinching my nipples, first one, then the other. "Harder. I need it harder." Heat flares beneath the next pinch, a drawn-out tug that brings tears to my eyes. "More."

"Fuck." His fingers steal over my clit, rubbing me hard and fast, the way he knows I need. "Fucking come all over me. Squeeze me with your tight little pussy."

Everything goes white as I tumble over, riding his hand and cock until I'm shaking from head to toe.

"Fuck, baby, fuuuck..." He sears my neck with a bite that makes me cry out. He fucks me like a feral beast, his hard thrusts filling the room with the wet smacking of flesh.

My desperate panting mixes with his rough grunts, as his fingers relentlessly draw a second orgasmic wave from my heaving body. Thank God he's a rock because I'm wrung out in his arms.

"I have no bones left," I say.

"Me either. But give me a few minutes to catch my breath, and I'm sure I can come up with another one."

Bliss. That's what this is. "Can we go to the bedroom for round two? If we stay in here, we might turn into wrinkly raisin people. We should save that look for our golden years."

He stiffens, and not in the good way he just promised. A quick kiss to my temple, then he's out of my body, out of my space, and out of the shower.

"What's wrong?" I shut off the water and follow him, leaving a trail of soggy footprints when I forgo a towel. I'm dripping all over his plush, cream carpet, and he's not batting an eye.

This time, my naked body doesn't affect him. He

doesn't even look at me while drying off and getting dressed.

"Answer me," I say, as he moves toward the bedroom door. "A few minutes ago, you were telling me you love being inside me, promising me more after you catch your breath. Now you can't get away from me fast enough. You can't just flip a switch like that and expect me not to demand an explanation. I'll chase you down the driveway, naked, if I have to, Troy."

From across the room, I see his knuckles turning white from gripping the door handle. He exhales, long and low, then turns, meeting my waiting gaze with a tight jaw and shuttered eyes. "I offered you support when you couldn't get it anywhere else, and that appreciation became attraction. It's understandable. But I had no right taking advantage of our situation."

"Are you kidding?" There's nothing funny about this conversation, but I can't help laughing. The kind that hangs in the air like an off-key note, and leaves a bad taste on your tongue. "First of all, you're full of shit. We both admitted to a mutual, longstanding attraction. One that started long before the stupid lump in my breast. As for taking advantage of our situation... *I'm* the one who used every opportunity to seduce *you*. And I'm not sorry I did, because we're great together."

"In bed. We're great in bed."

Even though he's seen every naked inch of me, from every imaginable angle, I've never felt more exposed. "I can't believe you said that."

"I hate hurting you."

"Then don't." I'm practically yelling now, but anger and desperation aren't enough to keep my tears at bay. Two fat ones roll down my cheeks.

"It doesn't feel like it right now, Cricket, but what I'm doing now...it's the right thing."

"For who, you? Because it's not the right thing for me."

He doesn't answer. Not with words. But his guard slips, revealing all the soul-deep emotions he's shared before this horrible moment.

Hope takes a beat in my chest. Then plummets to the depths of my churning gut as he turns and walks out the door.

I wait for the sound of his car leaving before I fall apart completely. Sobs rack my body as I pull on underwear and one of his t-shirts, then slide between the tightly tucked sheets of his bed. I'm not supposed to be here, as he so readily pointed out. Well, fuck that. And him.

"Hey." Gina's voice floats in from the doorway. "I heard everything. I'm not going to ask if you're okay because obviously, you're not."

I pull the duvet over my head as she sits on the edge of the bed. "I'm sorry."

She tugs the blanket to my chin, forcing me to meet her eyes. "For what? Having sex with my dad, not telling me you're having sex with my dad, or for scarring my eardrums for life when I heard you having sex with my dad, because you didn't give me a warning that I need to protect myself from that impending live-porn trauma?"

Miserable as I am, I can't help snorting. "No, yes, and yes. And thank you."

"You're welcome. Now, what can I do to help, because it sounds like my two most favorite people in the world have really made a mess of things."

The sheets are even nicer than the ones at the resort, but I use them to wipe my tears anyway. "Things shouldn't be a mess. We have a great connection. When we're together, it's—"

Gina stops me with a raised hand. "Nope. The first rule of 'You're Fucking My Dad Club' is, you never mention any details about fucking my dad."

Another snorted laugh bubbles out. I'm so lucky to have her as my friend. "I was going to say, when we're together, it's so right. As if nobody else exists, and there's no reason for us *not* to be together. I know he feels the same way, he said a lot of things while we were away."

"Did he tell you he loves you?" she asks, her eyes popping wide.

"Not in those words." God, I wish he'd said those three little words. "But I'm sure he wasn't lying when he said the other things."

"Solid assumption. My dad's a straight-arrow kind of guy. Sometimes he's guarded, sometimes he's a bit too direct, but he doesn't lie."

"Right. And after the stuff he said while we were away... I don't understand why he's backpedaling now."

"He told you why. He thinks he's doing the right thing, and my guess is, he thinks it's the right thing *for you*. And," her eyebrows rise, so do her hands, as if she's surrendering, "I know you don't want to hear this, but maybe he's right."

I sit up, pulling a pillow into my arms and squeezing it. "He's not."

Gina's lips form a wavy line. "He's almost forty, and you just turned twenty-three. You've got school to finish, a career to launch, and you might want kids someday. That's down the road for you, maybe in ten years? He'll be fifty by then. I know he's healthy and fit, but that's still pretty late in life to be starting back at square one with a baby. I'm speculating, obviously, but I know my dad. He's a planner, always thinking six steps ahead. He's had to, since my mother stepped out of the picture when I was still in diapers."

"That's part of why I love him, Gina. One of the many reasons I've been falling in love with him since the day I met him." A fresh stream of tears slides down my face. "I can't turn those feelings off. I don't want to."

"I know, sweetie." The fluffy pillow buffers the closeness of our hug, but not the length. She hangs on, letting go only when my sniffling ends. "You need to focus on *you* right now, and sort out this shit with him later."

I nod because she's right. That doesn't mean I'll be able to follow her advice, but I'll try. Starting with leaving the bed my heart knows I should be sharing with Troy.

The spare bedroom is across the hall. I've slept in it more times than I can count over the years. I always loved being that close to him. Now, it's entirely too far away.

eight

. . .

troy

THE TIME since returning from our trip has been the worst of my life. And that's saying something, because I've lived through some shit. The former times were a struggle because they were unplanned, beyond my control. This dumpster fire is my fault. One-hundred fucking percent. Knowing I did what's best for Cricket doesn't make the fallout easier.

I haven't had to shut her down again. Haven't had to see the pain I've caused reflected in her pretty eyes. The house isn't big, but our paths haven't crossed once since our blowout in my bedroom. She's only "home" when she has to be, and those hours are spent behind the spare bedroom's closed door, across the hall.

Every night, when it's late and the house is quiet, I hear her crying behind that door. That pain is my fault, and it fucking guts me. A lifetime of working hard to be the best man I can down the drain, because I couldn't keep my hands to myself and my dick in my pants. Because I stole her happiness and replaced it with a broken heart. I deserve every shitty fucking thing that happens to me, for the rest of my life.

She deserves the opposite. I'm not a religious man, but I've done some praying. I've offered my life and my soul— or what's left of it—to whatever power can get Cricket through this shit she's been dealt, as quickly and painlessly as possible. Haven't had any takers on my offer yet, but I keep sending up signals. Whatever I have to do.

For now, I'm silently taking care of her, and she's letting me. She's living in my house. Eating my food, even jotting things she wants on the grocery list. She took the insurance and credit cards I left on the kitchen table. Didn't take the note that went with them, but at least she took both cards. I wasn't sure how she'd feel about having *Mrs. Cricket Mannington* embossed on a credit card.

She hasn't used it yet, but I like knowing she'll never be stuck without the means to pay. For anything, ever, because I'll never ask for that card back. Even after the medical stuff is in her past. Even after I'm in her past.

As long as she lets me, I'm going to take care of her. And yeah, I like that if she pulls that credit card out, she's marked as my wife. I'm still a possessive bastard. I still want her, despite cutting her loose. It's fucked up. *I'm* fucked up.

"This is Troy," I say, picking up when the ringing phone on my desk snaps me back to the present.

"Hello, Mr. Mannington, this is John from credit services, calling about a pending charge on the new card issued to your account."

Could be a scam, but it'd have to be a good one for them

to get ahold of my direct line at work. Even if the call is bogus, it's still a hell of a coincidence. I lean back in my chair and tap the end of my pen on the desktop. "I'm listening."

"Thank you, sir. The card ending in 1396, issued to Mrs. Cricket Mannington hasn't been activated, but someone attempted to use it at Eastridge Hospital."

I'm on my feet so fast, my pen rattles to the floor, and the back of the chair thuds against the wall. "When?"

"Just now, sir. Would you like us to cancel the card and issue a new one?"

"No. Approve the transaction and activate the card." It's all I can do not to curse and bite the guy's head off.

"I'm sorry, the transaction was declined automatically. We can't approve it at this point. But I can activate the card for you now if you'd like."

Fuck. "Do that, thanks. Do you need anything else?"

"No, sir. That's all. Thank you for choosing—"

I hang up before the guy can finish his customer-service spiel. Then I'm out, tossing, "Family emergency, I'll check in with you later," to my assistant in the outer office, along with, "And find out why Cricket's benefits card isn't working."

Every eye in the room follows me as I storm toward the door. I hope my emergency comment is an exaggeration. I shouldn't be in the position of hoping, of not knowing why Cricket's at a hospital. Whatever the reason, I should already be there, by her side. I would be, if I hadn't pushed her away.

The second I'm in the car, connected to the Bluetooth, I call her. Four rings later, I get her voicemail. "End call," I say before her soft voice reaches the end of her recorded message. Either she's ignoring me, or she's unavailable to answer. I hope to fuck it's the first thing.

Traffic is thick, and it takes twenty minutes to get to the hospital. Another five to find a parking spot. I'm outside the main entrance when it hits me—I don't know where to go from here. In more ways than one.

I pull up Gina's contact and hit the Call button, barking at her the instant we get connected. "Cricket's at Eastridge Hospital. Do you know why?"

"Yes."

If she wasn't my daughter, I'd lose it. More than I already have. I close my eyes and take a breath. Regroup. Focus. If Cricket was hurt, or in trouble, Gina would have called me. I need to get my shit together. Everything is going to be fine.

Gina's heavy sigh drifts through the speaker. "She's there for a biopsy."

"What?" Everything is *not* fine. "Why didn't someone tell me about this? I had to find out she's at the hospital from the fucking credit card company. Do you know what time the appointment is, or what floor it's on?"

"Geez, Dad. For a guy who doesn't want to be part of her life, you sure are worked up about being excluded from it."

"Gina Marie, this isn't the time for your attitude. You're not too old to be grounded."

"And you're not too old to have a happy, long-lasting marriage with Cricket. Think about that on your way to the second-floor C-wing."

"Thanks." That's all I've got right now. There's no time to have this conversation with my daughter. I hope to hell there's still time to have it with Cricket.

troy

I'm grateful for Gina's hint, but there are a lot of doors in the C-wing, and I'm on the fourth one before I find Cricket.

Her eyes open wide at the sight of me. She doesn't speak when I take the seat beside her. Doesn't resist when I take her hand and thread our fingers together. But she doesn't smile either. Doesn't turn to look at me. Neither of which I deserve.

"I should've been here from the start," I say. "Here and any other appointments I've missed. I should've been with you every step of the way."

"It's fine." Her voice is quiet, her gaze focused on the wall across the room. "I didn't expect you to come to my appointments, or...anything."

Because I was a huge asshole. A stupid fucking bastard.

"Cricket," a nurse says, opening an inner-office door. "We're ready for you."

I rise along with Cricket, squeezing her hand tighter when she tries moving away. "Wait." Meeting the nurse's gaze, I ask, "Would it be possible for me to have a minute with my wife before she goes in? I'm sorry to hold you up, I was late getting here. I promise it won't take long."

"Of course." The nurse nods at me, then at Cricket. "Come back when you're ready."

There's a woman in the small waiting room, another behind the counter built into the interior wall. Not an optimal setting for what I need to say, but that's on me.

I take Cricket's second hand and bring us face-to-face. "I thought setting you free would be the best thing for you, in the long run. But I was an asshole, treating you the way I did, and I've spent every minute since regretting hurting you. I was wrong to take the decision from you. It's ours to make, not mine. I don't deserve another shot, but I'm asking for one. Let me be here for you. With you. As your husband, for as long as you'll have me."

"You want to stay married?" she whispers. "Really married?" Her beautiful eyes turn glassy when I nod.

I need to make sure that sheen is from impending happy tears. I drop to one knee and stare up at this woman who owns my fucking heart. "I love you, Cricket. I'm crazy in love with you. I'd be the luckiest man on earth if you'd marry me, again. Because you want to this time. Be mine. Every day, for the rest of our lives."

A smile that could light the world—it definitely lights up mine—breaks across her face. "Yes," she says, head bobbing. She gasps when I scoop her off her feet while rising. "Are you sure?" Her soft voice slides into my ear while I'm hugging her. "If this is because of the biopsy—"

"It's because I need you. I don't know how I lived without you before, but I don't want to do it anymore. Let me spend forever showing you how much I love you."

"I love you too," she says, burying her face against my chest when I return her feet to the ground.

It's not the place for the kiss I want to give her. *Need* to give her. I tip her chin up and settle for one that's PG-rated. Except, it's never settling when I'm with her. It's fucking everything. Even the small taste sends blood rushing to my dick. I press it against her, smiling against her lips when her breath catches.

Someone clears their throat behind me. A subtle time's-up.

I drop a kiss on her nose while easing back. "Can I go in

with you, hold your hand during the procedure?" I force myself to remain calm when she shakes her head. "Then I'll be right here, waiting to take you home."

To our home. To our bed. To our future.

epilogue

. . .

cricket

BEYOND THE HEAVY DOUBLE DOORS, the church's organist begins playing *A Thousand Years*. The notes tug at the corners of my mouth, drawing it into a smile that chases the nerves away.

"Whatever makes you happy, sweetheart," were Troy's exact words when I asked if he'd be okay with a non-traditional wedding march. That's his answer to everything. The best part is, he's not saying it out of disinterest. He truly means the words.

In the eight months we've been married, he's shown me, over and over, how much he values my happiness. How much he loves me. After my cancer diagnosis, he held me, let me soak him with tears, night after night. He was by my side through pre-op, the lumpectomy, and radiation appointments. The surgery hasn't changed the way he looks at me—or how much he wants me. He still worships my boobs every chance he gets. Both of them. The scarred, misshapen one gets as much of his hungry attention as its fully intact partner.

"It's time." Gina squeezes my hand before stepping forward to open the doors. She's wearing a pink bridesmaid dress this time around. Breast-cancer-ribbon pink, to be exact. Her choice. My best friend looks beautiful. I couldn't love her more if I tried.

Every eye in the packed church turns toward Gina. Then, once she's reached her position to one side of the altar, those eyes are all on me. The weight of their stares barely registers as I walk down the aisle. No, as I *float* down the aisle, toward my husband. He's all I see. The way he's watching me, I know I'm all he sees, too.

Some people think this wedding doesn't mean anything. They couldn't be more wrong. Our first ceremony was intense, exciting, and perfect. Today's is steeped in deep emotion. It's perfect too, in a different way. A celebration of our unexpected, resilient, unstoppable love.

"Jesus, you're so fucking beautiful."

I can't help giggling when the minister chokes at Troy's language. "You're pretty fucking hot, yourself."

Behind me, Gina mumbles something that sounds very much like, *Get a room*, before she reaches over to divest me of my bridal bouquet. Then it's showtime. But not for the dozens of family, friends, and whomever else Troy stuffed into the church because he wanted the whole world to see us this time. This showtime is for us.

The first time we swore our vows before God, we didn't expect them to last. Neither of us realized the other's true feelings, or fully accepted our own. We didn't appreciate the promises made in those vows. We do now. Saying the same words today, looking into each other's eyes, hearts, and souls, is a new beginning and a homecoming, rolled into one.

"You may kiss your wife," the minister says, adjusting the traditional statement to fit our situation.

"I love you, sweetheart." Troy cups my face, his clear, adoring gaze locked with mine. "Forever."

"I love you too." I barely get the words out before his mouth seals to mine. The rest of the world fades away with the first sweep of Troy's tongue. His moan rumbles through me, straight to my core. Arms twined behind his neck, I press myself against him, as close as two fully clothed people with a roomful of onlookers can get.

This time, Gina's, "Get a room!" is at full volume, and it evokes laughter, whistling, and clapping from our guests.

My face is flushed with heat when we break the kiss. Not from embarrassment, though. The heat is entirely Troy's doing. "What do you say, hot husband? Should we skip the reception and move straight to the honeymoon?"

To my surprise, he shakes his head. "No way I'm giving up the chance to dance with my beautiful wife in her fairytale-princess dress."

"I do feel like I'm living a fairytale. Thank you for being the handsome prince who swept in and claimed me."

His smile gets a wicked-sexy edge. "I've got a lot more *claiming* in store for you, Mrs. Mannington. It's going to be fucking hot in Jamaica next week."

"Then hurry up and take me to the ball, Mr. Mannington, so we can get to the hot honeymoon fucking."

His husky laugh ripples through me, then my feet leave the ground as my sexy, alpha prince twirls me around, right there in front of everyone. Happily-ever-after isn't just for fairytales.

**Join Karla's mailing list to stay up-to-date on all of Karla's new releases, sales, and more.
www.karladoyle.com/newsletter**

Thank you for reading Wedded Miss! I hope you enjoyed this steamy and sweet romance. I'd be so grateful if you have a few minutes to leave a review or rating BookBub, Goodreads, your favorite book retailer, or wherever you like talking about books!

Keep reading! **The Deal With Love** is next up and guaranteed to satisfy your craving for steamy age-gap romance!

the deal with love

THE DEAL
with Love

A HOPE HARBOR ROMANCE

KARLA DOYLE

the deal with love

They agreed to a hot summer fling.
Falling in love wasn't part of the deal...

adam

Fresh out of a bitter divorce, I jump at the opportunity to sublet my friend's rental in a sleepy, lakeside town. Four weeks in solo mode will reset my priorities to business, where they should have been all along.

That plan changes when I catch my pretty neighbor spying on me while I work out. Sparks fly when I accidentally see her naked. Suddenly, my stay in the quiet, slow-paced town has the potential to be a lot more exciting and a lot less solitary...if Allison accepts my proposal.

allison

A year after dumping my cheating, former high-school sweetheart, my heart has finally healed. I may never find true love, but I'm ready to move forward.

When the combination of my meddlesome best friend, unbelievably poor timing, and exceptionally bad balance leads to an embarrassing naked encounter with the attractive man renting my neighbor's cottage, I have a choice: Hole up in my house to avoid him, or accept Adam's invitation to be neighbors with benefits for the duration of his stay in Hope Harbor.

Technically, he's old enough to be my father, but he's the furthest thing from it. This is the perfect summer fling, until my heart wants more...

chapter 1

. . .

allison

"ALLY, come here. Quickly. There's a hot, half-naked man in your neighbor's backyard."

In the kitchen, I finish stirring sweetener into my coffee, then take my time rinsing the spoon. No need to hurry. The hot man my friend is currently ogling from the patio door will still be there when I reach the living room.

Esme blindly accepts the mug I place in her hand. "Oh my God, Ally, look at him."

"*Mmmhmm.* I have. I am." Together, we sip our coffee in silence while watching the hard-bodied specimen perform several minutes of intensive physical activity.

Esme sighs as the object of our infatuation switches from pushups on the patio to pullups at a steel bar attached to the shed. "Since when does the little old lady who owns the house next door have exercise equipment in her backyard?"

"Since the current renter mounted that bar, three days ago."

"If he's looking for something else to mount, sign me up."

My burst of laughter carries through the screen to the joined yards, drawing the man's attention. "Oh my God!" I jump aside, out of view, a move mirrored by my equally nosy best friend. "He saw us. He knows we were watching him."

"Maybe that's a good thing." Esme nods toward the sliding door we abandoned. "Now you have a reason to go talk to him."

"First of all, what makes you think I haven't talked to him already? Second of all, how does getting caught gawking at him while he exercises give me a reason to go talk to him?"

"Let's start with the 'first of all.' Have you talked to him yet?"

"No." Not a single word uttered. Merely waving in passing has rendered me tongue-tied. "He's only been there a few days. I haven't had an opportunity."

Esme smirks. Probably reading my mind, or, at minimum, the blush currently heating my face.

"Okay, fine. I've avoided talking to him because he's so good-looking, he intimidates me. Happy now?"

"I won't be happy until you're happy. And you won't be happy until you get some action."

"I don't need a man in my life to be happy."

"I agree. You don't need a serious relationship. But you do need some dick. Some short-term, no-strings-attached, sizeable dick." Esme peeks around the curtain, smiling as she nods. "And those sweat-drenched, gray gym shorts indicate your new, temporary neighbor meets the size criteria."

"Oh, he does." I wince as soon as the words leave my

mouth. I could say I also noticed the thick bulge in his shorts, but Esme would see through the lie. My best friend has one of the best bullshit detectors in Hope Harbor. I'd probably still be married to a cheating bastard if not for Esme's intuition.

"Tell me what you know," Esme says. "Describe every long, thick detail."

"I don't need to. When he's finished his workout, you'll see for yourself."

Not much shocks Esme, but her eyes nearly pop out of her head. "Are you serious—he's going to get naked out there? Does he think he rented a cottage at a naturalist resort?"

"He's doesn't strip outside." I swallow a mouthful of coffee to alleviate the husky rasp lacing my voice. "He takes his shorts off in the kitchen. Then stands there, naked, until he's finished with whatever post-workout concoction he drinks."

"Oh my God, you've totally been peeping this guy!"

"It's not peeping." The brilliant July sun might as well be inside my head, my cheeks are that hot. "I just happen to be standing at my sink, washing dishes, when he's in his kitchen, mixing his drink." Oh, the mixing. The way his biceps pop, and the subtle sway of his cock as he shakes the plastic tumbler. I could watch him shake those drinks all day long. Emphasis on long.

"Your eyes are all glazed over and you're drooling."

I slap a hand over my mouth—dry, by the way—then glare at my friend. "Jerk."

"Sticks and stones and all that." Esme shrugs, her gaze shifting to the neighboring yard. "Ooh, he's walking toward the house. Let's move this peeping party to your kitchen, so I can see the package that has you all worked up."

"I'm not worked up."

"And I'm not easily impressed, but after that exhibition in the yard, I'm sure as hell not going to miss the rest of the show."

I follow Esme to the kitchen, where we stand shoulder-to-shoulder at the sink. "Can you please be quiet, at least?"

"*Me?*" Her mouth falls open. "You're the one whose laughter got us caught."

"I know, I know. Him seeing us standing together at the patio door was bad, but it's believable that we were checking out my garden, or my new lawn furniture."

Esme snorts. "You have three tomato plants and a row of spindly lettuce. Your lawn chairs definitely aren't new, and they were scratch-and-dent when you bought them."

"Geez, Es. With friends like you, I don't need enemies."

"With a friend like me, you don't need any more friends."

True. But I'm not going to admit it while she's looking smug. "Mrs. Maguire rents her house for monthlong intervals, meaning I have to live beside him for the rest of July. I'd rather not feel humiliated every time we cross paths. If he sees us crammed together, staring out this small window, he's going to know we're checking him out."

"Does he have a woman staying with him, or is he alone?"

"Alone."

"Then I don't see the problem with letting him know you're interested," she says.

"Except that I'm *not* interested."

My bestie gives another shrug. "If that's true, then you won't mind if *I'm* interested, right?"

"Yes, I will mind. Since neither of our houses have central air-conditioning, the windows are open a lot. I don't want to hear you having sex with my neighbor, even if he is only temporary."

"Then I'll invite him to my house. You won't hear a thing from three blocks away." Esme waggles her dark-brown eyebrows. "Or, maybe you will..."

My temporary neighbor brings our conversation to a halt the moment he steps inside the small bungalow—and peels off his shorts.

Beside me, Esme sucks in a breath. "Oh my God, look at it."

As if I could do anything else when the most hung man I've ever seen in real life is directly in my sightline.

"How long do you think it is?" Esme asks, as Mr. Well-Endowed begins the process of measuring powder from a large, plastic tub into his clear, plastic shaker cup.

"Eight inches."

The weight of Esme's gaze bores into my profile. "You sure came up with that answer quickly. You've obviously given this some thought."

"I may have done some online research."

Esme snorts again. "I hope you used a private browsing window for that search."

Nope. I didn't think to do that. The recent crop of sexy ads in my Facebook feed and influx of spammy emails in my inbox make more sense now.

"I think you're probably right about the eight inches." Esme's focus returns to the scenery next door. "And that's just hanging around, minding its own business. I wonder how big it gets when he's not relaxed. Have you seen it hard?"

"No." Not for lack of trying. I've checked every window on the east side of my house since he unloaded his suitcases from the Lexus parked out front. The kitchen-to-kitchen access is the one-and-only vantage point. So far, all he's done in there is some very enticing beverage mixing.

"Well, one of us is going to find out. We both need the big D, but I'm giving you dibs, since you need it more urgently than I do. But if you don't go for him, I will."

Across the narrow buffer separating the houses, my personal July centerfold begins shaking his post-workout drink. The mesmerizing sway of his swinging dick brings a hush over my kitchen, giving me a reprieve from Esme's ultimatum.

"He has a great butt, too," Esme says, as he turns to exit his kitchen.

"Yup."

Great view gone, Esme shifts her stance, resting her hip against the counter, arms crossed over her chest. "He's got a lot of silver in his hair, but it's hard to guess his age with that body."

"Lots of guys go gray at a young age. Eddie Sherman was fully silver by the time he hit twenty-two."

"True, but I don't think your sexy neighbor is part of the early-to-go-gray group. I'd bet he's older. Like, silver-fox older."

"How old do you think he is?"

Esme's lips and nose scrunch up as she contemplates. "Fifty?"

My stomach bottoms out. "That old, really?"

"Fifty isn't *old*, Ally. It's middle-aged."

"My dad is fifty-six."

"Well, the guy next door isn't your dad. Though, if you want to call him Daddy, there's no shame in that, either." Esme laughs while ducking my playful jab. "Besides, you're only going to fuck him, not spend the rest of your life with him, so the age gap between you won't matter."

"It definitely won't matter, since I haven't agreed to approach him yet."

A wicked smile curves Esme's mouth. "You said 'yet.' That means you're calling dibs."

Crap, am I? Yes, apparently, I am. "Fine, dibs." I imitate her crossed-arms stance. "But I'm only calling it so you don't."

"The reason doesn't matter, only that you do it. And by 'do it,' I mean *do it*." Lest there be any doubt, Esme adds finger actions. "I'm serious, Ally. This is a prime opportunity for you to get back on the horse. Go fuck that stallion next door until you're walking bowlegged and can't remember your stupid ex-husband's name."

"Dennis really was stupid."

"*Is* stupid, Ally. Regrettably, all you could do was divorce him, not kill him."

I mimic one of Esme's patented snorts, laughing until I sigh. "The first year after I caught him was awful. I'm doing a lot better now."

"Damn right, you are." Esme nods. "Now get freshened up, put on your sexiest underwear, and march over there."

"What, like, *now*?"

"Exactly. No time like the present."

I shake my head as if I've been instructed to jump off the lift bridge. "I can't just knock on his door, out of the blue. I need an excuse. Or, I could find a way to casually and coincidentally be outside when he is, or—"

"Ally." Esme grips my shoulders and drills me with a stare. "You're a beautiful, intelligent, single woman. You don't need an excuse or a contrived meet-cute. You just walk over there and knock on his door."

"And then what?"

"Then he smiles at his gorgeous, surprise visitor. You

smile back. Introduce yourself. You offer a handshake, and when he accepts it, you hang on to his hand longer than a regular handshake would last. While you're holding his hand, you tilt your head a little and subtly bat your eyelashes."

Admittedly, it sounds like a good plan so far. But the plan only has me at his doorstep. "And when I have to let go of his hand—because if I don't, I'll look like a crazed stalker —then what?"

"Then, he'll either invite you inside, which you accept immediately, or you invite him for dinner and a tour of our quaint little town."

That doesn't sound too forward. Not at all. Just a friendly gesture, one I'd feasibly extend to anybody renting my neighbor's cottage, though I never have before. Yes, I can totally do this.

"Oh, and make sure you have a condom in your pocket, just in case he doesn't have any on hand."

And, I'm back to no, no way, not happening. I'll learn to embrace my single status eventually, but I'll never be the woman carrying a condom in my pocket, *just in case*.

"I'll think about it," I say, backing away from Esme, the window, and my momentary blip of courage.

Esme huffs and rolls her eyes. "Ugh, I pushed too far. You went all deer-in-the-headlights the second I said 'condom.' Forget I suggested it. If he doesn't have any, you'll wait until the second date to hide his salami."

"Oh, God."

"Hold on to those words. Maybe you'll be screaming them later."

I laugh because it's funny. My subsequent gurgle is because it wasn't. "I don't think I can do this, Es. I've only been with one guy, and the sex was never scream-worthy. I don't have the experience or confidence to do what you're suggesting."

"You don't need experience, and I know you've got the confidence. I've watched you work. You've been the top salesperson at the car dealership for the last two years. People walk in off the street with a 'just looking' mentality, then you send them out in a new car. You're magic, Ally. Nobody can say no to you."

"People come to the dealership because they're at least *curious* about the cars. I don't go out to the street and cold-sell to complete strangers who've shown no interest."

"Ah, I see."

"So, you understand?" The knot in my stomach loosens as Esme nods. "Thank you. I know you're trying to help me kickstart my love life, and I *will* get back in the saddle. Soon. It just has to be on my terms."

"And on your turf."

"Yes, exactly."

Esme nods again. "I'm going to head out. It's garbage night at my grandma's house."

"Your favorite."

"Ugh, it's so not. If she'd just let me load the half bag of garbage into my trunk and take it away, it'd be so much easier. But, no. Every week we go through the routine of her protesting that the bag will stink up my car, while also lamenting how embarrassed she'll be if her neighbors see how much trash she has. It's ridiculous. And I always end up taking the garbage." The warmth in Esme's tone overrides the mild annoyance in her words. "I should visit her more. Then garbage night could just be a quick task, not a drawn-out event."

"Good plan."

"Plans *are* good. Keep the one we discussed in mind, okay?"

"I will." I draw her into a besties-are-the-best hug. "Say hi to your grandma for me."

"Will do. Say hi to Mr. Well Hung for me."

"Haha, *won't* do." After Esme shows herself out, I head toward the bathroom, where I strip—in privacy, as normal people do—while drawing a bath.

Five minutes later, I'm chin-deep in peach-scented bubbles. Freshening up, but with a different endgame. The only action I'll get tonight will be courtesy of my vibrator. And maybe my dildo, too. Talking about sex—specifically, sex with a well-endowed man—rekindled some old longings. Orgasms are great, obviously. Those I can provide for myself. But the sensation of being filled with hot, hard, throbbing cock... My dildo can't truly replace that. I really should get back on the horse soon.

I pull the rubber stopper and step out of the old house's original, clawfoot tub. The loud, rhythmic glug of draining water replaces the sounds of a July evening that filtered through the bathroom window during my bath. I towel off, release my hair from the clip holding it in a messy heap on my head, and swivel to collect my robe from the hook on the door.

"Shit." No robe, yet again. I need to buy a second robe. Then I'll always have one waiting. Or, more likely, I'll leave them both in my bedroom, and still have to streak across the living room after a bath.

No big deal. It only takes a few seconds to cross from the bathroom to the bedroom. Unlike the guy next door, I won't be hanging out—and letting it all hang out—in front of the window.

I open the bathroom door and begin the dash, shrieking

at the sight of Mr. Let It All Hang Out, currently fully clothed and standing at my patio door. Distraction leads to panic, which goes hand-in-hand with clumsiness.

My shin connects with the coffee table in a solid *thwack*, and a stuck-pig shriek leaves my mouth. Face contorted in what has to be a wholly unattractive combination of pain and humiliation, I grab my throbbing shin, lose my balance, and pancake on the floor—right in front of the door.

Forehead pressed against the carpet, I send up a pointless prayer. *Please, God, let this be a figment of my cruel imagination.* Deep breath in, I turn my head to the side, and groan. Not my imagination, just my cruel reality.

"Are you okay?" he asks through the screen.

I'm not the only person to see their neighbor in the raw today. Mr. Handsome now has an up-close view of *my* naked ass. My white, untoned, pimple-on-the-right-cheek ass. I might never be okay again.

chapter 2

. . .

adam

I ALWAYS KNOW what do to. When to do it. The who, how, where, and why. About business. Investments. Cars. Women.

Now all I can do is stand here and gawk. Gawk and ask stupid questions. Time to take action.

Her pretty blue eyes nearly pop out of her head as I slide the screen door across its track. "Don't come in here, I'm totally naked."

"I noticed." My dick is currently showing its appreciation by pressing against my fly. I shut the door behind me and step around her to grab a thin blanket from the couch. I fan it over her body, the slinky material molding to her curves as if it can't get close enough. Lucky fucking blanket.

"Thank you." Her polite words are in opposition to her glare, as she stands while wrapping herself tightly enough to cut off circulation. "Now, kindly tell me why you were peeking through my patio door, then please turn around and disappear back through it."

I bite the inside of my cheek, but it doesn't fully conceal my amusement. My smile has charmed plenty of women over the years. It doesn't appear to be inspiring hot—or even lukewarm—feelings in the woman standing before me.

And damn, if that doesn't make her appealing. *More* appealing. Because...those curves. Her beautiful face. Consider me hooked.

"I'm waiting," she says.

So am I, though not for long. My spontaneous vacation now has a goal other than escaping judgmental looks from people who believe my ex-wife's bullshit, which seems to be just about everyone. "Sorry for startling you." I extend my hand. "Adam Foster. I'm renting the place next door for the month."

"I noticed." The tiniest hint of a smile pulls at her mouth. Her lips part as she slides her palm against mine.

"I noticed you noticing." Instinct demands I move closer, and I never argue with my instincts. "And I didn't mind you noticing." I sweep my thumb across her soft skin, my gaze dropping to the rise and fall of her breasts where she clutches a handful of pink material. "I know I should apologize for seeing you naked, but I can't be sorry for that, because you're unforgettably gorgeous and sexy."

A shade similar to the blanket tints the tops of her cheeks. "Are you hitting on me, after catching me naked and walking into my house uninvited?" The question might lean toward an accusation, if not for her hand, still willingly connected to mine, or the glassy quality of her gaze, as she continues making eye contact.

"I didn't intend to do any of those things tonight, but yes, I am."

"Well, I...I'm not ready. I mean, technically, I am. I just had a bath and I have the box of divorce condoms Esme gave me in my nightstand drawer. You're very attractive and fit, and, well...you know. Obviously, you know. It's your body. But I'm not mentally ready. So, I'm sorry, but my answer is no."

I've met some interesting women over the years, but the pretty brunette with the gift for nervous rambling is at the top of the list. "Thanks for the answer, but I haven't asked you anything yet."

She slow-blinks while jerking her hand away. "Right. Well...why were you staring into my house?"

"I'll answer that question if you will," I say, giving her a wink.

"You saw me through the kitchen window?" She stumbles backward as I nod, nearly tripping over the arm of the sofa in the process.

"Careful." I catch her elbow before she loses her balance *and* her blanket. Not that I'd mind seeing her naked again. Especially not with the electricity racing through me from the simple, innocent contact.

She feels it, too. No words necessary to relay that message, her jackhammering pulse and the deep blush painting her face give her away.

I release her arm and slide my hands into my pockets. Just because she seemed interested in watching me from across the yard doesn't mean she'll enjoy seeing the front of my shorts balloon up as if an airbag has gone off in there. Which is how it's beginning to feel. Things are getting pretty damn crowded.

"I wasn't staring through your patio door," I say. "I had just walked up when you streaked past."

"Why were you there at all?"

"Your friend stopped by a few minutes ago, and asked me to pop over here. She said you need muscle to loosen something up."

"Oh my God, she did that? And said that?"

"It's not a problem," I say, nodding. "What I lack in subtlety, I make up for with strength. Point me in the direction of whatever's tight, and I'll see what I can do."

Her *grrr* sounds more like a frustrated kitten than an angry bear. "I'm going to kill Esme."

"For trying to get you help?"

"For trying to get me laid!"

A gut-deep laugh bursts from my mouth. Not a welcome sound, based on the razor-sharp glare currently directed my way. "Sorry."

"I'm glad you think the prospect of me getting laid is amusing."

"Not amusing. The suggestion that a beautiful, sexy woman would need help getting laid is hilarious."

"Oh. That's not so bad." She exhales in an adorable huff, then extends her hand. "I'm Allison. Or Ally. Either is fine."

Taking her hand gives me the opportunity to close the distance between us by half a step. "Which would you prefer I call you? Because I do plan on talking with you as much as possible over the next three and half weeks. Assuming you're not completely pissed off at me for invading your privacy."

Her lips curve into a kissable smile. "Not completely."

I could stare at her mouth for the remainder of the evening and call it a good night. But I've never been one to settle for *good* when great is within reach. "What's your preference? Allison, or Ally?"

"Allison."

"Very pretty." I squeeze gently before releasing her hand. "It's nice to meet you, Allison."

"You too. And I didn't mean to invade your privacy, either. In my defense, I'm not used to having a neighbor worth gawking at."

I'm not arrogant, but I also don't do fake modesty, so I take the compliment with a laugh and a grin. "Now that we've got our naked-gawking apologies out of the way, how about we get to know each other better?"

"Are you hitting on me again, while I'm still basically naked?"

"Not with that simple invitation. Say yes and I'll up my game."

"And that's what it would be if I said yes, a game?"

"No. No games," I say, shaking my head. "Just a short-term, fast-paced, satisfying adventure between two people who've already been honest about their mutual, physical attraction."

"That's quite an invitation."

Might as well be completely upfront with her. "I'm a recently divorced, workaholic CEO of a multi-billion-dollar company. I'm in town for a month. At the end of July, I'll pack my bags and head back to Toronto, and the likelihood I'll come back to Hope Harbor is a slim margin I wouldn't advise investing in. If you're looking for somebody to get serious and plan a future with, I'm not that guy. But, if you're interested in a few weeks of good company and great sex, I'm your man."

Her eyebrows rise as she nods. "Wow, okay. That's... brutally honest."

"I prefer honesty in advertising."

"I prefer honesty in everything."

It could have been a general statement, but my gut tells me otherwise. "Then we can add honesty to the list of things we have in common. If I tell you something, count on it being the truth. There'd be a lot less disappointment in the world if everybody spoke from the heart—and also believed the words they heard."

"Sounds like my short-term neighbor has a long-term backstory."

"Don't we all?" I ask, and she nods again. "Anything you want to know about me, ask away."

"You're assuming I'm going to say yes to getting to know you better."

"I am." Another going-with-my-gut thing. "I'll head next door and let you get dressed, though I doubt anything you wear could look better than that blanket."

"Are you insulting my fashion sense, or do you have some weird blanket fetish?"

"Neither. I like the way the blanket hugs your curves. Plus, it's kind of see-through." I smile while taking the few required steps to the patio door, slide it open, and step outside. "I'll be ready when you are."

"Are you always this cocky?" she asks, moving closer to the screen as I close it.

"Confident. And yes."

"Confident, cocky, whatever. Different words that mean the same thing."

"Cockiness is bravado. Confidence is rooted in competence. Come knock on my door and I'll show you there's a difference."

"That sounds pretty cocky to me," she calls, as I cross the joined yards.

When I turn, I find her pressed against the screen, the dark mesh unable to mask her bright smile. Walking backward—with confidence—I raise one hand and make a knocking gesture. "See you soon, Allison."

allison

The hangers scrape against the wooden bar in my closet as I push the clothes back-and-forth for the fifth time. What to wear to an impromptu date that will undoubtedly lead to sex with an almost stranger? I have no idea.

But Esme will. Esme will have lots of ideas. *All* the ideas, in fact.

Since I'll end up telling my best friend everything about this night anyway, I might as well benefit from some guidance upfront. I abandon the closet to retrieve my phone from the bed, where it waits alongside the box of condoms. Yes, that's right, I'm going to be *that* woman after all.

> You are in so much trouble! My hot neighbor was standing at the patio door when I got out of the bath, and he saw me naked. Totally freaking naked! Luckily for you, he liked what he saw. Now he wants me to go over there and have sex with him. What should I wear?

I hit send on the message, then begin silently counting. *One Mississippi, two Mississippi, three Mississippi, four Mississippi*—

"Hello," I say, answering on the first ring.

"Oh my God, oh my God! He saw you naked? And you're actually going over there to fuck him? Like, right now?" An eardrum-piercing shriek follows, then one final, "Oh my God!"

"I guess you think I should do it."

"Of course you should do it. You should 'do it' as many times as he's physically capable."

"That could be a lot of times, since he suggested we be neighbors with benefits for July."

"He did? God, he's bold. Assuming he knows how to use what he's packing, you are in for one long—*ahem*—hot month."

"What if he doesn't know how to use it? Just because he's attractive and well-hung doesn't mean he'll be a porn star in the bedroom." Something I know from experience. My ex was one of the best-looking guys in high school, and while his cock wasn't as big as Adam's, it was a decent size. Neither of those attributes made him good in bed. Nothing did.

"Ally, anybody will be better than douchebag Dennis, the two-minute man. You're actually lucky he cheated on you. Otherwise, you would've spent the rest of your life having shitty sex."

True. But not what I want to talk about. "Okay, so what should I wear tonight?" I raise my index finger, even though my friend can't see it. "Keeping in mind that I haven't one-hundred percent decided if I'm going to go through with the doing *it* part. So, don't suggest anything *too* sexy."

Esme's snort rumbles through the line. "You don't own anything that falls into the 'too sexy' category. You own church clothes. Period."

"Not true. I have that one pink top with the lowcut neckline."

"I know the top you're talking about, and it's a regular V-neck, not something extra-lowcut. Plus, you own *one top* that shows your cleavage." Critique finished, Esme sighs. "If you don't want to wear sexy clothes, then don't. But we both know the real reason you've been shopping in the grandma section since high school. Dennis doesn't get to make you feel inadequate anymore. Not that he ever should have, but that's a pointless conversation now. The point that matters is—this is *your* life, Ally. Live it any damn way you want."

Phone pressed to my ear, I flop on the bed, turning to stare at the condom box. Again.

Esme's right. It's my life. I spent the past year recovering from his betrayal. Now, it's time to break out of the mold I allowed him to make for my life.

"Thanks, Es," I say, rising and moving toward the daunting row of hangers.

"Do you know what you're going to do?"

"Nope. But I know what I'm *not* going to do, and that's stay home alone, overthinking everything and doing nothing."

"Good." Esme's laugh drifts through the line. "I can hear you rifling through the closet. Since you're not going to waste time overthinking, just close your eyes, turn in a circle, then reach in and grab something. Whatever it is, just go with it."

"Alright, I'm going in. Hang on and I'll tell you what I pick." Phone clutched in one hand, I squeeze all the clothes tightly together, then turned a few circles. Sufficiently disoriented, I grab at air, until my fingertips connect with fabric. All traces of excitement shrivel when I open my eyes, and see the dress I randomly selected. "Best two out of three?"

"No do-overs. Just go with it, remember?"

"If you say so." I remove the dress from the closet, toss it on the bed, then switch to texting app and send a photo.

"Oh my God, I can't believe you still have that." Esme's riotous laughter rings through the call. "Okay, I'll let you go, so you can get dressed."

"Come on, you don't actually want me to wear *that* tonight."

"I made it, and you kept it after the event, so I say, go for it. It'll certainly make things interesting."

"You're a cruel best friend."

Esme snorts. "But still the best."

"True. Okay, then...wish me luck."

"Nope. You don't need luck. Whatever you want from this night, you just go out and get it. Got it?"

"Got it." Nobody's here to see me nod, but I do it. Affirmation required. "Bye, Es."

"Have fun, you lucky ducky!" One last laugh filters through the phone before Esme ends the call.

"Bitch," I say to the dead air on the other end, though I didn't really mean it anyway. It's not my best friend's fault I kept the duck-patterned dress she made for me to wear to a work event. Nor did I have to wear it tonight. As Esme had pointed out, this is *my* life. I answer only to myself now.

Time to get dressed. I have an adventure to begin.

chapter 3

. . .

allison

IF A LACE THONG can be considered "big girl panties," I've pulled them up, and I'm ready to go. Of course, my handsome neighbor might take one look at this dress, laugh, and withdraw his come-knock-on-my-door offer. I'll soon find out.

I lock my house and cut across the backyards, feeling sneakier than I have in...well, ever. Sneaking isn't my go-to. I've never had desire or reason to do anything I wouldn't be proud of, or that I wouldn't be willing to tell my parents. Until now. I'm definitely not mentioning *this* adventure over Sunday supper.

Heart pounding against my ribs, I give the classic triple-knock on Mrs. Maguire's legitimately vintage wooden door. Then I paste on a smile I hope doesn't look too crazy. I should've practiced in front of the mirror. Too late now.

Adam's tall, broad form fills much of the doorway when he appears on the other side of the screen. "Allison." He smiles while pushing the door open with one arm. "I was wrong about the blanket. You look even sexier in that dress."

"Patronizing me isn't a good way to start this arrangement," I say, narrowing my gaze while slipping past.

"I would never." Serious words, yet humor laces his smooth, deep voice.

"Mmmhmm. I'm sure."

He motions me to move deeper into the house. "I assume you know your way around in here."

"I've been in here a few times over the years. I'm familiar with the kitchen and living room. I've never been in the bedrooms."

"You haven't missed much." Hand spanning the small of my back, he leans in to slide the next word directly into my ear. "Yet."

A shiver ripples through me, raising goose bumps on my arms and tightening my nipples to hard peaks. Maybe this neighbors-with-benefits thing won't be so awkward after all.

He trails his fingers around the side of my waistline while walking away. "Would you like a drink? I have wine, Scotch, beer, or sparkling water."

"What are you having?" Ugh, such a wishy-washy-woman question. I need to work on that.

"Wine. It's a cabernet sauvignon, nice and full-bodied, if you enjoy a dry red."

"Alcohol has never been a great choice for me. I have a low tolerance, and tend to miss the 'do not cross' line until it's behind me, then end up regretting it the next day."

He nods and turns toward the fridge. "Sparkling water it is."

Karla Doyle

"You're not going to try to convince me to have an alcoholic drink, so I loosen up and we can have some fun?"

"Definitely not. I wasn't that kind of guy at twenty, and I'm sure not that kind of man at forty-six."

"You're forty-six." Well, poop. I really hoped Esme had overestimated his age, preferably by a larger margin than four years.

"I am." He doesn't ask the obvious return question. Just carries on with our evening, leaning into Mrs. Maguire's ancient, white Frigidaire, which hums louder than my dad at Sunday service.

At least Adam is younger than my dad. A full decade younger.

Adam's still in his forties. That seemed less...old.

I'm being ridiculous, worrying about the age difference. Adam is hot. Handsome. Temporary. So what if I'm twenty years younger? I have a full-time job, a crushing mortgage payment, and a divorce. It doesn't get much more adult than that.

"Wait," I say, as he reappears from the fridge with a bottle of Perrier in one hand. "I'm going to have wine instead."

He meets my gaze while setting the bottle on the counter. "There's no pressure to have alcohol. No pressure about anything."

"I appreciate that."

"No appreciation necessary, Allison. It's respect. You're a beautiful, sexy woman, and I think we'd both enjoy exploring the spark between us. But it'll only happen if you want it to, and it's a decision you have to make while you're sober."

"I want it to. I wouldn't have come over here tonight if I didn't."

"And my night is already better because you knocked on the door." Holding my gaze, he leans back and curls his hands around the laminate countertop. "Tonight, and anytime we're together, I want you to know I'll respect you. No matter how dirty things get, no means no, always. If your yes becomes no, I'll respect it. If you decide you're no longer interested, you walk out the door, and I let you."

"Simple as that?"

He gives a single nod. "Simple as that. I'm proposing we have a good time together—I'm not proposing. You exit as easily as you entered. No hard feelings."

"And no broken hearts," I say, because God knows, I can't handle *that* a second time.

"Definitely no broken hearts. I already like you, Allison, but this deal doesn't include love. I've been down that road, and I'm not planning to take it again."

"I am, but I'm not in a hurry. Your deal sounds like a fun side trip until I get back on the long road." There are no wrinkles in my dress, but I smooth the fabric anyway. "That said, I'd like a glass of wine, please. And...I'd like you to show me the bedroom." Not quite a fuck-me-now statement, but a step in the right direction.

Crinkles form at the corners of his eyes as he smiles, then moves to retrieve two glasses from an upper cabinet. "Let's start with a drink while we do some unpacking."

"You want me to help you unpack?" Good thing his back is turned, because my face has that scrunched-up feeling, as if I've sucked on a lemon. I really don't need another lemon in my life. Even temporarily. "That's weird foreplay, but whatever floats your boat."

Laughter ripples the muscles beneath his formfitting, white t-shirt. He recorks the wine bottle, still smiling as he faces me. "Not literally unpack. I had everything put away within ten minutes of getting here."

"That's efficient. I haven't been anywhere in over a year, and my suitcase is still standing in the corner of my room, with a handful of items inside."

"I couldn't handle that." He chuckles while crossing the room. A couple of long-legged strides bring him to the edge of my personal space, where he hands off one of the glasses. "Just knowing it's over there makes me want to go to your house right now and deal with it."

"I hope if you end up in my bedroom, the suitcase in the corner won't be your priority." And, bam! Flirt muscle has been flexed.

"If we're in any room together, I guarantee you'll be my sole focus." Okay, Adam's flirt muscle is pretty flexible, too.

I take a mouthful of wine, making an audible "*mmmm*" as the velvety liquid slides down my throat. "That's nice. I don't drink red wine often, but I would totally have this again. What brand is it?"

"Forty-Three Degrees. An old friend is the head winemaker. I won this bottle from him in a bet, a few years ago."

"So that's another thing we don't have in common. On the rare occurrence that I buy a bottle of wine, I open it the same day. I can't imagine hanging on to a bottle for a few years."

"Some things improve with age." He winks, then tips his glass to take a drink.

The Sahara Desert takes up residence in my mouth. Suddenly, I wouldn't mind if he taught me *all* the things that improve with age. I take another sip of wine, then another. For fortification. Also, because it really is good.

"Top up?" he asks, when I lower the nearly empty glass.

"Or should we look for that line first? I don't want you crossing it and regretting anything you do tonight."

My insides warm, a side effect of his genuine respect as much as from the wine in my belly. "The line is still in front of me. Besides, I'm positive I won't have any regrets about tonight. So, yes to a refill. Please."

"Coming right up." He doesn't have to go far to retrieve the wine bottle, but I admire the view for those few seconds. His thick, muscular calves. His broad shoulders. His butt.

Men's shorts aren't designed to show off their asses, but Adam's gray chinos obviously didn't receive that memo, because his butt looks damn good. Squeezable, but not in a squishy way. There's nothing squishy about him. Just solid, sexy man.

"Thank you." I swallow my Adam-inspired drool when he returns with the bottle. Tipping my head to read the pretty label as he pours, I choke on air when I read the vintage year. "This wine is sixteen years old?"

He turns the bottle as he finishes the pour, checks out the label, then meets my gaze. "So it is. That's quick math. I take it you're a numbers person."

"Not really. This was easy math for me, because I was ten years old when this wine was made."

He nods. "That would make it an easy calculation." Bottle in hand, he points toward the living room. "We can sit inside, or out back on the patio. Whichever you prefer."

"It doesn't bother you that I'm twenty years younger than you?" I ask, ignoring the choices he offered.

"Not at all." He maintains eye contact while taking a casual swallow from his glass. "Does it bother you?"

"Honestly?"

"Always, Allison."

"Okay, it's kind of weird that you're closer to my parents' age than mine. But you're incredibly attractive and super-hot, and those totally overrule the weird factor."

His eyes twinkle as he chuckles. "Glad to hear it."

"Let's sit inside. More privacy."

"Sounds good to me." Holding the neck of the wine bottle in the same hand as his glass, he places his other palm on the small of my back. Not a pushy touch, or overtly sexual, but firm enough to let me know it isn't platonic or innocent.

Is that what the sex will be like? Firm, without being forceful? Will he continue to give choices, then take charge of implementing them? That'd work. That'd work just fine.

He curls his fingers around my waistline, preventing me from turning left toward the living room. "How about on the screen porch out front?"

"It's not very private for our deal."

The space between us is minimal enough that his chuckle vibrates against my neck. "Did you think my invitation meant you'd walk in and we'd head straight to the bedroom?"

"You said 'fast-paced,' so I assumed I'd come over here and we'd have sex."

"Immediately."

"Well...yes."

Adam slides his arm around my waist. His hand spans my abdomen, and his solid body presses tightly against my back. "I think we have time for a glass of wine and conversation first, don't you?"

"I guess so," I say as he releases me. Why must I be so wishy-washy? I really need to get over that. Take charge, be bold. Reprogramming a decade of insecurity isn't a simple decision I can make, it's a process that'll take time. More than one night. More than the weeks I spend with Adam, I bet.

The porch floor creaks beneath our feet as we step out. The moment we're free of the narrow doorway, Adam bands his arm around me again, this time bringing us face-to-face.

"Fast-paced means we know where we're going, not that we have to sprint."

"So...you're not in a hurry to have sex?"

"I'm not impatient for sex," he says, chuckling when I huff and roll my eyes at his carefully chosen words. "But, for the record, I'd like to scoop you up and take you to the bedroom right now."

"I wouldn't object if you did. But we should set the wine down first, so your landlady doesn't hit you with a cleaning bill for the carpet."

His eyes twinkle as he smiles. "Beautiful, sexy, and a head for practical economics. You get hotter by the minute."

"And yet, I'm still on my feet, not up in your arms, headed for the bedroom." Look at me, being flirty and taking charge. *Raar!*

"That's really what you want?" he asks, sliding his hand downward to palm my ass. "Jump to the sex, don't get to know each other first?"

Is it? It'll have to be, because he made it crystal clear our time together is temporary. That when he leaves, it's over. No weekend visits. No further contact. We'll be strangers, once again.

I slip from his hold and place my wine glass on the nearby side table. "I know I want your clothes off. I know I want you to take mine off, too. So, yes, that's really what I want." I shake out my arms, positioning myself to be scooped up, as promised. "I'm ready."

Amusement flickers in his eyes. "Alright."

I exhale as subtly as possible while he sets his glass beside mine. In a matter of seconds, I'll be in his arms. Nobody has ever *literally* scooped me off my feet before. My ex wasn't motivated to engage in anything beyond lukewarm affection. Not with me, anyway. Lousy cheating bastard. Also, Dennis probably couldn't have hefted me up, even if he'd wanted to. He's kind of a wimp, and I've always been in the curvy category.

By the time Adam faces me, my pulse has shot up to cardio-day level. God, I might even be sweating under one arm. Not good.

"Changed your mind?" he asks, when I hold up one hand, halting his advance.

"Not about going to the bedroom. I'm just not sure about you scooping me up. I know you're strong. Seriously, those pullups you do are impressive. But I'm not built like a fairy, and you're—older. I don't want you to put out your back or something. That would really throw a wrench in our 'have sex throughout July' plan."

He laughs so loud, they probably hear him all the way to the lake. "I was moving in to kiss you, not pick you up."

"Oh, good."

"But I've changed my mind," he says.

"About kissing me?"

A mischievous smile curves his lips as he gives a single, side-to-side head shake. "About picking you up."

"What? No." I retreat until my back connects with the wall. "I told you why that's not a good idea."

"Don't worry about this *older man's* back. It's solid and capable of going for hours, just like my front."

My gaze drops to the front of his shorts. Briefly, yet obviously. Enough that my face blazes with embarrassment when I meet his eyes again.

The twinkle there became a smolder as he advances. Palms against the wall on either side of my head, he cages me, leaving only a breath's width of space between our bodies. "Allison." He catches a lock of my hair and coils it around one finger. "You're in the driver's seat, with the power to hit the brakes at any point. Don't use the brake because you're pre-judging what I'm capable of. If I tell you I can pick you up and carry you to the bedroom, I can."

"Okay, I'm sorry."

He shakes his head. Just one, small back-and-forth motion. "We have just over three weeks together. Let's not waste any of that time on unnecessary apologies."

I lift my chin, just slightly, enough to ensure he can see my smile. "You're right." I slide my palms up his warm, solid chest, then twine them at the back of his neck. "I can't guarantee I won't backslide into overthinking at some point, but tonight, this driver is taking her foot off the brake pedal, and her hands off the wheel. Somebody strong and sexy had better grab ahold and steer us in a good direction."

"Grabbing ahold," is all the notice he gives before doing exactly as he said—picking me up.

Despite knowing what's about to happen, I shriek as my feet leave the ground. Shriek louder still when he pretends to lose his grip, an action that has me clinging even tighter to his body. "You did that on purpose."

"Absolutely. Everything I do is intentional."

"Including walk past the bedroom?" I ask, as he continues toward the kitchen.

"Including that." In the kitchen, he returns me to my feet, but keeps his arms around me. "I don't want you to *decide* to have sex with me, Allison. I want you to *need* to. We're not going to that bedroom until you need my cock inside you so badly, you beg me to strip you down, eat your pussy, and fuck you until you've lost the ability to form words."

My eyes feel as if they're going to bug out of my face. "Nobody's ever talked to me so...graphically."

"You didn't slap me across the face or knee me in the balls. Either you're in shock, or you liked it."

My cheeks warm in the best way as I nibble my bottom lip. "Both?"

There's a sensual twinkle in his eyes as he traces the plump edge of my bottom lip. "Both works. For now."

"Why *for now*?" I ask when, instead of kissing me, he takes my hand and leads me to the door. "And where are we going?"

"It's 'for now' because you won't be able to claim shock again. Next time I talk dirty to you, you'll just like it."

"Oh," is the only word I'm capable of forming. There's going to be a next time. My synapses are melting just thinking about it.

"And I thought we'd take a walk on the beach," he says when I fail to produce additional intelligible words. "Enjoy the moonlight on the water while we get more comfortable with each other."

"That sounds nice."

"Good." He raises our joined hands to his mouth, and I swear I feel that innocent kiss all the way to my knees. "Ready to go?"

I nod, but it's a lie. I'm not ready yet. "For the record, I understand our deal. All the rules. And I don't expect you to woo me." I'm letting him off the hook, yes, but *I'm* the reason for my statement. I need to remember this limited-time relationship isn't real. Because every word from Adam's mouth makes me wish it could be.

"Allison." He cups my face in his palms. The playfulness is gone from his expression, replaced by a tenderness that unravels the defenses I'm trying to erect around my heart. "The deal I suggested wasn't solely for fucking your brains out, though once we get started, I am going to wring every orgasm I can from your beautiful body. I want us to have a great time every minute we're together, not just while we're naked in bed. I'm committed to you for the month. I have every intention of making our time together memorable in as many ways as possible."

My heart skips a beat, but it's no wonder. My ex wasn't always an asshole, but he was never romantic. "I like the sound of that," I say, sliding my hands up his chest. "I like the sound of all of it."

"Me too." Still framing my face in his hands, he dips down and seals his lips to mine. His lips are soft, but the kiss is firm, and oh, so good.

His tongue parts my lips, and a soft sigh escapes me. Each sweeping kiss stokes the fire low in my abdomen, a needy curling that demands I get closer. I haven't been kissed in so long. And even then, never this passionately. This...reverently.

His mouth is like magic, and I want it everywhere. On my nipples. Between my legs. God, I bet he knows what he's doing down there. I bet he loves doing it too. That'd be a welcome change.

Fueled by the libido I thought I'd lost, I grab his butt. Tug him closer, whimpering when his erection presses against my abdomen, instead of where I want it.

He responds with a growl I feel from my lips to my needy core. Then his hands are on my hips. He lifts me as if I weigh nothing, and presses my back to the wall, with my legs wrapped around his hips.

Pinned in place, I'm open to him, and it's the hottest thing I've ever experienced. He owns my mouth while grinding his thick, hard ridge between my spread legs.

Sparks race through me, zeroing in on my clit. I'm so close. The teasing tingle is right there, but just out of reach. "Too many layers between us," I whisper between hungry kisses. "Do you want to take this to the bedroom?"

"You know I do." His deep voice rumbles through me, and he nips my bottom lip playfully before returning my feet to the floor.

I gape like a fish as he leads me *out* the door, rather than away from it. "But—I thought... We're not going to the bedroom?"

"Not yet."

"You said you wanted to," I grumble, scuffing the sole of my sandal over the patio stones like a cranky child while he locks up.

"You asked what I want. Not good enough, beautiful. I told you what I need to hear."

My mind rewinds through our conversation, and my eyes open wide when I reach the part where he wants *me* to talk dirty, including several specifics. "I didn't think you were serious."

"Now you know I take your pleasure and satisfaction very seriously." He winks while catching my hand, smiling when I grumble again. "Come on, beautiful, let's go see where the moonlight leads us."

chapter 4

. . .

adam

IT'S a ten-minute walk to the beach, and my dick needs every one of those minutes to deflate after grinding between Allison's legs back in the kitchen. If I'd taken her to the bedroom instead of out of the cottage, I could be buried inside her sexy body right now. Balls-fucking-deep.

She was turned-on, no question. But ready in the moment isn't enough. I don't want her to have regrets. Not about me.

Do I want Allison in my bed? Damn right, I do. But not until she's sure beyond a doubt she wants to be there. We're temporary, but I'm not an asshole. I trust my gut, keep my word, and sleep soundly at night because of both things. So, I'll wait. A couple hours, days, a week or more… however long she needs to be completely comfortable.

Besides, I'm looking forward to getting to know her. My intention to hole up for a month of solitude took a backseat the first time I saw Allison. Pretty face, curves I'd happily get lost in, adorable mannerisms, and a laugh lighter than the summer breeze that carried it across the yard—I was hooked. New plan initiated, right then and there. I still owe her meddling friend a thank-you for expediting that plan.

Now that I've talked with Allison, started peeling back her layers, I want to know everything. What she likes. Dislikes. Her history, goals, and biggest dreams. As much as I can learn in a few weeks. As much as she's willing to share.

"Have you been to the beach since you got to town?" she asks as we trade sidewalk concrete for soft sand.

"I haven't. I did a quick drive around the day I arrived, but aside from that, I've spent my time at the cottage. I'm taking a break from the office, but I'm not technically on vacation. I'm just working remotely."

"You really hate vacations that much?"

I like that she's relaxed enough to tease. "Workaholic, remember? But I'm looking forward to my semi-vacation time with you." The sun has descended below the horizon, but the combination of streetlights and moonlight make it easy to see the kissable curve of her full, smiling lips. "You're incredibly beautiful."

"Thank you. You know, you've complimented me more in an hour than my ex-husband did in the last few years we were married. Or in the first few years we dated, for that matter."

"Then, be glad he's your ex, because he's obviously unworthy of you."

"I know I'm not hot or the most desirable woman around," she says, gently shaking her head. "But Dennis was—*is*—a jerk. I blame teenage naivete and living in a town with a very small dating pool. What's your excuse for marrying the wrong person?" It's self-deprecating humor, but combined with her other comments, it's more heartbreaking than funny.

Infuriating too. The bottom half of my shoes sink into the sand as I halt our forward motion. Still holding her hand, I haul her tight to my chest. "I'm more than happy to remind you how hot you are. Right here. Right now." I slide my hand down her back, then cup her ass and pull her closer. "Would you like that? For me to show everyone in that beachfront restaurant over there how fucking desirable I find you?"

Her lips part, but no words leave her mouth. Her big, expressive eyes have plenty to say, though. She wasn't fishing for extra compliments. Even in the dim lighting, the legitimate self-doubt she carries is unmistakable.

There's a small, empty booth nearby, and I walk her backward until she's wedged between its weathered wood and my steadily growing wood.

"*You* do this to me." I circle her wrist and cup her hand over my fly. "Not a little blue pill, or because I'm a horny creep who gets hard in the presence of any woman. You're beautiful, adorable, and sexy, Allison. I'm hard for you. I want *you*."

"I like the way you talk to me."

"Good. Because I'm not going to stop saying what's on my mind. The question is," I brush my lips across hers, "are you going to believe my words, or do you need hands-on proof to back them up?"

"My hand is already on the proof."

"Not yours," I say, gathering her dress in my palm and walking my fingers down her curvy backside. "My hands. Delivering the proof."

Our mouths are still touching, and when I slip my

fingers under the edge of her panties, her soft gasp mixes with my breath.

One arm braced against the empty hut, I claim her mouth while sliding two fingers lower. I groan at the slickness between her legs. The heat that's already there, waiting for me.

"*Adam...*" My name is a plea, and since she pushes her hips forward to meet my stroking fingers, it's not a plea for me to stop.

"We're alone, sweetheart. Masked by shadows. All anyone in the restaurant can see is a couple kissing under the moonlight."

"You're sure?"

"I promise. Nobody will see you come except me."

Her eyes open wide. "I can't...*come*."

It's fucking adorable that she's embarrassed to say the word *come*. I can't wait to make her say it again. That, and so many more words she's probably never said to a man. I want them all for myself.

"You will come, Allison. And when you're riding my hand over the edge, when you're fucking your pretty pussy onto my fingers, you're going to look into my eyes and say my name again, this time with, 'I'm coming.'"

"I can't, I...have to be lying down, and...I just can't do that here, like this."

Challenge accepted, even if she doesn't realize she issued one. "You will with me," I say, sealing our mouths in a deep kiss. Each sweep of tongue against tongue sends more blood to my cock. There's something about her mouth. So warm and sweet. Willing and open, despite her insecurities.

We're as close as two upright people can get. My chest is pressed to her perfect tits, my body pinning her in place as I roll circles over her clit. She's so fucking wet, so open for me. A couple quick adjustments and I could be inside her. Fucking buried inside her, skin-to-skin.

But this first. So she *knows* how fucking sexy she is, and what she does to me. So she knows I'll put her needs first. This time. Every time.

Her breath hitches as I match her body's cues. Give her more pressure, more speed, until she's panting against my lips instead of kissing them.

She curls her fingers around my biceps, pinpricks of pain shooting up my arm as her nails dig into my flesh. Her breathing is shallow and jagged, her thighs shaking. Her pussy's so fucking wet, my mouth is watering just thinking about it. *"Adam..."*

"Good girl. Now open your pretty eyes. Look at me and tell me you're coming for me."

Her body's rhythm falters, but only for a second. Then her eyelids flutter open, and she fucking slays me with her gorgeous, glassy gaze. Her lips part, a sexy, stuttering moan filling my ears as she breathes, "I'm—it's, oh..."

"For me, sweetheart. Say it."

"Adam," she whispers, clutching at me as she grinds and jerks against my fingers. "I'm coming..." Her breathy moan rises into the night air. "For you, I'm coming for you."

I crush my lips over hers, absorbing her sounds with my kiss. I won't share them with anyone else's ears. I won't even share them with the night. She's mine.

The thought slams into me. I've been with enough women in my lifetime to feel a lot of things, play a lot of bedroom games. Dirty talk is one thing. I've never wanted to claim and possess a woman. Not truly.

Until now.

Where the fuck is this coming from? It's not what I

want. Yet, the yearning tug radiating from somewhere deep inside me says claiming Allison is exactly what I want. Fuck.

"Better let you breathe," I say, breaking the kiss while withdrawing my hand from her panties. "And let some blood find its way to parts of my body other than my cock."

She laughs and buries her face against my chest. "That was just... I've never felt anything like that before."

"Me either, sweetheart."

She angles her head to peek up at me. "You don't have to say that. I don't expect you to. We both know you're more experienced than me. I mean, obviously. You really know what you're doing."

She's not wrong, I've been a student of women's pleasure nearly as long as she's been alive. That's certainly what I drew upon when I slid my hands between her legs. But not what inspired the following minutes.

I tip her chin up, stroking her bottom lip while holding her gaze. "I wasn't following a playbook when I touched you. That was me and you, nobody from our pasts. Just the two of us, moving together on instinct and igniting the spark we share."

"It felt amazing for me."

"For me too, sweetheart. I could get addicted to you. So easily."

She pulls back. Narrows her eyes at me. "You. Addicted to me."

"Sounds likes you don't believe me." I trail my fingers down her neck, over the swell of her cleavage, not stopping until I curl my hand around the sexy curve of her hip. "Need more hands-on proof? There's nothing I'd like more than to make you come again."

Her lips part, then snap closed when voices spill out

from the nearby restaurant, stealing my opportunity for a second round.

"Let's go for that walk," I say, stepping back and taking her hand. I can't help smiling while she smooths her dress down. "Sorry not sorry about the wrinkles."

Now that we're out of the shadows, the nearly full moon above us makes it easy to see her face light up. "I'm definitely not sorry."

"Good. But, if the wrinkles won't come out, I can buy you a new dress. You'll have to tell me where to get it, though. Can't say I've ever seen another like it."

She takes the gentle teasing in stride, playfully nudging me with her shoulder as we continue along the shoreline, away from the beachfront restaurant. "I assume that means you love my dress. It *is* a one-of-a-kind creation."

"Is that so?" is the best answer I've got about a custom-made dress with an all-over rubber-ducky print for a beautiful twenty-six-year-old woman who just came on my hand in a public place. Allison is one hell of an intoxicating combination.

She nods, her expression straight and solemn for all of about ten seconds, then she giggles, the genuine, joyous sound hitting me squarely in the heart. "Actually, it is. My best friend has a business making pet clothes and accessories. My work had a big 'Springtime Lucky Ducky Discounts' event, so I had Esme make a dress from one of her fabrics. I'm notorious for hanging on to things too long —as my marriage to douchebag Dennis can attest—so the dress was still in my closet. When I couldn't decide what to wear to your house, Esme told me to close my eyes and pick something. And here I am."

"And I'm the lucky ducky."

"*You?*" The gentle lapping of water onto sand is a great

sound, but it has nothing on Allison's laughter. "I'm the one who just—" Even in the semi-darkness, her blush is unmistakable.

"Say it, sweetheart."

"I'm the one who just came for you," she whispers.

My dick hasn't gone below half-mast since touching her, and it's on the rise again. "Fucking right, you did. And it was the hottest thing ever." Based on her previous comments, I expect her to dispute my claim.

Instead, she smiles at me. "It was." She's so pretty, so damn real, she cracks my heart open wider.

"Come here, I want you closer." I release her hand, wrap my arm around her shoulders and pull her tight to my side. She feels good there. A perfect fit. "Tell me about your job. I'm guessing some sort of sales, since you mentioned a discount event."

"I sell cars at a dealership."

I crane my head enough to get a view of her face. "Seriously?"

She nods. "You can't picture it, right? That's what everyone says. How can shy, unassertive Allison be successful selling cars?"

I feel her shrug. Physically, because she's snug beneath my arm. But I *feel* that shrug on a deeper level too. "I wasn't thinking those things, and shame on anybody who'd insult you that way."

"Then why'd you ask if I was serious?" she asks.

"Not because I doubted you could do it."

"Then why?" There's the boldness from our first meeting a few hours ago.

And my cock just got that much harder. Unfortunately, it might be hard and lonely once I tell her the truth. "I'm going to sound like a chauvinist asshole here, but I didn't expect you to be seriously interested in cars. I realize some women prefer a particular car's appearance or amenities, but I haven't known any who've given vehicles thought beyond the superficial, which you'd have to do to sell them. I apologize for being a sexist male. I promise to do better."

"You're already doing better than most men I know, just with that explanation and apology." One hand on my chest, she breaks our forward motion to push upward and places a kiss on my cheek. "Out of curiosity, what did your formerly sexist brain think I might sell?"

"Purely out of hope—lingerie."

She laughs and leans into my side, nudging me closer to the water's edge. "Oh my God, could you get any more cliché?"

"Probably not." Our mutual amusement settles into comfortable silence as we put more distance between us and the main portion of the beach. There's a metal retaining wall on our right, and the sand is narrowing rapidly. In a couple minutes, we'll be out of walkable space. "Should we turn around and go back?"

"There's an old access stairway not too far ahead. It's borderline sketchy, and we'll have to go through the water to get to it, but—"

"Let's do it."

"You didn't let me finish," she says, filling the night air, and my head, with more of her soft laughter. "What if I was about to tell you the water's waist deep?"

"Then I'd strip you out of your cute dress and suggest we take the long way so I make sure you *finish* again before we reach the stairs."

Her lips part, and her tongue sweeps across them, leaving them glistening. "The water's only ankle deep," she says softly. "Unfortunately."

"Then I'll improvise."

"How?"

"I love an inquisitive woman." I lead her to the retaining wall and press her back to the water-stained metal. Quick surveillance of our surroundings reassures me we're completely alone at beach level. Lights dot the houses on the escarpment above us, and there's no way to know if any of those windows are open, or any decks are currently in use. A chance I'm willing to take.

I dip down for a kiss, stroking my tongue alongside hers until she's grabbing handfuls of my butt and pulling me closer. "Ready to come for me again?" I ask against her lips.

"Yes."

"Good girl." Holding her gaze, I ease back. I take both her hands and guide them to the hem of her dress. "Lift it up. To the waist. I want to see your panties before I take them off."

"You're taking them off this time?" she asks while drawing the fabric up.

I nod. Loop my fingertips under the white lace and wiggle it downward. I've seen what's underneath, when I happened upon her naked. I've felt what's underneath, when I made her come on my hand. Now I'm going to taste what's underneath.

I lift one of her feet, then the other, then stuff the scrap of lace in my pocket. "So fucking pretty," I say, kneeling before her, stroking the soft pink skin that has my dick harder than the steel wall Allison is leaning on. "I've been thinking about this since the first time I saw you."

"Thinking about wha—" A throaty gasp takes the place of her words as I slide my tongue between her folds. "Oh, my God. I didn't think you'd do *this*."

I fuck my tongue into her sweet hole, lap at her again

before sucking her clit into my mouth. Then lick my lips, looking up her body while rolling slow circles around my favorite pearl. "Do you want me to stop eating your pussy, Allison?"

She shakes her head. Her bottom lip is caught between her teeth, and she's gripping the hell out of her dress. This is definitely uncharted territory for her.

I should take it slow, let her lead like I promised I would. Now that I've felt her come, now that I've tasted her... Fuck, now that something inside me *craves* her—there's no going slow. I won't break my promise. But I'm going to need her help to keep it *and* keep going.

"Then tell me you need my mouth on your pussy." I swear I can hear her heart pounding in her chest. Or maybe it's mine. I skim my palms up her legs, slowly mapping the curves from her calves to her lush thighs. "My mouth is fucking watering here, sweetheart, but I need you to say it."

"I need..." Her hips tilt forward to meet my fingers as I stroke the softest skin on earth. A throaty hum escapes her parted lips when I graze her clit with enough pressure to tease her higher, but not take her over.

"Tell me." It's a command, but I can't help myself.

"I need your mouth on my pussy," she whispers.

If everyone living above this stretch of beach doesn't hear me growl, I'll be fucking amazed. I grab her hips. Use my shoulders to nudge her thighs wider. Then fucking dive in and feast on her.

Her skin is soft as rose petals. And her taste...fuck, her taste. Spicy and sweet, fucking perfection.

My dick is ready to punch a hole in my shorts. I could bury my face between her legs for hours and it wouldn't be enough, but I can't wait to make her come. I need it like I need to breathe.

Her dress falls over my face, blocking my view. It's a fair trade for her hands on my head, pulling me in. For her fingers threading through my hair, her nails raking my scalp as her body jerks under my tongue.

"Adam, oh God, I'm coming... Oh, God, oh God, yes...*Adam!*" She's still rocking and shaking against my mouth when floodlights come on at one of the cottages above, bathing the hill—and us—in a swath of hazy white.

"Shit, sorry, sweetheart." I'm on my feet a hell of a lot sooner than I'd like, grabbing Allison's hand and running down the beach, as much as that's even possible.

"Oh my God!" Her laughter is as loud as her squealed words, and her smile puts the floodlights we escaped to shame.

Maybe it's the endorphins, or the combination of fresh air and judgment-free surroundings, but I can't remember ever feeling this light. And when I look over at her, I swear I've never seen a more beautiful sight.

chapter 5

· · ·

allison

A SNORT RISES from my coworker in the neighboring cubicle. "Incoming. This one's definitely for you, A-Game." Mike gifted me with the nickname three years ago, the day I sold a brand-new car to a customer with whom everyone else at the dealership had previously spent countless hours, yet failed to close a sale.

Sometimes, Mike uses the nickname with legitimate admiration. Most of the time, though, he loads it with sarcasm—and a hint of resentment. This time, his tone rings with amusement.

I turn from my computer to look out the showroom's front window. "Oh, my God." That seems to be slipping from my mouth a lot recently. Sometimes for better reasons than others.

"Is your friend still single?" Mike asks while I save and quit my work with harder keyboard pecking than necessary.

"Why?"

"Because I like a woman who's into role-playing. She can save a horse and ride me any day."

I shoot him a ha-ha-so-funny expression, then hustle for the door, beyond which, my best friend is dressed like a wannabe cowgirl. Or, a wannabe stripper in a cowgirl costume. She's been kind of over-the-top recently, but she's finally coming out of her lowest low, so I'll take it.

Plus, the flamboyant costume is another sign that her creativity has returned. Sure, it'd be better if she channeled it into marketable items for her business, but hey, it's a start. I just want her to be happy again. Truly happy. Not just happy-when-meddling-in-Allison's-life happy. Though her meddling did lead to meeting Adam, so I really can't complain.

Heat slams into me as I trade air-conditioned comfort for the thick, July humidity. Now, this, I can complain about.

By the time I reach Esme, a bead of sweat has trickled down my neck, creating a gross, moist path between my boobs. Lovely. "What are you doing here?"

"Getting all the deets about your date last night."

"I'm at work, Es. I can't just take a timeout to have a personal conversation."

"Ooh, so things *did* get personal with your sexy neighbor man. I knew it!"

"No, you didn't." A comeback with the sophistication of a grade-school kid. I might as well have said, *nuh-uh,* and stuck out my tongue.

Not to be outdone in the immaturity department, Esme pulls her phone from a back pocket, cues up our earlier text conversation, and waves the screen in my face. "I sent you the eggplant with a question mark. You sent back the shrugging emoji."

"And?"

"And it wasn't a question you shrug off. Eggplant, question mark? Either you got some eggplant last night, or you didn't. Thumbs up, or thumbs down. Giant happy face, or frowny face. I know you, Ally. If you didn't get any eggplant, you would have shot back an instant 'no,' and informed me that your self-imposed, eggplant-free diet was intact."

Having a friend who knows me so well is mostly a blessing. Except now, when it's a curse. Topic aversion required. "Why are you talking in eggplant code?"

"Because you're at work, so I'm being incognito."

"Incognito? You're wearing a pink cowboy hat, turquoise western boots, and your skirt is so short, it barely covers your...everything."

"It's not actually that short." A little tug on the hem brings the denim to a more respectable length. Marginally. "It just rides up when I move. And on the subject of riding..." Esme winks at her from beneath the brim of her not-incognito hat. "How was that eggplant last night?"

"I'm not discussing my sex life with you while I'm at work."

"Ooh, baby! That confirms you have a sex life to discuss. Finally!"

There's no withholding my groan. Or my grimace, as another disgusting bead of sweat rolls into my cleavage. "Unless you're here to buy a car, I'm going back into the air-conditioning."

"Fine, I'll leave. But Bluetooth me on your way home. I need details."

Heat floods my cheeks as images from last night flash through her mind. "Maybe."

"No 'maybe,' Ally. If it was horrible, I want to laugh

with you about it. We can dis the shit out of the silver fox. If it was awesome, I want to know, not only because I care about you, but also because I'm dirty-minded and horrifically undersexed."

"*Maybe.*" I toss the word over my shoulder while walking away. Pointless indifference I doubt I've pulled off, because I've never been good at faking.

Last night, I didn't have to fake anything. The orgasms with Adam were the real deal. Better than the best solo fantasies that run through my mind while I'm spending quality time with my battery-operated boyfriend. Adam was so much better than my vibrator. And that's without having any eggplant.

I pause at the showroom door. I've always shared the dirt with Esme. Until now, that dirt has all been about Dennis, and most of the details weren't particularly dirty. Sharing the bad stuff was a relief. I had nothing to be embarrassed about because the details after a "good" night were mediocre, at best. And "good" nights weren't all that common with Dennis. Pretty sure the total from a decade together would be a single-digit number.

Esme would freak out if she knew about last night. I should tell her. She could use the distraction, and she'll be happy for me. Besides, it's kind of killing me to keep it to myself.

I turn and find her leaning against her car, watching me. "I thought you were leaving."

"And I thought *you* were going back into the air conditioning."

There hasn't been anyone on the lot for hours. If someone comes looking, Mike can take them. I could always use more commission, but this month, he could use it more. Just because I indulged in public sex acts last night doesn't mean I'm not still a nice girl.

"How about mobile air-conditioning?" I ask, tipping my head toward a canyon-bronze-metallic sedan nobody wants to look at, no matter how great the sticker price. It's the duck dress of the dealership's closet. "Let me grab keys and a plate. We're going for a test drive."

adam

Focusing on work has been a struggle, and I never struggle with work. Business is second nature. My passion. Only today, it's not. My passion left for *her* job eight hours and forty-five minutes ago. The usual stream of acquisitions, proposals, and negotiations on my portable desk hasn't held my attention. Working out didn't distract me. Jerking off didn't satisfy me. I'm obsessed with Allison Anderson.

It's because we didn't fuck after getting back from the beach. Has to be. I'm thinking with my dick, that's all. Once I've buried myself deep inside Allison's body, branded her with the most thorough fucking of her life, my brain will kick back into gear. I'll be able to think about something other than her smile. Her eyes. The sounds she makes when she's coming. The way her laughter unlocks something inside me.

Shit. I'm lying to myself, thinking my head won't be filled with everything Allison after we fuck. Once won't be enough. Hell, a month's worth won't be. She's different from any other woman I've been with.

That's what it is—she's different. I've been surrounded

by intense, career-focused businesswomen for decades. Polished, driven. Assertive in the boardroom and the bedroom. Female versions of me.

Maybe it's Allison's girl-next-door goodness that's gotten under my skin. Stirred an innate need to protect and possess. To claim her by fucking her bare and coming inside her. That's the one really messing me up. I've never taken risks that could lead to procreation. My steadfast intent to *not* make Shauna pregnant cost me nearly half my life's work.

Yet, on the beach last night, if I'd had the chance, I would've fucked Allison bare. I would've come deep inside her, with zero regret. Fuck, it's more than lack of regret. Part of me wanted to knock her up. Right then and there.

The walk home gave me time to pull myself together—until I kissed her goodnight. Every urge rushed back the minute our lips touched. Standing outside her house, in the cover of darkness, I couldn't resist hiking her dress up, sliding my fingers between her legs again. If she hadn't stopped me out of fear her neighbors would see, I would've made her come again. If she'd invited me in, I'm not sure I would've let her get any sleep. Hell, if I knew which car dealership she worked at, I would've gone there today. Bought a fucking car if I had to.

I need to get myself in check. Enjoy this time with Allison without getting personally invested. I'm here for a good time, not a long time. Certainly not for a lifetime.

Good, it's all good. My head's on straight, and I'm sticking to the deal. No more caveman urges. I'm in control. A few weeks of sexy fun, that's what this is.

Sunlight glinting off glossy-red paint draws my attention to the street. Allison's car. My partner in fun is home.

I close the laptop I've barely looked at, set it aside, and head for the door. Allison enters my view the second I step outside. That control I just talked myself into reclaiming—it's nowhere in sight.

She's unloading groceries from her trunk. Innocent, everyday behavior. I haven't touched her, I'm not even close to her, yet my dick is thick and mission-minded. All I want is to scoop her into my arms, and march to a bedroom. I love sex, always have. But this is next level. I don't just want to have sex with her, I need to. Like a primordial mating urge only she can trigger—and satisfy. It's uncontrollable. Fuck, I don't even want to.

"Here, let me," I say, taking the shopping bags from her hands. Our fingers brush during the transfer, and I swear a jolt of electricity shoots through me.

Based on her parted lips and glassy gaze, she felt it too.

Tonight's the night. A nice dinner and good conversation—I can hold out that long. Then I'm going to fuck her six ways 'til Sunday. Pretty sure I'll lose what's left of my cognitive processes if I don't.

"Hello, beautiful." I dip down to kiss her, halting before our lips meet. "Do I have your permission to kiss you in public, in the light of day?"

She smiles while nodding, a pink blush tinting her cheeks. "Just kissing though. The other stuff needs to stay behind closed doors, at least around here."

"Deal." A word I need to keep in the front of my mind. Especially later, when we're behind a closed door. I lower my lips to hers and kiss her softly. That's my intent, anyway. My inner caveman has other ideas. Next thing I know, the bags are in the trunk, my hands are in her hair, and my tongue is in her mouth. I'm out of control. Again.

"Wow," she says when I force myself to break the kiss and step back. "You know how to say hello."

"Only to you."

Her lips curve into the sweetest smile, and it takes everything in me to keep my hands to myself. That has to be it—her sweetness has triggered these dormant, dominant urges.

I'm not a Neanderthal, I can control them. Starting now. I reclaim the shopping bags, close the trunk, then follow her into her house. "Good day?" I ask, watching her unpack the groceries and her lunch bag.

"Long day. Very few people on the lot. The only test drive was Esme, the friend that made my ducky dress."

"She's fortunate to have someone on the inside." Small talk is good. It'll help keep my mind off Allison's tits, which look ready to bust through the sunshine-yellow shirt she's wearing. Or her squeezable ass, currently on prime display while she bends to put canned goods in a bottom cabinet. "What're you selling her?"

"Oh, nothing. I won't sell cars to family and friends, it's a personal rule. Then there's no expectation of a discount, or blaming me if they're not happy."

"Sounds like you're speaking from experience."

She laughs while putting away the final items. "Are *all* 'I won't do such-and-such' rules rooted in bad experiences?"

"Valid point. Tell me over dinner. You pick the place, I pick up the tab."

From her position at the sink, rinsing her lunch containers, she looks over her shoulder at me. "You don't have to buy. I'm not the CEO of a multi-billion-dollar company, but I'm not completely broke."

"Glad to hear it. And letting me buy dinner will keep your money in the bank."

"I can afford to pay my own way, Adam."

Fuck, I do love when she says my name. I'll love it even more when she's saying it while coming undone for me.

"Are you in the mood for anything in particular?"

"Oh, yeah," I say, chuckling as I advance on her. There are enough restaurants in Hope Harbor, at least one of them must deliver.

"Sustenance-wise, mister. You can't just eat..." Deep-pink bathes her face as she whispers, "my pussy."

Hearing her say those words brings my need to claim her roaring to the surface. "Try me," I say, caging her against the edge of the sink, my cock pressing against her abdomen as I nuzzle her neck.

A throaty gasp escapes her lips when I slide my palms over her curvy body. "Okay, sustenance can wait until you're done with me."

"I'm never going to be done with you." The words are out of my mouth before I've had a chance to register the thought.

Instead of putting me on the hook for them, Allison laughs and gently pushes me away. "If I'm going to need energy to go all night, then you'd better feed me first."

It's a reprieve, and I take it. "Fair enough."

"I'm going to change and freshen up. I'll only be a few minutes."

I nod, but as soon as she's walking away, I know I can't let her. "Allison." I catch her hand, squeezing gently as she looks into my eyes. "It's pretty obvious that I want you, but I also want to know you. If I get too wolfish in my hunger for you, snap me back, like you just did by the sink. It's never my intention to disrespect or take advantage of you."

"I don't feel that way at all, and...I like that you're wolfish. Dennis is the only man I've been with, and he never wanted me the way you do. It's a nice change. Nice and dirty, but definitely nice."

"Any man privileged enough to lie beside you should be worshipping every inch of you," I say, winking as I add, "nice and dirty like."

"Is that your plan for later?"

"That's my plan for the rest of July."

"I approve of this plan." She gives me another smile that simultaneously makes me want to wrap her in my arms for safekeeping and spread her open for my taking. "I'll be right back."

"Take your time, sweetheart. We've got plenty of time." On tonight's clock. Not in the big picture. That was the deal, on my terms. Watching her walk away, knowing that in a few weeks, she'll walk out of my life for good... Suddenly, I'm less than proud of the deal I offered.

chapter 6

. . .

allison

BEFORE TONIGHT, I'd eaten in The Fischer Hotel's fancy dining room exactly three times in my life. To celebrate my first communion, my grandmother's seventy-fifth birthday, and the night Dennis proposed.

None of them felt as special as walking in on Adam's arm. Having the weight of every gaze in the room on us as my handsome date guided me to our table with his palm spanning my lower back. He's a stranger in Hope Harbor, yet he carries himself with a presence that demands attention. Once we were seated, though, every ounce of *his* attention remained on me. If he hadn't set out the terms of our deal, I might think he's falling for me.

I need to remember that he's not. He likes me, I can tell. Cares about me, even. He's most certainly attracted to me. He's an experienced, worldly man who knows how to make a woman feel like a princess and a sex goddess at the same time. I'm just his princess-goddess of the moment. The best thing I can do is enjoy everything he's offering and try not to cry too long when it's over.

Falling in love with him would be a huge mistake. It's only been twenty-four hours, and I already know I'm destined to make it. I'd have to be a self-centered, heartless bitch not to fall in love with him.

Dammit. I'm going to cry enough to fill the lake when he leaves. But I get three more weeks with him first, and I'm going to enjoy every minute.

We've shared a lot of life details during our meal. He listened intently while I told him about douchebag Dennis, from the first kiss at age fifteen to catching him kissing another woman at age twenty-four. Adam didn't call me naïve, or tell me I should've seen the signs, or ask me why I didn't give Dennis a chance to atone for his indiscretion—all the questions I'm tired of answering.

He didn't look down his nose at me when I told him I haven't been to college, or that I actually love living in my little hometown, and have no aspirations to do or become more than what I am, right now. Honestly, when I'm with Adam, I feel better about who I am than I have in a long time. Maybe ever.

No matter what I talked about, or divulged, Adam absorbed and accepted. He laughed with me, held my hand, stroked my leg beneath the table, and even wiped a tear from my cheek when I let my emotions get the best of me for a minute. He's a keeper. Too bad he doesn't want to be kept.

After listening to *his* stories, I understand why. His parents split when he was seven, and he spent the rest of his childhood bounced back and forth between two workaholics who didn't have time for him. At thirty-eight, he married a colleague believing they wanted the same things out of life. When it turned out they didn't, he divorced her so she could find a more fulfilling marriage.

Rather than be grateful for his compassion and the twenty-five percent share in his company laid out in their prenup, she sued for more, and ended up with forty-nine percent of Adam's company. A company he leveraged himself to the eyeballs to start, then spent a decade and a half building into a massive success. He's not hurting for money, and he's still the majority owner, but what a blow.

While listening to my Dennis stories, Adam said he might have to punch Dennis in the face if they cross paths. Then he chuckled it off as a protective guy thing.

I'm never going to be in a position to meet Adam's ex-wife. But if I were, I'd be tempted to punch *her* in the face too. Crazy how you can hate someone you've never met, but I do. The only good thing about Adam's ex-wife is the fact that she let him get away, so I could find him.

"What's going on in that beautiful head of yours?" he asks, melting my heart and panties with another of his twinkly eyed smiles.

Definitely not telling him I'm imagining decking his ex-wife, though I think it'd amuse him. "Just deciding if I should I tell you how amazing the homemade pies are, or try to sway you to skip dessert and take me to bed instead."

His eyebrows rise, then he's turning in his seat, one hand raised to flag our waitress. "Check, please."

"Are you sure? The pie really is delicious."

He leans in, close enough that I catch the scent of his cologne. He doesn't wear a lot, but it smells better than any food ever could. "Yours is the only pie I want to eat. And this time, I'm going to spread your legs wide enough to bury my face and eat my fill of your sweet—"

"Ahem." Our waitress clears her throat, cutting off

Adam's explicit plans for making me his dessert. Dressed in a formal, black-and-white server's uniform, she's nearly as vintage as the well-preserved décor, but the expression on her face indicates her hearing still works fine. Thank goodness she's not a friend of my parents.

"Thank you," Adam says, switching from wolf to silver fox in an easy beat. "Everything was outstanding."

Unimpressed, she hands off the bill, then walks away without another word.

The old me, the one before Adam, would've spent the rest of the night worrying I'd behaved badly, engaging in dirty talk in a public place. Current me just wants Adam to take me home and make good on his plan.

"I'll take care of the check, get the car, and meet you out front," he says, rising, then pulling my chair back.

"I don't mind walking to the car with you, it's not that far."

He shakes his head. Hand on my back again, he leans close while guiding me out of the dining room. "I want you to go to the restroom and take off your panties. By the time I'm at the car, I want a picture of your pretty pussy lighting up my phone."

"You—want me to send you nudes?" I've never sent—or taken—a nude photo. Not even to Dennis while we were married.

"One picture. Nothing identifiable. Just your bare pussy, waiting for my tongue. When you get in the car, you can watch me delete it."

"What if...I don't want you to?"

Stopped at the concierge desk, he pretends he's innocently kissing my temple, but his growl vibrates all the way to my clit. "Good thing you like the wolf, Allison, because he's starved for you. I'll meet you out front in five minutes."

My legs shake as I walk to the restroom. Locked inside, I complete step one, wiggling my panties down and off, then stuffing them into my handbag. I ruck my dress up, tucking the hem into the neckline to keep it out of my way. Good thing he only wants a closeup shot, because this is *not* a sexy look.

Taking the picture is more challenging than expected. My first five attempts look more like images of blurry fingers or the crack between sofa cushions, rather than sexy lady bits. Taking dirty pictures is more difficult than it seems, and I have a new appreciation for both photographers and models.

Wait—that's my problem—I'm trying to do both. I need to focus on being the model. Well, my pussy does, anyway.

I lay some tissue on the floor, set my purse down, then prop my phone against it until the angle is as good as it can get in a bathroom stall. Watching the screen, I practice a few poses, then take a deep breath and set the camera's timer. Heart pounding in my chest, I assume the position— one leg on the toilet seat, my index and middle fingers in a V that separates my pussy lips enough to expose my clit. I can't believe I'm doing this.

Click.

Oh my God, I did it. I scoop my things from the floor at the sound of voices outside the restroom. Whatever the picture looks like, it'll have to be good enough. I hold my breath and open it, a hot blush washing over me as I stare at the image. I'm too curvy to ever be a centerfold model, but I'm confident Adam will like this picture.

Dress back in its proper place, I hit Send. I haven't even

unlocked the restroom door when my phone rings. *Adam Foster calling.* And I thought my heart was beating fast before.

"Hi, I'm on my way," I say, heading for the building's front entrance. "It was harder than I thought it'd be."

"After seeing that picture, I'm the world record holder for 'hard.'" His chuckle becomes a low, appreciative whistle as I step out of the hotel. "Fuck, you're beautiful. I'm hanging up now so I can focus on watching you."

The call ends without another word, and I tuck my phone into my handbag before descending the long set of concrete steps that leads to the street, and to Adam.

Dennis would sometimes tell me I looked pretty or cute. Never beautiful or sexy. Adam is so different. Not just his choice of words, it's how he says them. With intent. With feeling. And that changes everything, including the way I feel about myself.

He's out of the car before I reach it. Instead of opening the passenger door, he snakes an arm around my waist and pulls me in close. There's no mistaking the thick ridge of his cock, but it's his soul-deep gaze that makes my pulse race.

"Take me home, strip me down, and fuck me until I forget how to make words," I whisper.

His eyes twinkle with equal parts smolder and affection. "Your wish is my command, sweetheart."

"And your command is my wish. That part about taking me home—I said it because you told me to, in your living room yesterday."

"I remember."

"I have a feeling there's not much you forget."

"Accurate assessment," he says, winking as he chuckles. "Let's go home so I can show you what else I remember from last night."

Desire flares low in my abdomen. My body's ready to go, but I shake my head and grab handfuls of his shirt when he makes a move to break our clinch. "Before we go home and start doing amazing naked stuff, there are things I want you to know."

"Sounds important."

"They are to me," I say softly.

"Then, whatever they are, they're important to me too."

I'm trying make this deal with Adam strictly about sex, but my heart knows it's more. For better and worse, I'm already falling in love with him. But that's not what I want him to know. I know I can never tell him that.

"I want you to know I've been tested for every possible disease, and I'm clean. I got checked after I found out my ex cheated on me, and he's the only man I've been with, ever. I have lab results at home I can show you."

His eyes are so kind, his smile so gentle. "I don't need to see your test results, Allison. I trust you."

"And I trust you." I take a deep breath, gathering the courage to see the next part through. "Which leads me to the other thing I want you to know. I like it when you tell me what to do. It's not something I ever fantasized about, or expected to enjoy, but when you get all alpha and bossy with me, it turns me on. A lot."

His nostrils flare, and his hold tightens, forcing a gasp from my lips. "Is there anything else you want to tell me?"

"No," I say, shaking my head.

"Then get in the car and pull your dress up, so I can look at my dessert on the way home."

My throat is like a desert. I nod and let him guide me into the car, staring up at him when he doesn't close my door.

"Your dress, Allison."

"Now?" I ask, and he nods. Just once. "But, you're not in the car yet, and—"

"Pull it up."

It's still light out, and while the street's not jampacked, it's not empty, either. I lick my lips and reach for the hem of my dress, my hands shaking as I draw it upward. My pulse is pounding in my ears by the time the fabric grazes my naked mound.

"Touch yourself." His voice is deeper than normal, husky instead of velvety smooth.

I pull my hands back as if he asked me to touch a red-hot kettle. "I can't do that here."

"If you don't, I will. I'll crouch beside the wide-open car door and finger your pretty pussy until you come."

If I called his bluff, would he do it? Part of me wants to find out. I don't even know who I am anymore.

"You know what else I remember from last night?" he asks, leaning in. "You waking the neighborhood above the beach when you came on my tongue. Do you think you can be quiet when I'm rubbing your clit?"

Oh, God. I slip one hand between my legs, biting my bottom lip when the first light stroke over my flesh sends sparks ricocheting through me.

"Fuck." His eyes don't leave me as he closes the door, or while he walks around the front of the car, or when he settles on the driver's seat and fires up the engine. "Keep touching yourself, but don't make yourself come. I want to taste the first one."

"Then drive fast."

The short drive from the restaurant takes half the usual time. It's still too long, because Adam didn't settle for watching me touch myself, he joined in, covering my hand with his and guiding my fingers. Only his repeated, "No coming, sweetheart" prevented me from tumbling over. But, God, did I want to. Did I *need* to.

Inside my house, the sound of Adam flipping the deadbolt barely registers in my ears. Blood rushes in my temples, and my heart is attempting to thump its way out of my chest.

I can't stop fidgeting as he stalks toward me, unbuttoning his cuffs and rolling the white sleeves to his very sexy forearms. "Do you want something to drink?" It's a stupid, nervous question, but he doesn't laugh at me.

"You're all I want," he says, pulling me close. His gaze drops to my mouth, then he brushes his fingers over the pulse hammering in my neck. "But let's have a drink if you want one. We don't have to rush to the bedroom. There's no pressure to do anything you're not ready for."

"I told you I want you to fuck me. I told you to boss me around."

"And I'll do both those things with more pleasure than you can imagine. But only when you're sure you're ready."

"You wouldn't be angry if I changed my mind? Even after the picture I sent, and...what we did in the car?"

He weaves his fingers through my hair, gently cradles my head in his hand while staring deep into my eyes. "Never."

"You must be the most patient man alive."

"Definitely not," he says, chuckling. "I just know you're worth waiting for." He's pretty romantic for a man who isn't interested in love and commitment.

Wishing he'd fall in love with me won't make it happen. I'll take his romantic side, though, and his other available parts too. "I don't want you to wait. I don't want *me* to wait. I'm just nervous because it's been over a year, and even when I had sex before, it wasn't adventurous. I don't want to disappoint you."

"Impossible, Allison. You're everything I didn't know I was looking for when I pulled into the driveway next door."

Oh, my heart. My silly, lovestruck heart that's going to break into a million tiny pieces at the end of July. "Then tell me what to do," I say, opening the top button of his shirt. "Because I want to do everything with you."

"Everything's a lot to offer, sweetheart, and once I have a taste of you, I might want to take it all."

All. My mediocrely sexed brain can only think of one thing that means. Something I've never done. Something I'd give him tonight, or any night, because I'd give him anything. "Then take it all," I whisper. "Make me yours."

chapter 7

. . .

adam

MAKE ME YOURS. She has no idea what she's offered.
The urges she's triggered in me.

I need to keep those deep-seated impulses in check. I
spent the entire day convincing myself last night was
strictly reactionary. Some kind of anthropological response
to pheromones. That it'll pass, that I can control it once I've
fucked her. Sticking to our deal—my deal—is a pipedream.
I'm not going to be able to let her go at the end of July. I
don't want to.

This time, she doesn't protest when I scoop her into my
arms. Her arms twine behind my head, holding me in place
so the kiss doesn't break. As if I'd let that happen. The only
thing that could stop me now is her.

There's one bedroom on the main floor, and I stride into
it, depositing her on the bed, and covering her with my
body. I need her naked, but I can't even wait for that. Her
mouth tastes like dry wine and sweet Allison, and I can't
get enough.

Her dress falls to her waist when she wraps her legs around my hips, spurring me to grind against her. She's breathing heavy against my lips within seconds. Whimpering when I push up to a kneeling position between her thighs.

"I know what you need, sweetheart. And I'm going to give it to you. I'm going to give you everything." I slide my hands up her body, over the light-blue dress with way too many buttons up the front. "Is this dress irreplaceable?"

Her eyebrows pinch together so fucking adorably, then her eyes open wide, as my unspoken question sinks in. "No. I don't care about the dress."

The caveman roars inside me as I grip the neckline in both hands and send those million little buttons flying in all directions. A pretty white bra is the only thing between me and the sexy tits I got a glimpse of during our naked introduction. The bra has to go.

I trace one lacy strap to the swell of her cleavage. "Take it off." A simple command that stirs my need to issue more. So many more.

She nods, opens the front clasp, then props herself up enough to wiggle out of the bra and what's left of her dress.

"So damn beautiful," I say, undressing as she lies back.

Her eyes open wide as my cock springs free. Then her tongue skates across her bottom lip, and it's all I can do not to bury myself inside her right fucking now. First things first.

"Open your sexy legs and show me my dessert."

Zero hesitation, she does what I say. Lies there, spread wide for me, her lush tits tempting me with their hard-peaked nipples. Later.

"Show me where you want my tongue." I fist my cock, my eyes glued to her hand as she slides it down her body, to her clit. "Rub it, sweetheart." I groan as her hips tip up to meet the press of her fingertips. "So fucking hot. But don't make yourself come, that's for me to do."

"When?" she asks, her tits rising and falling faster with each circle over her clit.

"Now, sweetheart. Starting right now." I shift closer, press the head of my cock against her opening, groaning at the welcoming slickness against my crown. "Going to eat your pussy until you come on my tongue, but I need to be inside you first." I press deeper, fire raging at the base of my cock as I watch my tip disappear into her tight heat. "You feel so good. So fucking good." I grip her hips, hold her just right and slide deeper. Deeper. All-the-fucking-way deep. So-fucking-good-I-could-come deep.

I fold myself over her, claiming her mouth, rocking into her so I'm grinding against her clit and stroking her G-spot. Lips parted beneath mine, her breath hitches as she digs her nails into my butt, pulling me even deeper.

"Come for me," I say between hungry kisses. My dick is throbbing and my balls feel ready to burst. Not going to happen. "You feel so fucking good, but I'm starving for your pussy. Come on my cock so I can make you come on my face." I stroke into her again, gritting my teeth to keep control as her body shakes and clenches around me.

Her sexy-as-fuck moan fills the room for what feels like eternity because I'm barely holding back, but it's still not long enough. The last shuddering tremor ends, and her eyelids flutter open as I pull out. "Did you come?"

"Not yet."

"I'm not on The Pill."

"I won't come in you without a condom." No matter how much my caveman would like me to. "Time for dessert." One last taste of her mouth, then I kiss my way down her body until I'm settled between her thighs. Arms wrapped around her hips, I tug her to my face. Breathe her in.

My dick is so hard, I swear it could punch a hole in the mattress. Because of her. My sweet Allison. One taste and I'm gone. No drawing it out, no teasing and retreating. Just me, licking, sucking, flicking. Me, humping the goddamn bed while devouring her sweet-and-spicy pussy like a starved beast.

"Oh, God, *yes*..." Fingers tangled in my hair, she writhes and bucks, her hips arching to meet my tongue as she comes and comes, her sexy moan filling the room.

A man has his limits, and I've reached mine. I grab a condom from my wallet and roll it on, then cover her with my body again. "Later, you're going to ride me so I can watch your tits bounce, but this time, I need to kiss you while I'm buried deep."

"I need that too."

"You don't know what you do to me," I say, filling her in one hard, fast thrust that forces a gasp from her parted lips. I hold myself in check long enough for her to catch her breath, then pull out and claim her again. "I touch you and I lose the ability to think." I draw her arms above her head, threading our fingers together and crushing my lips to hers. Over and over, I stroke into her. Deep thrusts that make her moan into my mouth and tip her hips higher.

Hot, heavy need licks at my balls, but I bite it back. I thrust deeper, dragging my cock over her G-spot and rolling my pubic bone against her clit until she's panting against my lips. "Come for me," I growl as her pussy squeezes me.

Her sexy-as-fuck, feminine moan fills the room again, stripping the last of my control.

"*Fuuuck*..." I slam into her, burying my dick so deep, I

can't tell where I end and she begins. I don't want to find out.

I roll to my side, groaning when I slide free of her body. Fucking condom. If I wasn't wearing one, I could stay buried inside her, where I belong.

Where I belong. The thought hits me hard, pushing the air from my lungs.

"Is something...wrong?" Her voice is soft and quiet behind my turned back.

I toss the condom in a nearby trash bin, then roll to her, covering her with my body again. "Only that I need to be inside you."

"Oh. Well, that's not wrong at all." She bites her thoroughly kissed bottom lip, before smiling up at me. She's glowing, and she's so beautiful, she takes my breath away.

"No, it's definitely not wrong." The opposite. Allison feels righter than any woman ever has. So right, I can't picture another night where I'm not balls-deep inside her, making her come, then lying beside her, in awe of my incredible luck.

"We should do that again," she says, giggling. "Tomorrow night?"

"Every night, sweetheart." Every damn night for the rest of my life. But it's too soon for that. Feeling it to my core is one thing. Saying it to a woman I met two days ago is another.

She wouldn't believe it. Hell, I can't believe it.

I lower my head and kiss her. Safer than staring into her eyes when my head's full of shit I can't say. One taste of her lips and blood rushes to my cock, making it thick and hard.

Her eyes pop open when I shift enough to notch the head against her pussy. "Already?"

"You do things to me, Allison." I slide home, groaning as I bottom out in her pussy. "Fuck, you feel so good." Buried to the hilt, I roll to my back, taking her with me, then setting her upright. "Your tits are as perfect as every other part of you." I cup them, stroking my thumbs over the nipples until they're hard peaks that demand squeezing. "Feel good, or bad?" I ask when she gasps.

"Good. It's just...different."

"Nobody's pinched your pretty nipples before?"

"No," she whispers, arching her back. "But I like you doing it."

One hand on her breast, the other thumbing her clit, I thrust my cock higher. "Ride me, sweetheart. Ride me hard and come on my cock."

"What about you—you're not wearing a condom."

"I won't come inside you." I increase the friction on her clit. Roll her peaked nipple between my fingertips. I can't take my eyes off her as she rocks back and forth on my cock. I'm steel-fucking-hard again. I won't break my promise, but fuck, I want to.

A rosy blush spreads across her chest, up her neck, to her cheeks. Her head falls back and her lips part, her breath coming in hitched moans.

"Tell me who owns this pussy I'm fucking, who you're coming for."

"You," she pants, grinding on me, squeezing my cock with her tight heat. "I'm coming for you."

Jaw clenched, I hold back. Resist the throbbing urge to unload inside her. Barely. I need to come, and I need to make good on another promise—to make her mine.

I lift her off my dick, reposition her so she's straddling my face. One hand on her back, I guide her down. "Wrap your pretty lips around my cock and suck me dry, sweetheart." I groan as she lowers her mouth onto me, one slow inch at a time, until my dick hits the back of her throat. "That's so good, baby. Your mouth was made for my cock."

She hums around me, and it's all I can do not to blow my load on her next downstroke. I need a distraction, and I've got a primo one right in front of me.

I band my arm around her hips and pull her pussy onto my mouth. She jerks against the first press of my tongue on her clit. Sensitive, probably, but I don't care. She's going to come again. I need her to.

I hold her hips, Frenching her entrance and sucking her clit until she's grinding her pussy onto my face. Her thighs shake by my head, and her moan vibrates around my shaft. The last of my control shatters. I slid one hand to her ass, pressing a finger against her pucker while I come down her throat. Marking her as mine. Mine to keep—tonight, and every night after.

allison

For what has to be the fifth time since we collapsed in a sweaty, sexhausted heap, my phone vibrates on the nightstand.

"Maybe you should answer it," Adam says while lazily tracing my spine. Though lazily isn't the right word. The man doesn't seem to have a lazy bone in his body, especially in regard to his *boner* bone.

I always believed that older men couldn't get as hard,

and couldn't go more than one round. Adam proved both of those wrong. Whew, did he ever.

I exhale when the silent ringing ends. Then groan when it begins again. "It's probably Esme, wanting details from our date. I'll shoot her a quick 'go away' text, then put my phone on Do Not Disturb."

"Do you always tell her the details of your personal life?"

"I always have." My cheeks burn as I reach across his broad chest to collect my phone. Partly because the stretch causes his hand to slide down my ass, between my legs. Mostly because I've essentially admitted to sharing the details of our sexy beach adventure. "I'm not going to tell her about tonight. Not the details, anyway," I say, meeting his gaze after settling in alongside his body again. "But she'll hound me to the ends of the earth if I don't confirm we had sex, so I'll do that."

His smile warms me more than his touch, and that's saying something. "Everybody should have a friend they trust that much. It won't bother me if you tell Esme about us. If sharing your feelings makes you happy, then don't hold back."

If only the advice applied to sharing my feelings with him. God, how fast would he shoot out of my bed, and out of my life, if I told him what's in my heart—that I've fallen in love with him.

"Do you have a best friend you talk to about your most personal details?" I ask, changing the conversation's direction.

"I do. Vince. He's been my number one since we met at University of Toronto. The cottage rental was his and his wife's, but he sublet it to me after the divorce made going into the office a shitshow."

"Wow, that's a generous friend, giving up his vacation plans."

"Vince would give you the shirt off his back if he thought you needed it more than him. I trust him with everything. He's the only person who knows all the ugly details about my divorce, and how much it ate me up to have my name dragged through the mud at a company I now own a hell of a lot less of, thanks to Shauna's lies."

"That's how she got forty-nine percent instead of the twenty-five from your prenup agreement? By lying?" My stomach knots when shutters fall over his eyes, and his lips flatten to a thin, tight line. "You don't have to tell me. It's your personal business, I shouldn't have pried, I'm sorry."

"You're my personal business now, Allison," he says, stroking my hair. "I'll tell you whatever you want to know, and hope to hell you don't think less of me when you hear the answer."

"As long as you're telling me the truth, I couldn't think less of you." Maybe I'm just naïve. Too trusting, even after having my eyes opened by Dennis's betrayal. Or, maybe I'm blinded by the flurry of feelings I have for Adam. "I understand if you don't feel comfortable entrusting me with personal information, though, since I won't be a part of your life once July ends."

Clouds roll through the gray-blue eyes locked with mine. "I was an asshole offering you that kind of deal. You deserve a hell of a lot more than a summer fling."

"You're right, I do. And, one day, I'll have more. A husband who adores me and would never want to stray, a baby we'll love more than life itself. But right now, I also deserve the chance to explore who I am, sexually, with a man I trust to take me everywhere I didn't know I wanted to go. I'm sorry crappy circumstances brought you to Hope Harbor, but I'm happy they led to our deal."

His brow line forms a ridge, and his jaw clenches. "You're really okay with it. The deal."

"Show me a deal with better perks, hmm?" I smile, forcing bubbles into my voice. I can do this. Tuck my big feelings into a box to deal with after he's gone. Because I don't want him to back out of our deal due to a guilty conscience. I'd rather have a month of todays with Adam than none.

The phone I haven't checked since retrieving it vibrates to life against my palm, startling me, and breaking the still that's fallen over us.

"Go ahead and check it," he says, pressing a kiss to my head, then extricating himself from our snuggled position, and the bed. "I'll grab us some hydration. We could both use it after all those *perks*." He's smiling when he says it, but the storm hasn't lifted from his eyes as he turns to leave the bedroom.

I shouldn't have asked about his real life. That's not a conversation for our sexy, temporary bubble. The tension will pass. I just need to stay in the casual zone, no matter how badly I wish we could be more.

I flip my phone faceup and unlock it, expecting a sea of text-message notifications from Esme. "Oh, shit."

"Everything okay?" Adam asks, returning to the room as what can only be bad news fills my phone screen.

"My friend only sent one message. The rest of the buzzing was my mother calling." Groaning, I flop onto my back, holding the evil phone above my face. "Somebody must've snitched on me."

His easy smile returns, along with a genuine chuckle.

"You're twenty-six. What could anybody 'snitch' to your mother about?"

"About you."

The mattress dips beneath his weight as he resumes his place on the bed. "You think your mother called about me?"

"I have eight hundred and twenty-six dollars in savings, and I'd bet every one of them." I sigh while opening the voicemail app, pausing to look over at him. "This could get embarrassing. I can go into the other room to listen to the messages."

"I'll leave if you want privacy, but there's nothing for you to be embarrassed about. Not around me."

"I suppose that's true. I am an open book, and you've, um, opened my book more than anyone has."

"It's a great book." His sexy grin sends an awakening tingle to parts that should be comatose from multiple orgasms. "Hurry up and listen to your messages so I can enjoy another chapter."

Just like that, we're back to fun and sexy. I didn't ruin anything by attempting to take things deeper. "Deal," I say, tapping in my passcode. "And you're right, it doesn't matter what you think of my mother, since you'll never meet her." I turn to face him while shifting the phone to my ear, the sour curl returning to my stomach when he doesn't return my smile.

"You have five unheard messages," the computerized voice says.

The first four are from my mother, each one a succinct, "Call me back when you get this."

I delete them in turn, my mind grasping for what could've flipped the switch on Adam's mood. My finger is poised to delete the final message just as quickly, but it's not short like the others. Not even close.

"Allison Renée, I don't appreciate that you're avoiding me. It's late, you should've called me back by now. Unless you're still out with that man I had to hear about from Melinda Brown, of all people. She called me up on the pretense of the church's pancake dinner, then drops in the question of whether you're dating yet, seeing as it's been a full *year* since you kicked Dennis out. Of course, I told her you're not dating anyone. Because surely, *I* would know. I *am* your mother. Imagine my *shame* when Melinda informed me she saw you at The Fischer Hotel, hanging all over some man with enough gray hair to make her think he's a friend of your father's." She pauses, punctuating the moment with a distinct cluck of disgust. "Don't get me wrong, dear, I want you to find a man. I won't get any grandchildren if you don't find one soon. But—"

I stab the End button, power off my phone and shove it to the edge of the bed. I pinch my eyes closed and drop my arm over my face, positioning it to hide my mouth. I wasn't kidding about being an open book. It's not only my heart that I wear on my sleeve. Even if I keep my words locked down, I know my expression would give me away.

"Hey, I'm here. Whatever that was, sweetheart, I'm here for you." Adam's tone is deep and soothing, the same as his touch when he gently peels my arm from my face, then slides his fingers through my hair like a comb, until I release the tension in a long breath.

I open my eyes, making a conscious effort *not* to worry my bottom lip. "Gossip spreads through Hope Harbor like a brushfire. Somebody called my mother after seeing us out for dinner. That message was just my mother being..." *Intrusive, insulting, judgmental.* "A worrywart. Nothing for you to be concerned about."

"You look concerned about it."

"It's fine." My shrug feels tense and jerky, and I close my eyes to regroup. "I'll call her tomorrow. By the time I see her for church and dinner on Sunday, she'll have calmed down." *I hope.* I open my eyes and find him watching me, his gaze brimming with concern. "It's nothing. Really."

"I heard every word, Allison. I know you didn't want me to, I saw you fumbling for the volume button, but your mother's words were loud and clear." He blows out a breath, and pushes his hand through the silver-dusted hair my mother mentioned. "I don't want my presence in your life to cause trouble between you and your family."

I bolt upright, pulling my knees to my chest for cover against the nakedness that didn't make me uncomfortable a few minutes ago. "What are you saying? Are you—" I don't even want to ask, but I have to. "Are you calling off the deal?"

"No," he says, pulling me into his arms. "Fuck, no. You think I could give you up that easily?"

I shrug again. Of course, that's what I think. Why wouldn't I? "I think you're a generous man with a conscience, and you'd do what you think is right. But I don't want that to be ending our deal." Burrowing closer, I take cover by pressing my face to his chest. "I don't want to give up the time we have together."

"Neither do I." He nuzzles my hair, hugging me tighter as he presses a kiss to my forehead. "I'm not generous enough to let you go just because your mother thinks I'm too old for you. You're the only person allowed to make that call. I'll only walk out of your life if you want me to."

My heart skips in my chest. I know they aren't, but his words sound like so much more than a deal. "I'll never want that."

"Good." He trails his fingers over my arms, my back,

every inch of skin within reach. "What time are we going to church and dinner?"

I jerk backward, expecting to find a grin on his face. There isn't one. "What—why?" I shake my head to loosen by bug-eyed stare. "You don't have to do that. I'll handle my mother. And any other gossipy people."

"Allison." He stills my fidgeting by cupping my face in his palms. "Our deal wasn't just about sex."

"It also didn't include Sunday service and dinners with my parents."

His smile is as warm as his touch. "I want to go with you. To both. Anywhere you go, I want to be with you."

"My parents will assume we're in a relationship, that you're my boyfriend. I won't be able to tell them the truth."

"Those things are the truth. We made a commitment, we're not seeing anybody else, and definitely seeing a lot of each other."

I can't help laughing when he waggles his eyebrows. I also can't prevent my heart from beating faster when he pulls me closer, and kisses me deep enough that I feel it all the way to my toes.

"You're where I want to be." He lays me back on the bed, sears me with the heat in his gaze, then fills me with one perfect thrust that steals my breath. "Right here, sweetheart," he says, retreating and stroking into me again. "With you is the only place I want to be."

chapter 8

. . .

allison

I NEARLY JUMP out of my skin at Adam's light tapping on the closed bathroom door. "I'll be out in a minute."

"Not rushing you. Just letting you know I'm loading the car, so I won't hear you if you're talking to me."

"Okay." I'm so *not* okay. Not only because there's less than a week remaining in July, and every minute that ticks past is like an attack on my soon-to-be-broken heart, but because of the white stick in my shaking hands. The reason I've been locked in the bathroom longer than my normal morning ritual.

A pregnancy test. One with two prominent pink lines.

I'm pregnant.

Five days from now, I'll be pregnant and alone.

It's too early to have morning sickness, but the breakfast Adam sweetly served me in bed races up my throat. I crank the water on full blast to cover my retching, then fold myself over the toilet and unload the contents of my stomach.

He's waiting, and he's on a schedule, so I wash up. Brush my teeth a second time. My pale-faced reflection stares back at me, wide-eyed and scared. I can't go out there looking like this. Adam will know something's wrong the second he sees me. I can't stay in the bathroom forever and I can't tell him the truth.

I rarely wear makeup, but today, I put some on. Lilac eyeshadow, lavender lip gloss, and soft-pink blusher. Now I have an excuse for the extra time in here and I look less like someone who just stress-vomited.

Even if he can't tell something's bothering me when I step out of the bathroom, I have to get through the rest of the day. Two hours in the car. Our fancy date night in Toronto. Then five more days together here. Adam has grown to know me intimately—body and soul. It won't take him long to realize something's on my mind.

If it comes to it, I'll have to tell him the *other* truth. That I fell in love with him, even though I said I wouldn't. And then hope it doesn't spoil the remaining time we have together.

He's waiting in the living room for me when I step out of the bathroom, and the sight of him stops me in my tracks. Charcoal suit, white dress shirt, royal-blue tie, and black shoes that are shinier than a freshly waxed, brand-new car.

"Wow." I scoop my jaw off the floor and check the corners of my mouth to make sure I'm not *literally* drooling. "Is this how you usually dress for work?"

Nodding, he pushes off the wall where he was leaning, and crosses the room to take my face in his palms, and kiss me breathless. "You're even more beautiful than you were an hour ago."

"I put on makeup."

"That's not it," he says, shaking his head. "It's something else. You're glowing."

God, I wish things were different. I want it so badly, it plays through my mind like a fairytale scene. Me, telling him I'm glowing because I'm pregnant. Him, smiling and sweeping me into his arms. The two of us, making plans for the family we both want.

"Sorry I took so long in the bathroom. I hope it won't make you late." *Late.* Like my period. The one that won't be back for another nine months.

"We're good. My meeting's not for three hours yet, and traffic should be moving steadily by the time we get to the city." Hand on the small of my back, he leads me out of my house, then into his car. "I'm glad you could get a couple days off," he says as we pull onto the street. "I'm looking forward to showing you a slice of my world, since you've shared all of yours."

"Yes, you experienced my whole world within three weeks." Another reality check for me. A glaring example of the gap between us. "You're probably looking forward to getting back to your life. The excitement, fast pace, and variety."

There are two stoplights in Hope Harbor, and he uses the first red to look over at me. "There are definitely things I've missed. That doesn't mean I haven't enjoyed every minute I've spent here, with you."

"Of course." I give the best smile I can muster. "It's been a fun few weeks."

The light turns green, saving me from the weight of his gaze. For the moment. It's going to be a long ride.

allison

Adam's private office is on the thirtieth floor of a building that looks as if it's made of mirrors. The inside is as slick as the exterior—dark wood, black leather, and polished stainless steel everywhere. The interior doors are ten feet tall, and his desk is as wide as my entire kitchen.

"Make yourself at home," he said when he dropped me off in here. Maybe he's already forgotten what my home looks like, because it might as well be another planet compared to this place.

When he said he needed to attend an important meeting, and asked me to join him so we could make it a big night in the city, I was excited. I envisioned the two of us cuddling in a private booth at some posh restaurant, sharing wine as smooth as velvet, and kisses as deep as the ocean. Maybe there'd be dancing. Or he'd take me to see a theatre show. Things I've never done, and likely never will again.

I expected to be out of my element, but in a fairytale way. Not a fish-out-of-water way.

Sighing, I drop into one of the seats on the outer edge of his desk. The luxurious chair welcomes me with cushy comfort. It's nicer than my couch, and probably cost four times as much, maybe more. For a secondary office chair. This world, Adam's daily world, couldn't be further from mine.

I remove my phone from my handbag and pull up the photo from my bathroom. I didn't imagine it, there's no mistaking the two pink lines. I wouldn't have thought to take a test if Esme hadn't mentioned Aunt Flow.

Our cycles have been in sync since the tenth grade. I hadn't noticed my absentee period until Esme texted about skipping our monthly ice-cream-sundae run to give me more time with Adam.

I wish I'd waited to take the test. Saying goodbye to him is going to be hard enough. Doing it while keeping this secret...

The door to Adam's office is whisper quiet, but the click-clacking of heels on marble tile is anything but. I sit straighter in the chair and turn toward the door, expecting to see the secretary he introduced me to upon arrival.

"Where's Adam?" A tall, blonde woman with as many polished surfaces as the building glares at me while crossing to Adam's desk. "I heard he's in the building, where is he? And who are you?"

He hasn't talked about her much, but there's no doubt in my mind this woman is his ex-wife. Who else would storm into a company owner's inner office and behave this way?

"I'm a friend of Adam's," I say, rising from the seat. "He's in a meeting."

Scowl firmly in place, the woman drills me with a frosty stare. "Adam doesn't have female friends. As his wife, I would know. Nor is he in a meeting, because there aren't any in progress that would involve him. I know that too, as I own half the company."

"Forty-nine percent, and, *ex*-wife. I know both those things because he told me what you did during the divorce." I give her the bitchiest smile possible, though I'm proud of the fact that it'll never come close to hers.

"Well, aren't you an interesting development?" She looks me over with an icy gaze that sends a shiver down my spine. "It seems Adam did a little slumming after tucking his tail between his legs and scampering away to hide."

"If that's how you see him, you don't understand him at all."

"And you do?" The contempt in her voice is as cold as everything else about her. "I've worked with Adam for ten years, and was married to him for seven. How long have *you* known him?"

Regret swirls in my stomach. This is the last thing I needed right now, and yet another thing I'm stuck with. "We haven't known each other long, but we know each other very well."

She cocks a cover-model-perfect eyebrow, then laughs. "Oh, sweet little naïve girl. Assuming you met him while he's been away, you've known him what, three weeks? You could probably tell me exactly how many days, hours, and minutes, couldn't you? You've obviously fallen in love with him. Don't expect him to reciprocate those tender feelings."

"I don't," I whisper.

"You obviously know who I am, and you've decided I'm a calculating bitch. I won't deny it, but I wasn't always this way. Did he tell you why he divorced me?"

"Because you didn't want the same things out of life."

"How perfectly vague. Just enough of a story to tug at your sweet little heartstrings, and open your legs in the process, I'm sure." She smirks when I don't answer. "Let me fill you in, cherub. I asked Adam for one thing, ever—a baby. All he had to do was take the condom off and get me pregnant. The idea of fatherhood was so repugnant, he chose to divorce me instead. That's what loving Adam brings."

My stomach lurches again. This time, there's nothing to throw up, and nowhere to hide. I won't give this woman the satisfaction of seeing me cry. "Thanks for the warning, but I don't love Adam. I just love having sex with him."

Shauna's eyes widen, then she laughs. "I hope you don't expect him to believe that lie. He's an asshole, not an idiot." She's still laughing as she heads for the door. "Good luck, tender heart. You have no idea how much you'll need it."

adam

Something's wrong, and as much as I'd like to pin it on the run-in with my ex-wife, I know it's more. Allison has been quiet since we left her house this morning. Not angry quiet, just...distant.

One of the things I love about Allison is her heart. How she's not afraid to show it. To share it. Watching her retreat behind a wall today, I nearly turned the car around and went back to Hope Harbor, so I could take her to bed and knock that fucking wall down.

I wanted to make tonight an occasion she'll remember forever. Something she can tell her best friend about, because I know how much she values that relationship. Now I couldn't care less about the plans I lined up. I shouldn't have waited. Wouldn't have, if I'd been able to get my hands on the ring sooner.

Fuck, I should've bought something from the little jewelry store in Hope Harbor. Whatever they had in stock. We could be well into celebration mode by now. Fuck, we could've started planning the next chapter of our life two weeks ago.

Add it to the list of wrong decisions I've made. There's no going back, and I'd rather go forward with Allison than dwell on past mistakes, large or small. No more waiting for a fabricated perfect moment. To hell with the restaurant and her ring in a champagne flute. Now's the time.

"This is it." I gently squeeze her hand before releasing it to open the door of my twelfth-floor condo.

"It's beautiful." She glances around the space while walking to the floor-to-ceiling window overlooking the Toronto harbor. "Wow, that's breathtaking."

"Couldn't agree more," I say, sliding my arms around her from behind and nuzzling her ear. "You're the most beautiful, breathtaking view I've ever seen, no matter where you are."

She doesn't answer. Doesn't turn or smile up at me.

"Allison." When she doesn't respond, I turn her in the circle of my arms, and gently tip her chin up. "Whatever's bothering you, you can tell me. I'm here for you."

"For now." She blinks fast and swallows hard, unmistakably forcing back tears. "Less than a week."

"For always. I'll always be here when you need me." I dip down and kiss her, drawing back when I taste the tears that've rolled down her cheeks. "You're crying. Sweetheart, don't cry."

"I'm sorry," she whispers, burying her face against my chest. "I agreed to our deal, to keeping my heart out of it. But I couldn't. I fell in love with you." Sunlight streaming through the glass bounces off her hair as she shakes her head. "The deal, I just can't anymore. I can't pretend I'm okay having short-term fun with you. I can't pretend it won't break my heart when July ends. Don't say you'll be there for me once the deal is over. I know you mean well, but I can't be in casual contact with you. Please take me home. And after you drop me off, come back here, to your life. Forget about me."

"I could never forget you."

"Then, remember me fondly, but...let me go."

I hold her tighter when she tries to back out of my arms. My heart's pounding as if I'm running for my life. It's not wrong. If I don't catch Allison before she writes me off, I can't picture what my life will be like. "You really think I was going to let you go at the end of July? That I could *ever* let you go?"

"That was the deal. Your deal. You never said you wanted to change it."

Eyes pinched shut, I press my lips to her hair. Breathe her in, let her scent, her soul, roll through me until my pulse fades from my ears. "I've fucked this up from day one, but I'm going to make it right."

"You never promised me more than you gave. There's nothing to make right."

I step back, cup her beautiful face in my palms. "I was an asshole, offering you that deal. An idiot to think I could stick to it. I fell in love with you the first night, Allison. The things I felt—they scared the shit out of me. Then those feelings got bigger, and the fear shrank, until it was gone. I've felt love before, but nothing like what I feel for you."

"If that's true, why didn't you tell me? We slept together every night and woke up together every morning. Why would you let me continue thinking it was just part of our deal?"

"At first? Fear. I'd told you I had no interest in love, that you shouldn't count on me for more than a fling. Then everything flipped inside me. How could I tell you I loved you within days of giving you that asshole speech? I didn't think you'd believe me. Worse, I was afraid you didn't feel the same way, that you'd call off the rest of our time together before I could convince you to let me into your heart."

"You were already there," she says softly.

I want to kiss her, but once I start, I won't be able to stop. And there's still more to say. Important things that can't wait. "I started planning this night two weeks ago. Seeing you so upset today, knowing that I caused it—" I exhale, long and slow. "I should've said it already, a hundred times, but I'm telling you now. I love you. I know we've got things to work out—where we'll live, how much time we'll spend here, and in Hope Harbor—but those are just details. I love you, Allison. I'm not letting you go."

"You have to." A fat tear slips from her eye as she takes a step backward. "Love isn't enough, we don't want the same things out of life. I want to have a family, and I know that you don't."

Fuck. I only left her in my office for twenty minutes. I met my lawyer, signed papers that'll give Allison everything if I'm ever stupid enough to cause her pain, then got the ring I'd ordered from the main vault at the office. Not a long time, but too long. "You talked to Shauna."

Allison nods. "She heard you were in the building, and stormed into your office."

"And decided to give you her side of the divorce."

Another nod, this one accompanied by more tears. "She said all she wanted was a baby, and you hated the thought of kids so much, you divorced her instead."

Blood rushes to my temples again, and I have to consciously unclench my jaw. "I did divorce her instead of fathering her child. We went into our marriage with our eyes wide open. Two workaholics with no desire for a family. When Shauna changed her mind, I said I'd divorce her, so she could find someone who'd make her happy in a way that I couldn't. I offered to buy the twenty-five percent stake in the company I'd written into our prenup, if continuing to work there would be uncomfortable for her. Instead, she took me to court for 'emotional abuse.'"

"How is not wanting to have children considered emotional abuse?"

"She claimed I'd promised we'd have kids, and that I'd forced her to take The Pill every day so she wouldn't get pregnant."

"But that's just one person's story against another."

"It would've been, except she'd been secretly seeing a therapist, feeding them bullshit lies that substantiated her claims. She waived her patient confidentiality rights, and authorized the therapist to release her session history as part of the record. She now owns forty-nine percent of my company, and she's doing her best to turn as many of its employees against me as possible. That's why I took a break from the office. I don't know if she ever loved me, or really wanted a baby, or if the whole thing was a very calculated setup."

"Oh, my God, Adam." Allison throws herself into my arms, making the world better with a simple embrace. "You could've told me the whole story. Why didn't you?" she asks, looking up at me with lingering sadness I'd do anything to erase.

"You might not have believed me."

"I would have."

"Not a chance I was willing to take. Even if I had, I didn't want to waste time or energy rehashing the past, when I was so fucking happy in the present, with you."

"I was happy with you too. More than I dreamed possible, but—"

"No 'but,'" I say as she pulls away from me again, shaking her head when I try to draw her closer. "I love you, Allison. Do you still love me?"

"So much."

"Then stay with me, whether it's here, or in Hope Harbor, or both. There's nothing we can't figure out together."

"Except a family. You don't want one, and I'd never try to change your mind or force you into a situation that'd make you unhappy. But I'm going to have a baby one day." Her face is red with restrained emotion. Distress she shouldn't be feeling. Wouldn't be feeling, if I'd been honest with her from the beginning.

I'm ready to be honest now. "That's it, you don't want to hear my thoughts on the subject? Because I have some. Fuck, do I. If you knew how I truly feel—"

"I'm pregnant." The dam breaks on her tears, and she spins away, sobs racking her body. "I don't expect you to stay with me, or be in the baby's life. I know you didn't want this."

Instinct demands I wrap my arms around her, scoop her up and take her to bed, where I'll show her exactly how much I want her, want this. But first things first.

I pull the ring from my pocket as I make the space between us disappear. Standing in front of her, I go down on one knee, take her hand, then open the velvet box. "I'm in love with you, sweetheart. So fucking in love with you. I'm with you until the end of time. You and our baby, or babies. As many as you want, or you'll let me give you, because I've been thinking about it—fuck, I've been obsessing about it—since the night on the beach."

"You've been obsessing about getting me pregnant?"

"You wouldn't believe the stuff that's gone through my head." Revisiting those thoughts has my cock pressing against my fly, ready and desperate, the way I always am for her. "I don't want to keep anything from you again. I swear I didn't consciously set out to get you pregnant, but on a subconscious level—maybe. All the times I was inside you without a condom... I knew there was a chance, even though I didn't come inside you. I should've taken better care of you, protected you, but I was selfish. I wanted every part of you for myself. I still do."

"I wanted to give you every part of me," she says softly. "I still do."

My heart's on par with my cock—ready to explode. Because of her. Only for her. "And I want to give you everything. Everything I have. Everything I am, and ever will be. Honor me with the privilege of being your husband, and I promise I'll spend the rest of my life making you happy. Marry me, sweetheart."

"Yes," she whispers, fresh tears rolling over her cheeks as I slide the ring onto her finger. "Oh my God, Adam, yes."

"Some of my favorite words," I say, standing and pulling her in tight. "Think I'm going to need to hear you say them a little louder, Mrs. Foster."

"Only a little?" She giggles when I scoop her off her feet, into my arms. "Are the walls thin in this fancy condo of ours? Are you worried the neighbors might hear us?"

Condo of *ours*. I fucking love that. "If they don't hear you screaming my name while you come, I'd better step up my game."

"Is that what this is, a game?" There's a smile on her beautiful face as she asks a question similar to one from the night we made our deal.

"No games necessary, sweetheart. I'm already the winner."

"We both are," she says, as I lay her out on our king-size bed.

Settled alongside her sexy body, I splay my hand across her abdomen. "We all are."

adam

THE LATE-DAY SUN hangs above the horizon, bathing the sky and sand in peach, pink, and gold. It's warm but not uncomfortable, and there's not a hint of humidity, which I'm told is a miracle for Hope Harbor in August. Yesterday's downpour disappeared with today's dawn, leaving the beach dry by afternoon. A few dozen white chairs are arranged to face the lake, but when the guitarist starts playing, all the guests' heads turn in the opposite direction.

Allison steps out of the white cabana, and none of the other details matter. The soft white dress, the tiara made of flowers, a pair of flip-flops with blue bows on top—all perfect. None of those things make her beautiful. She glows from within, because of who she is. So damn beautiful, it's like looking at the sun. She is my sunshine. The center of my world now, and there's nothing I want to do more than revolve around her for the rest of time.

Her father steps to her side, and she loops her arm with

his. He whispers something to her, and she smiles, then hugs him tight. Had to be his blessing. I'll thank him later for giving her the one thing she wanted that I couldn't provide.

He didn't wholeheartedly support Allison's decision to marry a man almost his age, and I get it. He's worried about her future, the inevitable years after I'm gone. He's not alone, I worry about that too. But it's the faintest dot in a far-off future. Allison and I have a lifetime together before that day comes, and we're going to fill it with friendship, love, adventure, and our family. She'll never be alone.

My heart takes off at a cardio clip as she walks toward me. Hush falls over the guests when she reaches me, and when I finally get to take her hands, it's all I can do not to skip to the kiss.

"You're so beautiful."

"Thank you," she says, unleashing the full power of her breathtaking beauty when she smiles at me.

"I can't wait for the vows, and they aren't enough anyway. You complete me, Allison. Your heart and soul fill every space, you make my life overflow with more happiness than I imagined possible."

Soft *awes* rise from the nearby seats, but the words weren't said to impress anyone, even my glassy-eyed bride.

"Thank you for making every dream I didn't know I had come true," I say, raising our joined fingers to my mouth and pressing a kiss to her fingertips. "I promise I'll spend every day making yours come true too."

"You already have." A tear slides down her cheek, toward her rosy, kissable lips, and I use the pad of my thumb to gently wipe it away.

The minister clears his throat, his eyebrows rising when we tear our gazes from each other to look at him. "You're a tough act to follow, but whenever you're ready, I'll do my best."

Light laughter fills the warm, summer evening air. The happy noise tapers off to peaceful silence, leaving only the sound of water lapping the shore, and my heartbeat, as I look into the eyes of my bride. My soulmate. The mother of my unborn child.

"I've never been more ready," I say.

The minister nods, draws a breath, then the ceremony begins, along with the rest of forever.

Thank you for reading **The Deal With Love**! I hope you loved Allison and Adam's summer-fling-becomes-forever romance as much as I do. If you have a few minutes to write a review at your favorite book retailer, BookBub, or Goodreads, I would be ever so grateful.

Allison's best friend Esme gets her
happily ever after in **Doggy Style**.

There are more feel-good romances in
the Hope Harbor Series, too!

hope harbor series

Hope Harbor is a fictional small town on the north shore of Lake Erie, in Ontario, Canada. There are other real-life cities and towns mentioned in the Hope Harbor books. With a little geographic investigation, you might be able to pinpoint Hope Harbor's location on a map.

All books in the Hope Harbor series are standalone stories focused on a different couple's romance. You'll visit the same settings across multiple books, and there may be some character crossover pop-ins, but there's no reading order. Start anywhere in the series, and follow whatever path you choose in Hope Harbor! They all lead to a satisfying happily ever after.

hope harbor series books

Dad Bod Wingman
Heart Beats
Last Call Casanova
Fleshing It Out
The Deal With Love
Doggy Style
King of Her Dreams
Her Pipe Dream
12 Days

These books are linked to the Hope Harbor Series, but take place in a different location:

Resorting to Love
White Lie Christmas
Heart of Texas

Check Karla's website for the most up-to-date list of Hope Harbor Series books.
www.karladoyle.com/books/hope-harbor-series/

gingerbread man

gingerbread man

Man of the Month Club: Candy Cane Key

A town that celebrates Christmas year-round is the perfect place for a newly divorced, six-foot-four ginger-haired baker to open his new business, The Ginger Bread Man. Too bad he doesn't share the community's love of everything ho-ho-ho. Fake it until you make it, right? Or hire someone who has enough holiday spirit that nobody notices your lack thereof. Enter Honey Golding, the sweetest little thing Cal has ever laid eyes on. His much-younger new employee is off-limits, but his sweet tooth might overrule his common sense... and his willpower.

A small town, grumpy + sunshine, steamy age-gap romance with a guaranteed Happily Ever After!

Celebrate National Gingerbread Day (June 5th) with this sweet-and-spicy treat!

one

Monday, May 15th

cal

WHEN LIFE HANDS YOU LEMONS, you make lemonade. Whatever rose-colored-glasses-wearing optimist came up with that bullshit didn't walk in on their wife fucking their business partner. Assholes.

It's been a year since I packed a bag and exited that life. Winona and Shaun didn't stay together, and I didn't give my ex the time of day when she asked me for another chance. Once burned is enough.

As for my former business partner... Last time I checked, my old bakery's former five-star rating had dropped to a measly three. Lots of comments about favorite items no longer available and the new product being subpar. With reviews like that out in LA, it's only a matter of time until the place flatlines. Am I happy knowing my previous business is in the shitter while my new place is selling out every day? Fucking right I am.

I thought I had it all back in Cali. Prominent business, gorgeous wife, slick car, condo overlooking the beach. Living the fucking dream, right? Turns out I was living in dreamland instead.

The Ginger Bread Man is small potatoes compared to my old business. I'm serving a small Florida community and its Christmas-crazed tourists now, not high-profile Los Angeles clientele willing to spend more for baked goods than some people earn in a week. My new prices aren't jacked because they don't have to be. Also, because I'm not that guy anymore.

Small-town living and a slower pace are changes I didn't expect to enjoy. What my apartment above The Ginger Bread Man lacks in modern style, it makes up for in comfortable charm. Same with the bakery's storefront. Plus, all of it is solely mine. Nobody chews me out if I leave the toilet seat up during the night or load the paper roll in the wrong direction. At work, I bake—or don't bake—whatever the hell I want, without having to justify my choices. I have complete control over every aspect of the business.

Unfortunately, that currently includes customer service, since I haven't hired anyone for up front yet. I'd rather be behind the kitchen door, not in front of it. And playing along with people who love Christmas in an extreme way, when it's not even June yet...

Yeah, I knew the "celebrate Christmas every day" thing was Candy Cane Key's tourist trapping before I moved here. I thought that's all it'd be—a gimmick. Unfortunately, I couldn't have been more wrong.

Even the locals who come into the bakery seem to be perpetually hopped-up on holiday spirit. I've been playing along, but I'm a certified master baker, not an actor. Not a salesman, either. And I'm sure as hell not the six-foot-four Christmas elf everyone seems to think I should be.

Job number one—hire a fucking elf.

I slice the top off a takeout box, grab a fat black marker and scrawl "Help Wanted: Friendly Customer Service Elf" on the white cardboard, then tape it to the front window. Not the way we would've done things back in LA, but this is Candy Cane Key. Everything's different here. Including me.

By late-afternoon, my shelves and cases are long since empty, but the stack of applications is a hell of a lot fuller than I expected. Seems like that slapped-up sign on the window was a beacon to anyone and everyone looking for a job in Candy Cane Key. Too bad not a single one of them is the right person for the job.

As much as I want to hand over the service side of the business, I can't hire someone for the sake of being done with it. The bakery is my livelihood. My passion and my reputation. So I'll wait it out. Keep pretending I'm a merry motherfucker, though I doubt I'm fooling anyone.

I'm finishing the daily cleaning in the kitchen when I hear light tapping from the storefront. This isn't the first time. Until I get more employees hired, there's a limit to how much product I can make, and it's not enough. The bakery opened a few weeks ago, and I've sold out of every last item by mid-afternoon. No product, no point in staying open.

Not everyone agrees with that practice. I answered the first few times someone knocked. Figured they must have a reason for rapping on the glass when the place is clearly closed. Wrong again. Apparently, if my posted hours run until six, I should stay open until six. Guess I'm supposed to just blink and make more breads and baked goods magically appear, while I'm standing there with my arms crossed over my chest.

Yeah, not acknowledging that knock. Whoever it is will have to wait until tomorrow for their freshly baked carbs.

Except they don't want to wait, because they're knocking again. Louder this time. The kind of knocking that says they're not leaving until I answer.

Yet another reason I need to hire someone ASAP—to deal with this kind of shit in a way that won't permanently cost me a customer. Because right now, I want to storm out there and give whoever can't read the *Sorry, We're Closed* sign hanging at eye level a free sample of my ginger temper.

Tension tightens its grip on my trapezius muscles when my persistent would-be customer settles in for round three on the glass out front. I set aside the cleaning spray and paper towels, then head out of the kitchen.

The scowl on my face is probably as wide as the Key itself. That doesn't stop the cute brunette from smiling and waving as I cross the storefront to the door. No, not smiling—that doesn't adequately describe it. She's beaming. Practically glowing. Not from the sun at her back, either. It's her. The kind of beauty that's irresistible. Or would be, if she hadn't pissed me off with all the damn knocking.

"Sorry to bother you," she says when I unlock and open the door. "Your hours say you're open until six, so I thought I had plenty of time to catch you."

"I close when everything's sold."

Little Miss Sunshine doesn't flinch at my grumpy tone. She just stares up at me with the prettiest green eyes I've ever seen. "You don't have anything left to sell? By quarter after four?"

"All gone. Every last loaf and cookie." An apology would be appropriate here, I know. Not my style. Hence why I need an elf. "Come by in the morning if you don't want to be disappointed." Shit, even I can do better than that. I huff a miserable-sounding sigh. "I tell you what—I'll put something aside for you, and you can pick it up whenever you get here. The door will probably be locked, but I'll wait for you. Best I can do. So. What were you hoping to get today?"

"A job." No tapping on the glass this time. She pushes past me to reach in and pull my makeshift sign from the inside of the window, then hands it to me. "This job. You won't find anyone better. What time should I be here tomorrow?"

I grunt a laugh. Even smile a little. She's spunky, confident, and yeah, very easy on the eyes. Too easy, considering she's gotta be in her early-twenties, and I'm knocking on forty's door. My attraction is irrelevant. She's applying for a job, not a date.

Right now, she's my top candidate, simply because of her personality. But this is my business, and despite feeling like the stupidest man alive for being blindsided back in Cali, I'm not foolish enough to hire anyone on impulse. Not even the irresistible brunette.

"Got a resume?" I hook a nod toward the cash counter. "I'll add it to the pile and look it over later." When she's not standing in my personal space, looking and smelling like a sweet treat I could sink into. My second head doesn't get to do the hiring.

She breaks eye contact only long enough to pull a sheet of sunshiny-yellow paper from her bag.

Despite my comment about reviewing it later, I scan the page after she hands it to me. "No bakery experience," I say, pointing out the only fault I find.

Her genuine smile doesn't waver, not even for a moment. "Don't worry. I'll have your buns and baguettes figured out in no time."

If she knew how much *my* baguette liked the sound of that, she'd snatch her application from my hand and never come back. "I'll be in touch—" I glance at the paper again, as if I didn't already have her name and number committed to memory. I'm so full of shit. "Ms. Golding."

"It's Miss, and call me Honey."

Another grunted laugh slips out. "Hoping to *sweeten* me up so I give you the job, *Miss* Golding?"

"I always put Honora on formal or professional documents, but everyone in town calls me Honey."

Shit. I've got big feet and an even bigger mouth to shove them in.

She raises one eyebrow over eyes the color of moss and shiny as sea glass. "Don't worry, boss, I'm not offended. What time should I be here in the morning?"

"I haven't offered you the job." A smile forces its way past my resting grump face as I accept the hand she extended, awareness rising to riotous levels throughout my body the instant we make skin-to-skin contact.

"You will," she says, holding my hand and my gaze. "I'm exactly what you need."

She's right. I know it with every cell of my being. Trouble is, I think she's exactly what I need in more ways than I can have her.

two

. . .

honey

"HEY, MOM," I answer when my phone rings while I'm walking through town. My mother will read texts, but she refuses to have a conversation that way. "Just dropped off my resume at The Ginger Bread Man."

"Oh, good. I wasn't sure it'd be open by the time you got over there. The shelves were almost empty when I stopped in to get a treat, and he just up and closes once everything's gone. I realize the business is new, and he's still getting everything in order, but that's not going to help him build a loyal clientele in Candy Cane Key, no matter how delicious his products are. He really should have done his hiring before opening."

The critique is enough to make me hold the phone away so she doesn't hear me snort. If organization and preparation were competitive categories, my mother would come in last. Honestly, she wouldn't even want to enter the race. She prefers to live in the moment rather than to plan for one. Still, she has a point.

"I told him I'd start tomorrow, so that'll take a chunk of responsibility off his plate," I say, giving a friendly wave at a driver who stopped to let me cross the street.

"He hired you? On the spot?"

"Technically, no. But when I said I'd see him tomorrow, he didn't tell me *not* to come in, so I'm taking that as an indirect, 'you're hired.'"

"That's my girl." The smile in her voice is as clear as the water surrounding the beautiful Key. "You should stop by the house during book club tonight and try the treats I picked up, so you can compliment him on it tomorrow."

Book club night. The one thing my mother organizes. She's hosted her reading group once a month for as long as I can remember. That's at least sixteen years, because my first vivid memory happened when I was ten years old. My parents had sent me to bed but I couldn't sleep because of the voices from the living room, so I crept downstairs. Turned out, it wasn't a roomful of school moms fighting about some hot-button PTA issue. They were passionately discussing which "team" they were on, regarding a romance novel love triangle. Anyone who assumes book clubs are boring has never been a member of Fay Golding's Fiction Fay-Natics.

"What time do you bring out the treats?" I ask.

"Everything's set out for seven o'clock, when the meeting starts. And no, you can't have anything beforehand."

Damn it. She knows me so well.

"Then I'll be there at seven." Can't have those bookish buddies of hers gobbling all the dessert before I have a chance to snag some.

"Or you could join us for the entire meeting." It's not

the first time she's tried to lure me into her book club. Or the twentieth. "It's going to be a fun one."

Closing my apartment door behind me, I smile and shake my head. "You always say that."

"And I'm always right. But this one might interest you, since you're going to work for Cal Smith."

"Why, is this month's book a cozy mystery with a male baker?" I ask, taking a can of diet soda from the fridge, then tipping it to my mouth.

"No, darling. It's a forbidden romance with a very large, very handsome ginger who likes to restrain the heroine with various things while they have very vigorous sex."

Soda splatters from my lips and I choke on the little bit I didn't just spit all over my kitchen. "Seriously, Mom?"

"For goodness' sake, Honora. You're twenty-six. Surely, you're not still embarrassed about sex. It's the most natural thing in the world. How do you think you got here?"

"If it was through vigorous sex while you were restrained, Mom, I *really* don't want to know. Like, ever."

A resigned sigh floats into my ear. "Drop by the house this evening. You really ought to know how tasty Cal's goodies are."

"As long as that's not a double entendre, Mom, I'll be there."

"It wasn't," she says with a light laugh, "but since you're thinking it, there's hope for you yet. See you tonight, darling." She's gone before I say goodbye. My mother isn't one to linger—on a call, a hobby, a job...

The apple didn't fall far from the tree. Like my mom, I crave change. Hence why I'm in the market for a new job.

Don't get me wrong, my previous job was fine. Those forty hours a week staring at a computer screen and the surrounding drab gray walls of my cubicle more than paid the bills. For the first time since graduating college, I was able to pay off my credit card instead of digging myself deeper into debt. If I'd stayed there, I could have saved up for the down payment on a house.

But, God, it was boring. Monotonous. Every day, another piece of my soul disappeared into the void. Endless cold calling and script reading beneath fluorescent lighting just wasn't for me. I tried taking a practical job instead of jumping into a fun opportunity. I thought it might have a different ending than all the jobs before it. That maybe it would stick. I couldn't get bored with a job I never loved in the first place, right? Of course, it wasn't that simple. It never is with me.

I need variety. Scenery. Face-to-face interaction with people—even grumpy ones like Callaghan Smith.

When my mom called me about the *Help Wanted* sign she spotted in the window at Candy Cane Key's newest bakery, she also warned me that the owner isn't the most congenial person. As if that would dissuade me. I never met a person I couldn't win over. My future boss will be on the "everyone loves Honey" list in no time.

And he will be my boss. Starting tomorrow morning, when he unlocks the door and sees my smiling face waiting on the other side. The ginger baker is about to have his goodies rocked. No double entendre intended, even though my mom is right about Cal. The man *is* very large and very handsome. I may have been there looking for a job, but I'd have to be blind not to have noticed the manliness of the man. I recognized him immediately, even though I've only seen him from a distance, and not in daylight. The closeup view was *not* disappointing. It certainly won't hurt having him in my workday scenery.

I had no intention of hanging around for Mom's book club meeting. Arrive a respectful fifteen minutes after the meeting began, so I don't appear greedy. Grab some dessert, say a polite goodbye, then head out the door. That was my plan. I would've stuck to it if they'd been talking about their monthly book selection when I walked in. But no. They were discussing Cal. In detail.

"Last week, I bought bread for each of my neighbors—one loaf per day—just so I had an excuse to go look at that fine-ass man. And Lord, he does have a fine ass."

"I 'accidentally' spilled my coffee on the floor so he'd come around the counter to clean it up. *Mmmhmm*, that man can bend over in front of me anytime."

"Tall, big hands... you know what that means. You can tell just by looking at him that he's big *all over*."

"I'd like to unzip those white work pants and suck the scowl right off his growly, handsome face."

"Do you think he's ginger *everywhere?*"

And it just kept going. There are eight women in the book club, and every single one of them had something inappropriately favorable to say about the ginger giant. Their nickname, not mine. Even my mom joined in.

"My husband ensures I'm very satisfied in every way—and I'll leave it at that since my darling daughter is in the room," she said, giving all her pals a you-know-what-I'm-talking-about smile. "But if I were single, ginger would be my new favorite flavor." Thank God she kept it relatively clean in my presence.

I'm very aware that my parents are still madly in love. That doesn't mean I want to know the gory details. Nor did

I want to hear the inner workings of her mind where my future boss is concerned. It's fine when we share an opinion on a sexy celebrity. Knowing we're both thinking R-rated things about Cal just feels...weird.

Tucked inside the quiet solitude of my apartment, I can't resist Googling him. One of the book club ladies said he's originally from Los Angeles and that he was kind of a big deal there. I didn't know bakers could *be* a big deal. Chefs, yes. But bakers? Also a yes, apparently. The search results populating my screen confirm it.

Callaghan Smith co-owned a hoity-toity bakery in LA. The high-end place catered to celebrities and other well-to-do types. Everything about it was sophisticated modern glitz. The Ginger Bread Man is cozy and quaint—the total opposite of his old business, which is still open. What spurs a person to make such sweeping life changes?

I'd rather get that information from the source. And no, I won't be sharing my findings. Not with my mother or her book club cronies.

I'm sure an attractive man like Cal can handle female attention. It's me with the issue here. The idea of seeing one of my mother's friends flirt with him, or the thought that he might date one of them... I shake my head to clear the images from my mind. The job description said "friendly customer service elf," not "Cal's personal life manager" but I'm adding that to my duties anyway. A good employee looks out for her boss's best interests.

That's all this is—me, planning on being the best employee Callaghan Smith ever had. Making myself irreplaceable. It has nothing to do with his broad shoulders, strong jawline, or the tingly feeling I got as he towered over me. Nothing at all to do with the way his blue eyes twinkled during my persistence.

Shit. I'm blaming those horndog book club women for the thoughts flowing through my head. Yes, I noticed Cal is attractive all on my own, but hearing them verbally ogle him... It's their fault I'm thinking about what's beneath his tight, white work pants and the T-shirt that showed every bulging muscle of his lean upper body. This is a temporary train of thought, like most of mine are. It'll pass. It has to. I cannot have the hots for my future boss.

Tuesday, May 16th

cal

THE APARTMENT above the business is one of the things I liked about the building when I saw the real estate listing. I don't need to live somewhere big or showy. That was my ex's thing, not mine. Being a staircase away from work is a hell of a lot better than a commute. Plus, the views are incredible. Ocean on one side, cute little town on the other. What more could I want?

Someone to share the view with.

I growl at the unwelcome thought and swallow the remaining coffee in my mug. The only way I'm sharing my view with a woman is if I have her pressed up against the window and she's breathing hard enough to fog the glass. Then she can do the well-fucked walk right on out of here.

But a relationship? Hell no. Not interested in getting burned again. Something casual would hit the spot, but in a place as small and gossipy as Candy Cane Key... probably not a good idea.

That's a bullshit excuse and I know it. I'm just not a casual guy, in any aspect of my life. Maybe one day, I'll wake up and feel ready to open the door to another relationship. Maybe. Not holding my breath though. The only door I need to think about right now is the one for my business. Time to open that one.

After quickly brushing my teeth, I jog downstairs and through the prep area. The kitchen assistant I hired doesn't even look up as I pass. Joe knows my routine. I've got shit well underway by the time he gets here at five a.m., then we both bust our asses until eight-thirty, when I head upstairs to quickly shower and eat. Doors open at nine on the dot, and there are always people waiting.

Even after only a few weeks, the bakery has regulars, and a good chunk of them have learned to get here early. It's not their faces I see through the front window when I'm crossing the storefront to the door. It's my number-one applicant for the customer service job. The cute little brunette I had no business thinking about while stroking my cock last night. Did it anyway. Chances are pretty damn good I'm going to do it again.

I flip the sign and unlock the deadbolt, then greet the customers who stream through the doorway. Miss Sunshine hangs back, watching me with those pretty green eyes I could fucking get lost in. A couple of golden-brown curls frame her face. The rest of her hair is tucked up inside an elf hat. Doesn't matter that I only met her yesterday, I can already tell she has more personality than anyone I knew in LA. She's perfect for the job. Perfect for a lot of things.

"Miss Golding," I say, once it's just the two of us at the

door. "Nice hat." Now that we're up close, I can see it's not a generic elf hat from a discount store. The cone part is the standard red, but instead of a furry band around the bottom, it's flat white material with loaves of bread printed all over it. Cute and unique, like the woman wearing it.

"One elf, reporting for duty. And call me Honey." The smile she beams up at me is brighter than the Florida sunshine. She smooths one hand across the top of her short-sleeve, tapered-fit, white golf shirt, essentially drawing my attention to her tits. "I hope this is okay for now. You can give me a uniform or tell me what to wear later."

Now, I'm smiling too. Legit smiling, and it has nothing to do with business. That hasn't happened in a hell of a long time.

"Come on." She tilts her head as she slips past me. "We have customers to serve."

"We?" I ask, following her as she walks behind the bakery counter, where she stows her purse on an empty shelf near the cash register. "I haven't hired you."

"I handed you the *Help Wanted* sign and told you I'd start today. You didn't say no."

"And you took that as a job offer?" Damn, she's a piece of work—in the best kind of way.

"Good morning! I'll be right with you, Mrs. Halston," she says to the woman standing at the till, then steps close enough to me that she has to tip her head back to meet my eyes. "You didn't put the sign back in the window."

"Maybe I ran out of tape."

Without breaking eye contact, she reaches for the small dispenser I keep beside the register and holds it up in front of my face. "Here you go."

When I curl my fingers around the tape, capturing and

holding her hand in the process, the jolt that races through me is electric. "Congrats on your new job, customer service elf."

Her perfectly kissable lips curve higher. "Congrats on the best decision you ever made, gingerbread man."

Wild as it is, I think she might be right. "Let's get to work." Releasing her hand, I move to the cash register, where I give the woman who's waiting the most authentic smile I've given anyone since I opened. "Just the loaf of pumpernickel for you this morning?"

"Yes, thank you. And if you don't mind me saying, you made a smart hiring choice. Honey is a wonderful young woman." Mrs. Halston turns her attention to Honey, a gentle, maternal smile on her face. "Maybe this will be the one that sticks."

A hint of pink creeps across Honey's tanned cheeks. "I hope so."

Based on the number of jobs on Honey's resume, Mrs. Halston's comment clearly refers to Honey sticking it out at the bakery. But the way Honey's eyelashes flutter when she gives me a little peripheral glance, I can't help wondering if she might be hoping something else about this opportunity sticks.

She's my employee, not to mention being significantly younger. That doesn't stop me from wanting her to stick around as more than just my customer service elf.

Honey was a quick study with everything. She had all the frontend tech stuff down before she'd been here half an hour. The assortment of jobs she's worked gave her enough familiarity with the machines and apps I use to make training almost unnecessary.

As soon as we got through the initial rush of customers —all of which she watched and helped with from a position close enough to my side that our arms brushed repeatedly—she pulled a notebook from her bag and started jotting down names, info, and pricing for every product I make.

Her exact words after jotting something about the last one: "I won't need these notes tomorrow. I just have to look at something once to remember it."

Bold promise, yet I don't doubt her for a second. She never stops going. Never turns it off. Just buzzes around, smiling and chatting through everything she does, all of it looking comfortable and natural.

After a quick tour of the facilities and a lightning round of Q & A, Honey shooed me into the kitchen to "make more stuff to sell." She didn't care what, though I fully expect that to change as she settles in. The woman is a snack-sized force of nature. And every minute with her just makes me hungrier for a taste.

I haven't had the opportunity to bake during business hours since opening the shop. Joe's head snapped up the instant I set foot in the kitchen, his eyes going wide as I scrubbed up at the sink, then tied my apron over my baker's jacket and wrapped a scarf around my head. It felt great.

When I emerge from the kitchen with the first tray of cinnamon buns, Honey literally cheers. After the clapping and squealing ends, she checks the time, then looks me in the eye. "I'll have it all sold in an hour."

"Think so?" I ask, then head back to the kitchen for another tray, then another. "Still think you can sell it all in an hour?"

She tips that pretty chin up and arches one perfect dark eyebrow. "Is that all you've got?"

So bold, my little elf.

I nod. Just once. "Don't want to overwhelm you on your first day." Let her think I'm talking about baked goods. I'm the only one who needs to know what's running through my filthy mind about how much I'd like to give her.

"Are the bakery's social accounts logged in on this terminal?" she asks, pulling up the internet browser on the computer.

"They should be." I move closer, watching her fingers fly over the keyboard as she opens a line of tabs long enough to make my head spin. "I don't have accounts set up on all of those."

"Oh, I know. You think I showed up for work without doing my research?" She smiles up at me, and it takes all my willpower not to taste her blossom-pink lips. "But you will."

I will what—kiss her? Is she reading my mind? Fuck, my attraction is probably written all over my face.

"You're okay with me taking control of the front, right?"

The question makes my dick grow another size. The thought of Honey on her knees, taking control of *my* front... "Sure," I say, forcing myself to step away.

"I realize you only hired me to work the counter, but I'm positive we can grow the walk-in business with a stronger social media presence. Or maybe that's not what you want, since you're already getting more customers than you have products for. And I don't mean that negatively. There's nothing wrong with staying small." Her gaze flicks up and down my body. "Not that you'd know anything about that. How tall *are* you?"

"Six-four."

"A full foot taller than me."

Not touching that one, even though I've already thought about how she'd fit against me, tucked nice and close under my chin. "Growing the business is good," I say, directing the conversation to appropriate ground.

"Then we need to be on more platforms," she says, tapping away, oblivious to the hard-as-fuck state her boss is in. "Be active daily and with recognizable branding."

She's right. One hundred percent.

"I understand the power of social media, it's just not my thing. I'd rather be in the back." And there goes appropriate, because now I'm thinking about bending her over and spreading her round ass. I shove my hands in my pockets in an attempt to hide the biggest hard-on I've ever had during a workday. "I had a marketing team back in Los Angeles."

She gives me her attention long enough to issue a single word. "Fancy."

A grunt pushes past my lips. "Necessary. But that was a totally different marketplace. It didn't cross my mind to hire someone here."

"Don't underestimate Candy Cane Key. You're already tapping into the Christmas theme with the business name. And word around town says your product is ten out of ten. If you want The Ginger Bread Man to explode, we can make that happen."

We. She keeps using that word. Because she's a team player, the best kind of employee. No other reason.

"If you want to take on the social media stuff in addition to working the counter, the job's yours. On that subject, we ought to discuss your pay expectations, now that you're officially my employee." Saying the last part out loud has no effect on my cock. It doesn't care that she's completely off-limits.

Pausing her busy-bee activities, she turns to fully face me. "I don't have a number in mind. I'm not motivated by money. I trust you to pay me whatever you think is fair, and that you can afford, because I think I'm really going to like it here and don't want you to go bankrupt from overpaying me. If you want to wait until you've watched me work for a couple of weeks to decide my salary, that's fine by me."

Who makes an offer like that? Nobody, that's who.

"Why'd you leave your last job? Or any of the ones before it?" I ask, giving in to temptation and moving closer. "It won't affect my decision. Just curious. You're obviously smart and a go-getter, and well-liked by everyone in town. If money's not your motivator, what do I have to do to be the last on your list, instead of an entry on your resume?"

The prettiest twinkle lights her eyes. "Not even one day on the books, and it sounds like you've already decided you want to keep me."

Definitely not touching that one. "Sounds like *you're* avoiding my question."

"Maybe I am," she says, her expression taking on a serious quality I haven't seen yet. "Not because I'm trying to deceive you. I guess I'm just embarrassed to answer honestly, which is the only way I ever answer anything."

"Then we have that in common." Since the shop is empty except for us, I unbutton my jacket and lean on the backside of the counter, hoping the casualness will put her at ease. "Everyone has stuff in their past that's embarrassing. I sure as hell do."

"That's hard to imagine," she says, gravitating closer. "You seem so established and self-assured."

"I'm both those things. Still have embarrassing shit behind me."

"Like what?" When I fail to answer, she shifts closer, nudging my arm with hers. "You might as well tell me now. You've already as much as admitted you want me to stay here forever, which means we're going to do lots of talking. And I'm very persistent, if you hadn't noticed."

"I noticed," I say, grunting a laugh. "I'll tell you, but then it's your turn. And for the record, I'm a firm believer in 'ladies first,' so plan for that from now on. No exceptions."

Rosy pink floods her cheeks and her lips part. She pulls the bottom one beneath the top, then lets it slide back into place, all shiny and plump. She's not thinking about future conversations. She's thinking about sex. About me making sure she *comes* first.

The fact that I'm considering throwing her over my shoulder, taking her upstairs, and making it happen should be at the top of my embarrassment list. I'm her boss, for fuck's sake. Maybe throwing my pride under the bus will deflate my goddamn cock. "A year ago, I caught my wife cheating on me with my business partner. Doesn't get much more embarrassing than that."

Honey's face scrunches with a mixture of pity and repulsion. "Yikes. I'm so sorry."

"Wasn't the best day of my life, but I've moved on. Your turn."

"Yours doesn't really count, Cal."

It's the first time she's used my name, and hearing it in her soft, feminine voice is going to be on a continuously replaying loop until I fall asleep with my cock in hand.

"It wasn't within your control," she says. "You shouldn't be embarrassed about someone else's actions."

I'm not telling Honey what Winona said to me the day I

caught her riding Shaun's dick. That my focus on the business and the long hours I put in resulted in me neglecting her wifely needs. When your beautiful wife looks you dead in the eye—while she's still impaled on another man's dick—and says you didn't give her enough sex, that's pretty fucking embarrassing.

"Matter of opinion," I say, clamping the lid on my personal shit. "Your turn."

"I—" One word is all she has the chance to say before the bell over the door chimes as it opens. She gives me a cute little shrug and smile before turning toward the incoming customers. "Perfect timing!"

"For them, or for you?" I ask loud enough for Honey's ears only.

She gives me the briefest peripheral glance. Just enough to acknowledge me—as she ignores me. "Cal just brought out a freshly baked batch of cinnamon buns. How many can I box up for each of you?"

My little elf may have been saved by the bell, but my memory is as long as my ability to hold a grudge. In this moment, though, I don't give a fuck about any of the shit that's inspired my perpetually grumpy mood for the past year. The new sunshine in my life is bright enough to chase away any clouds. Now I just have to figure out how to keep her in my orbit.

four

. . .

honey

EVEN WITH THE extra batch of cinnamon buns Cal baked, we still sold out of everything by mid-afternoon. I tried to convince him to bake more and stay open until six, like the business hours state, but he wasn't having it. Said he'd rather sell out early than have leftover product because he refuses to sell "day olds" or throw food away.

Apparently, he's used to disappointing customers. His LA bakery always sold out. It was a much larger operation in terms of facilities and employees. They intentionally made less than they could sell to drive up the demand—and the prices. That's not his business model for The Ginger Bread Man. He assured me of that when I wrinkled my nose at his admission.

The problem—if selling everything you produce can be called a problem—here is understaffing. Insufficient market analysis and preparation before he opened the business. He admitted that, too.

Though he didn't say it in exactly this way, Cal moved

to Candy Cane Key purely to escape his shitty situation in California. He just wanted a quiet, fresh start. He didn't expect business to boom.

I'm not even sure he wants it to boom. But I do. I want The Ginger Bread Man to be *the* place for must-have baked goods, for tourists and locals alike. Achieving that goal will benefit Cal, but he's not why I have it. It's for me. A challenge to occupy my inescapably squirrel-like nature, hopefully for a very long time. I know it's only been one day, but I can picture myself staying here. At the bakery. With Cal. I don't want to *want to* leave.

But it could happen, because I'm me. I go whole hog on every new thing. Then, one day, bam! I'm checked out and there's no getting the enthusiasm back. The worst part is that I never see it coming. I just wake up one morning missing the passion and focus of the day before. It's a shitty way to feel and an even shittier way to behave because I let people down. Every time.

So, when Cal asked why I left my other jobs, and how he can avoid being another entry on my resume, I really didn't want to give an honest answer. I don't want to lose the job or his trust. And...I don't want to lose him.

Yes, it has only been *one day*. Not long enough to really know him or develop true feelings. But there's something there. Between us. Chemistry that makes the air crackle and my body tingle. A connection that could set fire to the mattress—or anywhere else he wants to fuck me. I know he wants to. It was in his eyes every time he looked at me, even though I could tell he was fighting it.

After grabbing a coffee from Tranquili-tea on my way home, even my phone's vibrations on the desktop startles me. I should know better than to caffeinate late in the day. Honestly, I should probably avoid it altogether. There's no hard, scientific data about the effects of caffeine on brains like mine, but it's not like I need the extra stimulation in the cranial region.

"Hey, Mom," I answer, after her name lights the screen a second time. Of course, she's returning my text with a call. This is our dance.

"Since your message said you're 'home from work,' I guess that means you're officially hired at the bakery. Good for you, darling. I knew he wouldn't be able to resist your charm."

I bite my lip as my mind returns to the moments we were in each other's personal space. Yes, we were working, but there was something more simmering just beneath the surface. We're obviously very different, but we click. It's comfortable and magnetic at the same time. A connection. Definitely an attraction.

Mom and I are close, but it's too soon to tell her any of those things. Plus, there's really nothing to tell—yet.

"He likes me, I'm sure of that. But I also think he was relieved I pushed my way into the position, saving him the trouble of interviewing people."

"Give yourself more credit. No employer, and certainly no man, ever views your presence in their life as a relief. You're a rare gift."

"A gift that rarely sticks around long," I say with a sigh. "I really like the bakery, the job, and Cal. I want this one to last. Do you think I should give medication another try?"

Silence goes on long enough that I might think she ended the call, except I know she's there, carefully assembling her words, rather than the usual blurting out of whatever comes to her mind. We have that in common, along with the squirrel thing.

"I think you should do whatever makes you happiest. In

the past, that hasn't been taking medication, but if you're inclined to go that route again, maybe you should..."

"Should *what*, Mom?" I ask after seconds tick by without the rest of her sentence materializing.

Her huff fills my ear. "I hate to even say any of this. You know how I feel, darling. Just because your brain operates differently from someone else's doesn't mean it needs fixing. But if you decide to try medication again, you might want to let your boss know. He hired the Honey Golding you are today, and she's not who'll be working for him once the medication takes effect."

She's right—I won't be the same. At least, I haven't been the other times I took medication. Even if I ask the doctor for a different drug or dosage, there's no guarantee it'll be any better. Hell, it might even be worse.

"Thanks," I say, trying to keep the defeat out of my voice. And failing miserably.

"I love you, Honora. I support whatever decisions you make because you're smart, thoughtful, and deeply kind. Just remember to treat yourself with the same generosity you give to others." And then she's gone, because like me, she's not the type to stick around.

God, I hope I can stick around this time.

cal

After a lifetime in Cali, I knew I had to find someplace warm year-round and right on the water. When the realtor I hired sent me the listing for Candy Cane Key, I pulled the trigger immediately. No flying out for a viewing, no third-party inspection, no haggling on the price. Just signed on the dotted line and wired the money. Boom, done. I didn't care if the new bakery made a lot of money. If I sold enough to pay the basic bills, it'd be enough. Glad I trusted my gut on this one.

This small section of beach is nearly empty as I cross to the water's gentle edge. It's just me and a couple lying on a blanket, tangled up in each other almost to the point of public indecency. Lucky bastards. I hadn't given my self-imposed post-divorce abstinence a thought until yesterday. Since last night's jerk-off session had no effect on how hard Honey made me today—all fucking day—clearly, I need more than my hand.

I could get one of the apps geared to hooking up. Find someone on the mainland who only wants a hot, sweaty night. But that's never been my thing, even before I married Winona.

Dating in a small town, especially one that's semi-isolated, when I know I can't offer the kind of commitment most women want... also a pass. I'd rather women think I'm a grumpy loner than end up on the local shitlist because I'm an emotionally unavailable, anti-commitment asshole.

Doesn't matter anyway. There's only one woman I'd want to date, and she's out of bounds.

Guess it's just me and my hand—and it's getting a workout as soon as I'm home. Close proximity to Honey today made me hard for more hours than I wasn't. Now, the couple on the blanket behind me sound like they're doing a hell of a lot more than making out, and I'd be a liar if I said the live-porno soundtrack wasn't affecting me. Since I've reached the end of traversable beach, I either have to turn around and walk toward them, or stand here and stare at the ocean until they finish. Not the greatest choices.

I tip my head to the side and rub the knot in the back of my neck. "Fuck."

"Not yet, but I think they're getting to it."

I turn toward the voice I've been thinking about since she said goodbye and essentially skipped down the sidewalk—but see nothing.

"Over here." She pokes one arm out of a nearby mangrove, motioning me toward her as she whispers, "Come hide with me."

This option isn't great either. I'd seem like the biggest asshole in the world if I didn't take it though. Shit.

Walking toward the mangrove doesn't require I look over at the couple on the blanket. Curiosity gets the best of me and I turn my head. Really bad idea. Even with the sun dipping below the horizon, there's no mistaking what's happening over there. The woman is on her back, her dress up around her waist. The guy is on his side, leaning over her, his hand between her legs with his arm moving in a fast, short, sawing motion. I'm looking at strangers but my mind is full of me and Honey.

I'm now hard as a rock and I'm about to climb into a grove of close trees with the woman I want to fuck until she's moaning loud enough for everyone on this island to hear. So much for unwinding at the beach.

"What are you doing in here?" I ask as I join her in the darkness of the mangrove. The reduced air flow makes it even thicker and hotter, and the closeness of her body just cranks both dials higher.

"This is my hideaway place," she says quietly as I settle beside her on a curved section of tree root. "I like to sit in here and watch the sunset. Lots of people come to the beach, but nobody knows I'm here. I get to just...be. Try to get out of my own head for a while."

Something else we have in common. "I walk down almost every night for the golden hour. Have you seen me before?"

"Yes." One word, that's it. And she's fidgeting, too.

"What—have you seen me picking my nose or scratching my ass?" I don't think I've done either, but I'm human, and humans do a lot of involuntary shit.

She giggles softly, the air that pushes out from her lips teasing my nose because she's that fucking close. "No, Cal, I haven't witnessed you doing anything embarrassing."

"Good. You had me worried with that one-word answer."

"Oh. That was me trying not to make things awkward. Like you might be wondering why I didn't mention that I've seen you before. But how could I have?" More fidgeting, this round causing her tits to brush my chest. "What was I supposed to say? Oh, by the way, we've never met, but I've been unintentionally stalking you at the beach for several weeks?"

My grunted laugh is a bit too loud, and Honey leans in, placing her fingers over my lips. Mutual moaning from the couple on the blanket carries in the still air, and it takes everything in me not to slide my tongue between the V of Honey's fingers, up one side, then down the other.

"Oh my God, are they—"

I turn my head in the same direction as hers. "Fucking?" I swallow hard as the guy settles between the woman's legs, his thrusting hips moving her up the blanket. "Yeah, they are."

"But his pants are still on," she whispers. The hand that was on my face is now pressed flat to my chest and her other one lands high on my quadriceps as she angles to get a better view. "I guess that's so they're less likely to get arrested."

"Likely." Filling my lungs with her scent is a bad idea. I can't help it. She's so close, and she smells so fucking good.

"I've never seen actual people having sex before, have you?" She makes a little noise in her throat. "Sorry, that was a super personal question."

"It's fine," I grind out, as her fingers curl around my leg, so close to my ragingly hard cock, it'll be a miracle if she doesn't feel it throbbing against the side of her hand.

Less than twenty feet away, the writhing, grunting, and moaning picks up speed. Honey's attention is glued to the action, but her body is far from still. She's fidgeting in place and I can tell from the changes in pressure where her leg touches mine she's squeezing her thighs together. Even if I couldn't feel her doing it, I can smell that she is. A man doesn't forget the scent of pussy, no matter how long he's gone without.

Her hand moves higher up my leg and I swallow a groan when her fingers curl over the ridge of my hard-on. She probably isn't aware she's doing it. It's her body's involuntary response to the live porno we're watching.

I turn my head just enough to watch her from the corner of my eye. It's too dark to see if her cheeks are flushed pink, but her eyes are open wide and her lips are parted. She's turned-on. So much so, I could kiss her and I bet she'd let me. Kissing would lead to touching, and she might let me do that, too. But it'd be permission based on a moment of excitement and wildly heightened arousal. Not because she wants me.

Her breath hitches as the couple on the blanket come together in a series of jerky movements and passionate moaning. As soon as the show's over, Honey's gaze drops to my chest and lap. "I'm so sorry!" She jerks her hands away, then uses them to hide behind. "I was totally groping you."

"Not totally."

She groans against the screen of her palms. "Are you going to fire me? That's sexual harassment, right? Oh my God, I just sexually harassed my boss in a mangrove."

Part of me wants to let this play out because she's fucking adorable. But the part that remembers her hesitation to tell me something embarrassing earlier wins out. "I'm not firing you or letting you quit," I say, gently peeling her fingers from her face. "And you didn't sexually harass me."

"But I groped you. My hand was on your—"

I wait, hoping she'll say the word. Probably good that she doesn't. It'd only make me harder, if that's possible. I nod toward the beach, where the couple is shaking out their blanket. "Looks like the show's over."

"And it had a happy ending," she says, her voice returning to its usual vibrant tone.

"Two of them, I'd say."

"True." She giggles. "Unless she was faking."

"A woman should never have to fake an orgasm."

"Oh, come on. Men don't really care."

Is she serious? "Any man who doesn't make sure your orgasms are real doesn't deserve the privilege of being between your legs." The words come out rougher than I intended. Hell, they shouldn't have come out of my mouth at all. I'm her employer, nothing more. "I shouldn't have said that, it was inappropriate."

"But true."

"Definitely true."

Silence wraps around us as we sit in the darkness of the mangrove. The sun is long gone, replaced by the moon, and slices of its light bend around the trees, painting her face with dappled silver.

"Thanks for sharing your hideaway," I say, instead of telling her she's beautiful. Enough bad-boss behavior for one night.

"You're welcome to use it anytime. Though I can't guarantee there'll be X-rated entertainment again. I didn't recognize the couple, so they're probably tourists enjoying a romantic holiday, or checking something off their sexual bucket list."

There's no safe response to that. But you can bet I'll be thinking about Honey's sexual bucket list when I'm lying in bed tonight. "Time for this old guy to head out," I say, hooking a thumb toward the beach. "Three a.m. alarm shows no mercy."

"I'm going home, too. But not to sleep. It's an early night if I'm asleep by midnight."

"I can't remember the last time I saw midnight."

"My brain refuses to shut down any earlier, so I just keep going until exhaustion takes over." Her soft, bubbly laugh runs through me like an adrenaline rush. "I bet that couple from the blanket won't have any trouble falling asleep."

"It is the best natural sleep aid." Any more talking about sex and I might do something there's no going back from, so I extricate myself from the grove, offering my hand to Honey when she follows.

"Thank you," she says, sliding her palm over mine.

I don't let go once her feet are on solid ground. I should. Even after our very personal moment, I'm still her boss. But I don't feel like her boss right now. And the way she's looking at me, she's not thinking about being my employee. I reposition our hands so our fingers weave together. "I can walk you home if you want, since it's dark."

"Candy Cane Key is pretty safe, but I'd still like it if you walked me. Just because."

"Good enough reason for me." We're still holding hands as we reach the street. That's when it hits me that I've assumed a hell of a lot. "If this is a problem..." I say, raising our joined hands.

"Not for me." She smiles up at me while we walk past shops, some of which are still open. "Is it a problem for you?"

Only because it makes me want more. "Not at all."

"So, there's nobody new on the horizon?" The streetlights make it easy to see the blush on her cheeks. "A little less personal than the question I asked earlier, but if it's too much, you don't have to answer. I can't promise I'll stop asking them, though. My brain works faster than my filter."

"I haven't been with anyone since my marriage ended. And don't hold back or change on my account. I like you the way you are."

She breaks our eye contact to stare straight ahead. Silently, too.

Is she weirding out because I said I like her? It's an innocent enough statement on its own. Not to mention pretty tame after everything that happened in that mangrove, and her open willingness to hold my hand in public.

"Remember earlier, in the bakery, when you asked about my previous jobs?"

"Yeah. And you don't have to answer. I didn't ask when you brought in your resume and it doesn't matter now."

"But it does," she says, looking up at me again. "I've

never been fired from a job. I quit them all. Full disclosure —except for the most recent one, I quit every one of those jobs because I lost my passion for them. I'm... well, some people call it flighty, but I hate that word because it makes it sound like I don't care that I flake on things. And I do care. A lot. If I could change just one thing about myself, it would be this. My inability to stick to something."

Her admission makes it feel as if I swallowed a rock. I met her yesterday. She's an employee, and I've had dozens over the years. They come and go. It's part of being in business. I shouldn't care if she's a long-hauler or a job jumper. I shouldn't care if she gets bored and leaves her position at the bakery.

"And remember in the mangrove, when I told you I go there to try to get out of my own head sometimes?" she asks, slipping her hand out of mine.

I know where this is going. Shit. "I remember."

"Well, the thing on my mind tonight was whether to go back on medication that helps regulate the squirrels in my brain. Because I don't want the bakery to be just another line on my resume. I want it to stick."

All right. Good news for a change. I'll take it. "Have people made you feel like it's weak or shameful to take medication? Because it's not. And I'll need their names, so I can knock on some doors, maybe knock out some teeth."

Her laugh is short and soft, but it lightens the cloudiness in her expression. "Unnecessary, but thank you. My dilemma is strictly internal. And I'd like to keep all my teeth, please," she says, leaning sideways to bump arms.

"Definitely." This isn't the time to tell her she has a beautiful smile. She's worried about who she is on the inside, so that's where I'll focus my attention. Easy to do, since I already like that part of her as much as the outside.

"If medication makes a positive impact on your life and helps you achieve things you want, it seems like an obvious solution, not a dilemma."

"You would think so, right? But the truth is, I like the way I feel, squirrels and all. And when I take meds, I feel... less like me. It's not that way for everyone, but it is for me. So, it's a tradeoff. One I haven't been willing to make, long-term."

"I understand." And the damn rock in my gut just doubled in size. She's letting me know she won't be sticking around. I should be grateful for the heads-up. Knowing the day will come when she walks out the door for the last time should make it easier to distance myself from her now. Only, it fucking doesn't.

She meets my gaze as we turn a corner toward a residential neighborhood. "I'm not sure what I'm going to do about meds, but I know I want to stay with The Ginger Bread Man for as long as possible."

Much as I'd like her to be referring to me, I'll take what I can get. "Glad to hear it."

The rest of the walk is silent, ending a few minutes later, when she stops in front of an older, two-story house with a bright-yellow front door.

"This is me," she says. "Only the front lower part of it. I rent. Not because of the squirrel thing. I've lived here six years, since I moved out of my parents' house, and I've never had the urge to go anywhere else." The information feels like subtext. Like she's trying to tell me something without saying it outright.

Or maybe I'm just looking for hope when I shouldn't be.

"I'd invite you in but..."

"But I'm your boss. And a lot older than you."

The front light is on, giving me a clear view of her pretty eyes blinking up at me as she shakes her head.

"But you said you want to go home and sleep," she says as a big smile curves her tempting lips.

Shit. I'm making an ass of myself. "Right. Of course. I'm going to go do that." I turn and take a couple of steps, then stop.

She's still standing on the stoop when I look back. Still smiling. Still looking like everything I didn't know I wanted, all wrapped up in one adorable, sexy, off-limits package.

"No matter what you decide about medication, you have my support. Do whatever makes *you* happy, and don't worry about anything else."

"Thanks, Cal."

Crazy how hearing her say my name makes me instantly hard. "See you tomorrow, little elf."

"I'll be there will bells on," she says, giving me a wave.

It wouldn't surprise me if she literally shows up with bells on. And I can't wait to find out.

five

. . .

Friday, May 19th

honey

"WHAT'S THIS?" I ask when Cal hands me an envelope on my way out the door Friday afternoon.

"First week's paycheck."

"But I've only been here four days." Four amazing days. "And the week's not over yet."

"I don't expect you to work Saturdays."

"You work Saturdays. Why wouldn't I?"

Cal has his moments of loosening up, but mostly he wears a semi-scowl. That's how he looks right now. Borderline grumpy with a side of uncomfortable. "You're young, single, and free-spirited. Your Saturdays should be filled with fun."

"Then I'll see you first thing tomorrow morning, because I have fun when I'm here."

"Real fun, Honey."

A little shiver ripples through me. My nipples are

probably poking up like two little points, too. Cal doesn't call me by name often, but I sure do like it when he does. "I'd love to hear your definition of 'real fun.' Care to enlighten me?"

He grunts at my tilted head and exaggeratedly cocked eyebrow. "I think the statute of limitations on that kind of conversation ended when we climbed out of the mangrove."

Finally, we're getting somewhere. I've spent the last three days trying to get back to the dynamic we shared that night. Cal hasn't been cold toward me, but aside from brief, subtle glimpses of Tuesday-night Cal, his "I'm your boss" wall has been firmly in place.

I guess I can't blame him. First, I unintentionally—okay, subconsciously—grabbed his cock. His totally hard, really huge cock. Then I kind of forced him into a conversation about orgasms. All of which miraculously ended with him walking me home while holding my hand —until I ruined it by burdening him with my life-with-ADHD story.

"I'll be watching the sunset from the beach tonight," I say, tapping the envelope on his broad chest. "If you want to join me."

Heat dances in his blue eyes, and I'm sure I see his nostrils flare. But he doesn't accept, decline, or acknowledge. He just says, "Have a good night."

"I will. I might even have a great one." I wink while walking backward toward the door. "See you later, Cal."

The sun has already begun its descent when I hear the crackle of footsteps on the stony portion of the beach behind me. My pulse picks up speed, as it has every other time I've heard footsteps. The beaches always get more traffic on weekends, and Friday night counts as the weekend for most people. Cal isn't most people. Saturday is one of his busiest days at the bakery. It wouldn't surprise me if he skipped the sunset tonight so he can get extra rest. Or he might skip it to avoid the employee who's hitting on him...

Groaning, I flop backward on the blanket. Only, it's not the clear twilight sky I see when I open my eyes. It's a six-foot-four hunky ginger. And he's smiling down at me.

"Did somebody steal your mangrove hideaway?"

"No," I say, scrambling to sit up as he drops onto the blanket. "I thought this would be more comfortable for you. It's tight in the hideaway, and you're pretty big."

"We fit together last time."

Is he disappointed we're not wedged in there again, or is that wishful thinking on my part?

"This is good, too." He arranges his arms behind him—which involves planting one palm directly behind my ass—then unfolds his legs that go on forever, crossing them at the ankles. The position is casual, probably for comfort. He might not even be aware that it shows off the bulging package nestled atop his thighs.

I force my eyes from his lap, heat flaring in my cheeks when I realize he's been looking at me the entire time I've been ogling him. Should I apologize? Probably. But it'd be a lie. I'm not sorry for visually appreciating him. I'm not sorry for wanting to grope him again—this time, intentionally.

"Pretty dress." His gaze travels over the yellow-and-white floral material that ends above my knees. "Decided to take my advice and have some real fun after watching the sunset?"

"Depends. Would you walk me home again?"

"Of course."

"And would you come inside if I invite you?" My heart's pounding so hard, he can probably see it thumping beneath my breasts.

"I'm your boss, Honey."

"That's not an answer," I say, despite barely being able to breathe.

"I'm almost forty."

"Still not an answer." I shimmy closer, so our hips and legs are touching. Then I really touch him. I put my hand on his leg, as high as I can without making contact with his growing bulge. "And I don't care about your boss status or your age."

"I do."

"Oh." The bottom drops out of my stomach. "I'm so sorry. I totally projected my feelings onto you."

"You didn't," he says, trapping my hand beneath his when I begin to move away. "I was attracted to you the second I saw you, and it gets stronger every minute I'm with you. With every smile, every laugh. With everything I learn about you."

"Then you'll walk me home and... come inside? Show me what a real man does with the privilege of being between a woman's legs?"

His deep groan sends a streak of need straight to my core, and I squeeze my thighs together to try to get some relief. The self-administered kind might be all I get tonight, because he still hasn't answered.

"I'm not trying to make things hard—"

"Too late," he says with a husky laugh. "Way too late."

"Well, I'm not apologizing for *that*, but I'll reword what I was going to say. I'm not trying to make things *difficult*. The way my brain works, with everything moving super-fast, I just... well, I jump in when I want something. Then I figure out how to make it work as I go. I wanted the job at the bakery, and you have to admit that I'm perfect for it."

"Better than perfect."

"I don't think that's a thing, but I'll take it anyway." I smile and lean against his strong, solid arm. "And I want you. I might not be perfect at everything right away, but you can teach me all the stuff I'm not experienced in."

"You think your new boss is the best person to help you with your sexual bucket list?"

"That's not what this is about," I say, moving away and taking my hand along with me. "I want to have sex with you, yes. Lots of it. All the ways I know about and the ones I don't. Not because I have a list. There's no list, and even if there were, it'd be new, since I met you."

The sun has almost disappeared from view, but enough light remains that I can see he's closed himself off again. The shutters are up and his smile is gone.

He shifts position, pulling his knees up and resting his folded arms across them. "I get it. And I'm flattered—beyond flattered, because you're a beautiful, sexy, smart young woman. But I don't do casual."

"I never said I wanted casual."

"No, but you said you don't stick around. Kind of the same thing. It's going to suck when you get bored with the bakery and follow your squirrels to the next thing. It's going to suck exponentially, because in four days, you've already made your mark, and I can see how much that's going to snowball because of your passion and innovative mind. The business won't be the same without you. But it's business, it'll adapt and carry on. Me, though?" He grunts and shakes his head. "If I got a taste of you, I'd be all in. Completely addicted. And when you move on from me because I work too much or my routine lifestyle is boring..."

My chest tightens, and I hug myself to try to soften the sting. "I shared that private information about myself with you so you'd understand me better. Not so you could use it to make predetermined judgements about me."

"I'm not judging you, Honey. I told you I support you and I do. I told you I like everything about you and that gets truer with every minute. But I can't go full speed down a road that I know is going to end in a drop-off."

"Then why'd you come here tonight?" I whisper.

"To share the sunset with you. Have a few minutes of being close to you, even though I know I shouldn't."

He said he *would* be all in with me if we started something, but I think maybe he already is. I feel like I am. No other man has ever embedded himself in my brain the way he has. And I'd tell him that if I thought he'd actually hear it.

"So, where do we go from here?" I ask, following his lead when he rises to his feet.

"I go home to sleep because the three o'clock alarm still rings on Saturdays. You should go somewhere fun where lucky men your age can appreciate how great you look in that dress."

"I wore the dress for one lucky man only, and since he's unavailable, I'm going home to make a new elf hat for the bakery. But that's not what I meant and you know it."

The corners of his mouth tick up. It's only a small smile, but better than the stone wall of seriousness. "Another new hat?"

I shrug. "I enjoy making them. Plus, people seem to like them."

"Of course they do. People like everything you do."

"I could make hats for you, too. Customers would eat that up. We could take a picture of you wearing one and—"

"No." Just like that, all traces of amusement are gone. "No hats for me, no pictures of me. You're the face of the bakery."

"But you're literally *the* ginger bread man, Cal. If you didn't want to be part of the marketing, you should have chosen another business name. It's a great gimmick and we should be utilizing it."

He doesn't argue, nor does he have to. The scowl on his face says it all. He knows I'm right, but he thinks he's immovable. On not wearing my fun hats and posting his picture. On his decision not to get involved with me. Cal is big and solid and steadfast. And he's my boss, but he's not the boss of me.

Squirrels might zigzag, but they're determined, and they always get the nut. This little squirrel is no different. I know what I want and I'm not giving up because the first try failed. I'm coming for you, Cal. No matter how many zigzags I have to make.

six

. . .

Monday, June 5th

cal

"HAPPY NATIONAL GINGERBREAD DAY!" Honey says as she bounces into the kitchen via the delivery door, half an hour before opening time. "Wash your hands so you can open your present!"

"Can't. Busy." Not even going to ask why she got me a present for a made-up holiday she found on the internet.

She'll tell me soon enough. That's how she is. *Who* she is. Full disclosure, all the time, about every subject.

It'd annoy the shit out of me if anyone else constantly bombarded me with *everything*. More than that, I would've fired their ass long ago.

It's different with Honey. I'm different. I bend for her without giving it a thought. I go along with shit I *never* thought I'd agree to.

Like painting the storefront to look like a gingerbread

house. I didn't even blink when she asked. Just gave her my credit card to pick up supplies, then spent an entire Sunday alongside her, with a paintbrush in my hand.

Then, she wanted to continue the Christmas theme *inside* the bakery.

I'm probably the least jolly person in Candy Cane Key, and I like my bakery clean and lean. Always have. Yet, I handed her my credit card again and gave her carte blanche. Now we have white and gold fairy lights, and a potted mini pine tree decorated with gingerbread ornaments and complimentary candy canes. She was right about customers loving the Christmas vibe. The unexpected part is that I don't hate it. I even smile when I turn on the damn fairy lights every morning.

On the subject of smiles, the massive one on her face right now should mean whatever's in the bag is a good present. In her beautiful, busy mind, it's probably the best present ever. But Honey's idea of *good* doesn't necessarily align with mine.

Case in point—she thinks it's a good idea to invite me to watch the sunset with her every damn night. She thinks spending personal time together is a good idea, even though I've told her repeatedly that it's not.

Yes, a lot of those repeated conversations took place while watching the sunset together. Because my willpower bends where Honey is concerned. One day, she'll get bored with watching sunsets with me and the invitations will stop coming. That'll be the day I stop bending for her because I'll break instead. If I'm lucky, it'll be a small break. One I can recover from. That's the only thing keeping me on the outside of her front door when I walk her home at night. If I get in any deeper with her, she'll break me apart when she walks away.

"If you don't wash up and open the present, I'll open it for you," she says, standing behind me and shaking the bag in front of my face. She's close enough that her tits are brushing the back of my right arm.

Now I'm frozen in this position until she moves. I can't have more than this with her, so I soak up every second of innocent contact.

The Christmas gift bag shakes in front of my face a second time. "I made it and you're going to love it."

My grunt earns me a tits-to-arm nudge. Not complaining about that. "What about Joe? Does he get a present for National Gingerbread Day? I think he lost count of how many gingerbread cookies he made about two hours ago."

"More like, I can't count that high," Joe says from across the kitchen.

Honey's laugh floats up, filling my head and further fueling my endless craving for her. "Of course, Joe gets a present." Rather than move toward Joe, she brings her left arm around to dangle a second bag in front of my face. "This one's his." Her current position has her body fully pressed against my back. Her softness makes me harder, her warmth spreading through me like a caress. Then it's gone, as she removes Joe's gift from my view and shifts to a position at my side. "But yours first."

When I don't stop working, she gives a cute little huff and moves away. I miss the contact immediately, but it's for the best. I need to distance myself from her. My daily goal, the one I never meet. The one I'm happy to fail at.

Paper rustles behind me, then I feel her hands at my lower back, untying my apron. "Move back a little," she says, reaching around to free up the apron where it's sandwiched between my hips and the table. She tugs at the sides of the fabric. "Come on, humor me."

As if I'd do anything else. I shift backward enough to create a gap for the fabric to slip through, not more. Not enough for her hands to get close to the hard bulge in my pants.

"God, you're tall," she says, stretching up to get the neck strap over my head.

I could crouch to make it easier, but then she wouldn't have to press her body against me. I'm a glutton for the soft, warm punishment. I glance down as she drops the new apron into place. "Where's the gift I'm going to love?" I grunt as she cinches the ties extra tight at my back.

"Don't be a grump. It's just for the holiday promo."

"Looks good, boss." Across the kitchen, Joe is barely holding it together.

No wonder. The apron Honey has me wearing is the shape and color of a gingerbread man, complete with three big white dots for his buttons and the customary rickrack trim. If anyone else suggested I wear this, it'd already be in a ball at my feet. I can't hate the atrocity tied around me because it came from her brain. From her hands.

"Joe's turn." She bounds across the kitchen and sets his gift bag on a nearby non-prep surface. "Here you go. Spoiler alert, it's the same thing." Then she's back in my space, leaning in close. Exactly where I want her. "I know you hate the apron. But I have another present for you. One I hope you actually love."

Looking into her eyes is guaranteed to make me bend. "Then I'm sure I will."

"Can I give it to you in private?" she whispers.

There's no office area on the main floor—I didn't want

to waste space on one since I could just as easily do my administrative shit upstairs. It's close enough to opening time that there's probably a small crowd outside the front windows. Especially with all the hype Honey has put into our National Gingerbread Day promo.

"Yeah." I nod and motion toward the door that leads to my apartment. I haven't taken her up there, and the intimacy of it builds with each stair she climbs.

"This is nice," she says when she reaches the top.

"Thanks." I step around her and watch her visually cataloguing the details of my open-concept main living area.

It's what she does. Her first day on the job, she told me that once she sees a thing, it's committed to memory. That's why she makes notes of new things, then throws them away just as quickly. She needs the visual snapshot.

I'm pretty sure she's a literal genius. Equally sure she'd deny it's even a possibility. One thing I know without a doubt is how much I like having her here. In my apartment. In the bakery. In my life.

She crosses to one of the large windows and leans over the back of the couch to look through the glass. "The view is incredible."

"Sure is." There's no controlling the huskiness in my voice, or my eyes from checking out every inch of her curvy little body.

"You can see our beach from here," she says, smiling at me over her shoulder.

Our beach.

That's how I think of it, too. It's how I'll always think of it, whether she stays in my life or leaves me behind.

"Cal?" Her soft voice snaps me out of my head, a place

I'm spending too much time. Time I could be sharing—really sharing—with her.

"I'm an idiot."

Her lips turn down. "You hate the apron that much? I just thought it'd be fun promo for the day. I know you haven't fallen in love with all things Christmas the way Candy Cane Key does, but—"

"I wasn't talking about the apron." I glance down at it, a semi-smile pushing its way onto my face as I think about what I must look like—a six-foot-four ginger-haired baker wearing a cutesy gingerbread-man dress-up apron. Do I look like an idiot? Maybe. Do I care? Not anymore. "The apron is great. Customers are going to love it."

"Do you mean that?"

"Yes," I say, crossing the room to stand in her space. "And I appreciate everything you do. You see things from a different angle, a place I'll never get to because it's outside my safety zone. Your perspective makes everything better."

"Business would still be booming if you didn't let me follow my whims."

"But it wouldn't be as fun. I'd still love the baking, but I wouldn't love all the other stuff. You make that happen."

"Thank you," she says, raising her hand toward my chest but stopping before she touches me.

I catch it before she pulls back, bring it to my mouth, and place a kiss on the inside of her wrist. Her eyes go wide and she blinks up at me, lips parted, and uncharacteristically speechless.

"If you're available later, I'd like to watch the sunset with you. And after the sunset, I want to take you home."

"You always walk me home," she says quietly.

Holding her gaze, I shake my head. "I'm not talking about walking you home. I said I want to *take* you home. No goodnight on the doorstep. A good night on the other side of the door."

Pink floods her suntanned cheeks. "I'd like that," she says, then giggles. "And here I was, worried that you wouldn't even *like* the apron, but it got me a date."

"It wasn't the apron." Not fighting it anymore, I let the smile spread across my face. "It's me, finally getting out of my own head enough to see that I'm an idiot keeping you at arm's length, when what I really want is to get as close to you as possible."

"Finally," she says, wrapping her arms around my neck and pressing her sweet, soft warmth against me. "I want that, too. Let's not wait for sunset."

A shiver runs through me when her fingers find the edge of my hair. "I can't kiss you now. I won't be able to stop, and we've got a holiday to celebrate."

"To profit from, you mean."

"To celebrate, Honey Golding style. Profit is just a perk." I slide my palms down her back, barely biting back a groan as I reach the swell of her ass. "I enjoy watching you do your thing. Seeing how your special magic makes a simple transaction into a great part of someone's day."

"You really think that?"

"I do. You're a gift, Honey. To everyone you meet. To me."

"Oh!" She's out of my arms as quickly as she entered, snapping her fingers, then pulling a small, tissue-wrapped item from her bag. "Your other gift. Good thing you reminded me after totally making me forget about it."

"Maybe I shouldn't have reminded you," I say, pointedly glancing at the apron I'm wearing.

She giggles at the teasing, the sound tapering off as she offers me the present. "This one isn't for National

Gingerbread Day. It's just something I made for my favorite ginger bread man."

Crafting things is one of Honey's nighttime activities. She says it keeps the squirrels busy until they finally knock off and let her get some sleep. Whatever the reason, it's another thing she's great at. She hasn't made a new elf hat for *every* day she's worked in the bakery, but damn close. They're all detailed and unique, like her. Aside from today's gingerbread-man aprons, she hasn't made anything for me. Probably because I shut her down when she mentioned making a hat.

No more shutting her down. About hats. About anything. She can dress me up or decorate me however she wants, as long as I get to keep seeing her smile.

I tear through the tissue and let it fall to the floor. The material I'm holding is folded into a small rectangle. The background is white, and it's covered in a ginger-colored, fine-lined pattern.

"Hey, this is all our stuff." I turn it around in my hands, then shake it out to get the full effect. "All the different breads and cookies we make here. And our logo. And my ugly mug," I say when I spot the tiny outline of what's obviously supposed to be me. "Is your beautiful face on here?"

She points to a small area of the pattern. "There."

"Should've been bigger." I look up from the fabric to meet her eyes. "This is amazing. You made this?"

"Only sort of. I drew the pattern and had it printed on a baker's headscarf like the ones you wear. Yes, I creeped your stuff, so I knew exactly which brand you like. But no pressure. I tried to keep it subdued, but I know it's not what you're used to, so you don't have to actually wear it."

"I'm wearing it," I say, pulling the plain white scarf off

my head and tossing it aside, then folding the new one and tying it in place. "I love it."

"I hoped you would. If not right away, then eventually."

I get the feeling she's not talking about the headscarf anymore. And tonight, when I take her home, I'll tell her everything else I love.

seven

. . .

honey

WHEN I REACH our little beach, there's only one person on it, and he's standing at the water's edge, looking out at the water. Cal turns at the sound of my feet on the stone. He's been smiling more since we started meeting to watch the sun go down, and the one on his face tonight is the best yet. He looks relaxed. Not only in his smile, but also in the set of his broad shoulders. Even in the hazy light of the golden hour, I can see he's at ease as he walks toward me. He looks…ready.

God, I hope he's ready. Holding back is unnatural for me, and pulling it off for hours on end, day after day, for weeks, has *not* been easy.

"Hello, handsome," I say as I meet him at the blanket he spread out—in the exact same spot the couple used to have sex a few weeks ago. "I approve of your blanket placement."

He gives one of those sexy grunted laughs that makes me need to squeeze my thighs together. "We're not giving anyone that kind of show," he says, pulling me into his arms as if it's the most natural thing in the world. And it should be. It is, as of now. "If exhibitionism is on the sexual bucket list you *don't have*, it'll have to wait. Tonight, I'm going to need you stripped bare and spread wide for my eyes only."

As good as it feels to be cradled beneath his chin, I pull back enough to look up and meet his gaze. "I hope you use more than your eyes."

"I'm going to give you everything I've got, sweetheart." His hands leave my back to cup my face. A tender touch, yet there's no mistaking the possession in it, or in his eyes. "Be sure, Honey. Be sure I'm who you want."

"You are," I whisper.

"Thank fuck."

My giggle becomes a sigh the instant his lips seal against mine. There's no more hesitation, just warm, delicious urgency. I open for him, moaning at the tease of his tongue along my lips, inside my mouth.

His hands travel over me, one threading through my hair, then using it to hold my head exactly where he wants it while kissing me senseless. He cups my breast with the other hand, kneading and swiping his thumb back and forth across my nipple, making it hard and sensitive, even through layers of material. Then both his hands are on my hips, on my ass, mapping my every curve and valley.

The hard ridge of his cock pushes against my waist—not where I need him. I tug at his waist, trying to guide him down onto the blanket with me.

He breaks the kiss, shaking his head with his lips against my forehead. "Not here. Once I get horizontal with you, there's no more polite. No holding back and sure as hell no going back."

"Then take me home right now, because I'm done holding back with you."

I don't know how many poles and trees there are between the beach and my apartment, but I can now say I've been kissed against all of them. Okay, not *all* of them. Cal's back was against some, too, because I did my fair share of shoving and demanding kisses. Thank God it's a Monday night without too many people milling around. I don't care who sees us. But Cal might. He's a business owner—and I'm his employee.

If there's gossip around town, we'll deal with it. I won't let anyone drag Cal's reputation through the mud. Whatever I have to do, I'll do it.

Right now, I just want to *do it*.

The apartment door slams shut from Cal's kick. Then it's his mouth on mine. His fingers threading through my hair. My hands squeezing his firm butt. Zippers down, buttons open, clothing off. His shirt, shorts, shoes, socks. My sandals, dress, bra.

"These." His fingers hook over the elastic strings at my hips. "Sexy as fuck, but they need to come off."

"So do these," I say, sliding my fingertips under the waistband of his packed-to-bursting boxer briefs.

He shucks his first, then crouches in front of me and slowly wiggles my panties down, groaning when my pussy is revealed. Reverently, he traces my seam with one finger before sliding it inside me. "I can't wait to find out what you taste like when you come."

Even as my body clenches around his finger and need tugs beneath my clit, my brain won't shut off. Won't stop reminding me of the times before. "I don't want to disappoint you, but I might not come like that. Or...at all. I never have," I say when he looks up, meeting my gaze. "I haven't been with many people—four, to be exact—but it didn't happen. As in, I couldn't come. And it wasn't for their lack of effort. It's me. I can't stop thinking, even when I shouldn't be thinking at all."

His smile gentles. "Okay."

"That's it? Just...okay? What does that mean?"

He places a single kiss over my clit, then rises to a stand and pulls me into his arms, with his fingers tipping my chin up. "It means I hear you and I understand. I know there are a lot of tabs open in that beautiful brain of yours, and it might take a while to get them all closed so you can get out of your head and let your body take the wheel. No pressure. No hurry. I'm here for it, sweetheart. I am here for everything you are—head to toe, inside and out. Okay?"

I nod because I don't trust my filter-free mouth not to ruin things some other way.

Cal dips his head down and kisses me again. Not a crushing, urgent kiss. This is a deep, intentional kiss that slowly turns up the heat building inside me. Cupping my face, he kisses as if it's the only thing he wants to do. As if he could do it forever, taking me from simmering to boiling and ready to climb him like a tree.

"Tabs are closing," I say against his mouth. "Bedroom, please."

Chuckling, he picks me up, wrapping my legs around his waist. "You feel that, sweetheart?" he asks, moving me up and down against his cock, where it's wedged between us. "One of the benefits of age is patience. We'll take as long as you need to get there, and I promise you I'll love every fucking minute of the journey. And along the way, you tell me what you like and don't like. Tell me anything and everything you want me to do. Whatever your sexy mind comes up with, I'm in."

"Even if it's kinky?" I ask as he lays me out on the bed and cages me beneath his big body.

"You label it however you want. If it makes you feel good, I'll do it. But—" He catches my chin in one hand and looks into my eyes. "Don't open tabs thinking about it."

"Yes, sir."

His gaze darkens and he smiles—no, no—he smolders. A smile so hot, it'd melt my panties, if I were wearing any. "Good girl." He steals any opportunity to answer with a hungry kiss. His tongue strokes into my mouth in a rhythm that matches his hips as he rocks his cock over my clit with the perfect amount of pressure and speed.

The familiar tingle of need grows stronger with each pass, and I wrap my legs around him to try to get more of... something. "I want to come, but I can't," I say when my frustrated groan breaks our kiss.

"We're not in a rush, sweetheart."

"Speak for yourself."

The rumble in his chest vibrates through me, then he presses his forehead to mine and begins rocking his cock against me again. "Remember the night we were in the mangrove, watching that couple on the blanket?"

"Yes," I whisper as the images flood my mind.

"You liked watching him rub her pussy, didn't you?"

"Yes."

"And when he started fucking her." Cal's mouth drops to mine, his words brushing over them like the tease of a kiss. "You were so turned-on, you would've let me do anything to make you come, wouldn't you?"

"Yes."

"I wanted to fuck you, Honey. Being close to you, the

scent of your pussy surrounding me, seeing you squeezing your legs together... I wanted to drag you onto my lap and pump into you, deep and hard, while I rubbed your clit."

I'm panting too hard to speak. I'm so close. So close.

And he knows it. "I wanted to feel your wet pussy squeezing me tight when I made you come all over my big, fat—"

"Yes!" I cry out as the light of a million stars flashes behind my eyelids. I grab him as if I'm hanging on for dear life, jerking and moaning beneath him as I come. "Oh my God, that was so good," I say as the world comes back into focus. "And so hot. Did you really want to do those things to me in the mangrove that night?"

He grunts against my breast as he kisses his way down my body. "And more."

"I would've let you."

"I know," he says, pushing my legs wider and settling between them with his mouth hovering above my pussy. "It wasn't our time."

"But now is."

His eyes glint with a smile as he takes a long, leisurely lick up my pussy. "Now is."

My eyes roll back in my head with his next pass, which ends at my clit. I'm still sensitive from the first orgasm, but the stuff he's doing with his tongue... his lips... Oh God, his fingers, too, sliding inside me, pumping me like his cock would. *Will.* Tonight. Soon.

I grab his head as the orgasm hits, holding him tight. I can't speak, can't tell him what I want or need, but I don't have to. He knows. He just knows and does it all. Sucking, flicking, sucking more until there's nothing left for my body to give.

His breath wafts over my sensitive skin, making me

shiver, then he crawls up over my wrung-out body. "Never going to get enough of that," he says, then kisses me, sliding his tongue along mine.

I reach between us and curl my fingers around his cock, guiding it to my entrance. My hips have a mind of their own, tilting upward the instant his tip notches into place. "I'm all in," I say when he breaks the kiss to look into my eyes. "And I want you all in."

Kissing me deep, he rocks forward and back, forward and back, until every long, thick inch of him is buried inside me. His hungry moan vibrates through me, and I hook my legs around his waist to take him deeper.

I'm so full, so happy. I don't need to come. This, just like this, is more than enough.

But not for him. "I can practically hear you thinking," he says, changing position to look into my eyes. "Time to get you out of that pretty head." He drops a kiss on my mouth, then he's gone. From my body. From the bed.

I cover my eyes as the light comes on, watching him through the screen of my fingers as he lights the candles on my dresser, then drags my freestanding floor mirror over beside the bed.

The overhead light goes out, and he lies beside me on the bed, propped on one arm. "Look in the mirror."

I turn my head toward it, gasping as his fingers slide between my legs.

"Watch us the way you watched them." His fingers quickly find the rhythm my body likes—hard pressure, medium speed, constantly circling. "You liked watching him play with her pussy. It made you wish someone was touching yours."

"Yes," I whisper, my hips rocking to meet his touch. "I wanted to be her. I wanted you to be him."

"You smelled so good that night, just like you do now. I wanted to touch you so bad. Rub your wet, warm pussy until you were panting and moaning, begging to come."

I whimper, pushing higher, desperate to get the little bit more I need. *"Harder."* My eyelids flutter closed as he gives me exactly what I need.

"Watch," he commands, and my eyes pop open, immediately drawn to the scene in the mirror. "Watch how sexy my good girl is when she comes."

I tumble over as he hits my perfect spot. The woman in the mirror bucks against his hand, her breasts jiggling and heaving as a full-body tremor rolls through her. Then she melts into the bed, her skin glistening. She's me. I did that. He made me do that.

"Now it's time for you to get into *my* head," he says, moving to sit on the edge of the bed and hauling me onto his lap, my back to his chest. Holding me with his big, strong hands, he guides me onto his cock. In front of the mirror, so I can see my body stretch around him as every thick inch disappears.

I moan at the rush of fullness as he thrusts up into me.

"Look at that beautiful pussy." He bands one arm around my middle, his fingertips curling into my side as he holds me tight so he can fuck me deep. His other hand finds my clit, rubbing it perfectly, mercilessly pushing me toward another orgasm.

"Cal..."

"They hear you moaning, baby. Hear all the sexy fucking sounds your pussy's making for my cock. They're watching *us* now, sweetheart. I'm fucking you in that mangrove and they're watching, waiting to see you come."

"Yes." My head falls back against his shoulder and I dig my nails into whatever part of him I can grab while I ride

his fingers and cock through a wild wave of orgasmic euphoria.

Cal's arm tightens around me. "*Fuuuck...*" he groans, his cock throbbing deep in my body. Aftershocks ripple in his muscles as he bows his head, pressing his lips to my neck.

"Will it be like that every time?"

He raises his head to meet my eyes in the mirror. "It'll be anything and everything you want. Less, more, anything."

"Would it be greedy of me to say I don't want less?"

"No," he says, his chuckling vibrating through me.

"Good, because I loved that."

Hugging me tight, he presses a kiss to my shoulder. "I loved it, too."

There's a shift between us as our gazes hold. We just did something big. Potentially, really big.

Cal is a confident man, but I can almost see the questions in his eyes. He won't ask them. He's afraid to hear the answers.

But I'm not afraid to give them. I reposition so I'm facing him and slide my arms around his neck. "I didn't just love the sex, or that you made me come four times. Four times!"

He winks. "Didn't want to set the bar too high the first time."

"You think there could be more?"

"I think the possibilities are endless," he says, sweeping the pad of his thumb across my lips. "And as long as you want to share them with me, I'm here."

And there's the question, even though it's not one.

"You're worried about my squirrels. I've lived with them long enough to know they're crafty and unpredictable, and I never want to be untruthful and make a promise I'm not sure I can keep, especially if it could end up hurting you."

He presses a kiss on the inside of my arm. "I know."

"I don't know if I'll stay at the bakery forever. I can only tell you it feels different from any other job. All the shiny new excitement is there, but I also feel...grounded. Kind of like a bunch of helium balloons tethered to a really solid weight. They get to flutter and bump and maybe even get tangled up, but they aren't going to fly away—and they don't want to." I touch my nose to his. "It's a metaphor."

"A good one. New tab you just opened, or a saved one?"

"Brand new. Just for you. A lot of things I'm feeling are like that." I'm a blurter by nature, but for this, I need a deep breath first. "I've never been in love before. I think I expected it to feel similar to any other 'shiny new thing,' but it's more like... without you, I'm a wild, floppy string, but with you, the ends connect, and I'm a whole circle, with all my *me*-ness free to float around happily, but in a safe place. You're my safe place, Cal. I never want to leave. That's all a very long way of saying I love you."

"It was the Honey way, which is my favorite way. For everything. You're everything I didn't know I needed, and all I'll ever want."

"Is that your long way of saying you love me, too?"

"You'd prefer the short version?"

"I think so, because I've never heard it before. Even girls with busy brains dream about the day their perfect man says the three special words. Though, maybe just this one time. You are pretty great at the extended version of things."

"Noted." His eyes twinkle as his gaze travels over my face and he gives me the best smile yet. "I love you," he says, tucking a strand of hair behind my ear. But instead of releasing it, he threads his fingers through the rest, cups my head and holds me in place for a long, soul-seeking kiss that leaves me breathless. "Good short version?"

"Definitely worthy of a replay. And if it leads to the extended version of other things, well..."

His chuckle vibrates through me, then he brushes the words, "I love you," over my lips, and shows me again how much he means every word.

Two-and-a-half years later
December 25th

cal

When you've spent eighty-five percent of your adult life waking up for a three-a.m. alarm, sleeping in the other fifteen percent of the time doesn't come naturally. I never minded. I rolled out of bed and got to work. When you're a business owner, there's always shit to do.

Since Honey moved in, lingering in bed on my days off is a lot more appealing than getting out. Most mornings, I just hold her while she sleeps. Bury my face in her hair, listen to her breathe. Sometimes I can't resist waking her up, but I haven't had a complaint about that yet.

This morning, I don't get to do either thing because her side of the bed is empty when I open my eyes. The sheets are pulled up to her pillow, and when I slide my palm over

Karla Doyle

the place where her body should be, I can tell she's been gone for a while. Not surprising. It's Christmas Day, and she's been even more excited than usual this year.

I get out of bed and creep to the living room as quietly as possible. It's still dark outside, and the Christmas tree lights cast a soft, colorful glow over the immediate area, including the couch where Honey's sitting. Her legs are tucked up beneath her and she's looking out the window that faces the beach. Our beach.

She's so fucking beautiful, I'm tempted to just stand here and look at her for as long as I can. My need to touch her wins out, as it always does. She turns at the sound of my footsteps, giving me a heart-stopping smile as she rises from the couch. She's dressed in an elf outfit—of course. A different one from last year. No surprise there. Last year's was damn near X-rated. This year's is less revealing, but still sexy as hell because it shows off all her soft curves I love worshipping.

"Merry Christmas, my little elf," I say, pulling her into my arms. "Too excited to sleep?" Even tucked in under my chin with her arms around my waist, she's practically bouncing.

She pulls her head back to look up at me. "More excited than any Christmas ever."

"Me too." It's true. The holidays were never important to me before Honey bounced into my life. A lot of things weren't.

Her joy and enthusiasm are irresistible and contagious. I didn't grumble even a little bit when she suggested we dress as Santa and Mrs. Clause for work yesterday so we could hand out free gingerbread men to all the kids who came into the bakery. The truth is, I loved pretending to be her husband.

I'd love the real thing even more. Never thought I'd want to get married again, but everything is different with Honey. I promised I'd never pressure or rush her, and I'll keep my word. I'm just grateful to wake up with her every day and fall asleep holding her every night. For as long as she wants me.

Stepping out of my embrace, she gives me a long, heated look, head to toe and back again, with a noticeable stop at cock level. "First, you need pants."

I take my hard-on in hand and give it one slow stroke. "Are you sure about that?"

"If you want to be gloriously naked in the pictures I show everyone..."

Now, I grumble. Pictures of me still aren't my favorite thing, but for her, I bend. I even smile when she points the camera at me.

"Here." She hands me a package from the pile beneath the tree. "Spoiler alert, it's pants."

Not just any pants, though. Red sleep pants that feel like butter when I pull them on. If I can't be naked with her, these are the next best thing. "They're great," I say, helping myself to a handful of her squeezable ass when she leans down to rummage through the pile of presents.

She giggles and jumps, smiling at me over her shoulder. "You need to be sitting down for this one."

"You gave me the pants. Shouldn't it be my turn to hand out a present?" Just because I'll resist the urge to get down on one knee and ask her to commit to forever doesn't mean I didn't buy her a ring. It's hidden in my desk because my excitable little elf has been shaking every gift under the tree for weeks. Still, I do what she wants and take a seat. Whatever makes her happy, I'm all in.

"The pants don't count." Still holding one arm behind

her back, she joins me on the couch, snuggling in at my side. "My holiday, my rules. Plus, you believe in 'ladies first,' remember?"

"Always." I lean over and kiss her until I feel her soft little hum against my lips. "If you'd stayed in bed, I would have put you first a couple of times already."

"We have all day for that," she says, giggling.

"We have forever for that."

"Do we?" Seriousness tints her tone. "Is forever what you really want?" She knows all the details of my previous marriage and the depth to which my ex-wife's betrayal broke me.

I've told Honey many times the past doesn't cross my mind anymore. That I'm happier than I've ever been, now, with her. Because of her. But if she needs to hear it again, I'll tell her. I'll tell her every damn day. "You're the one for me. The only woman I want to love, and I love you so fucking much. I'm not sure you'll ever really know. But I'll spend forever telling you and showing you, if you let me."

"I'll let you," she whispers, shifting off the couch to kneel in front of me. The hand behind her back comes forward, offering me a small, open jeweler's box with a flat, gold-band ring. "You're my home, Cal. I know in my heart, mind, body, and soul that I want to be with you for the rest of my life. No matter what direction the squirrels go, they always want to come home to you. If you ever want to get married again, I want it to be to me."

The smile on my face has to be as wide as the Key. No, that's not enough. As wide as the horizon we watch together every night. "Are you proposing to me, sunshine?"

"If you say yes, then yes. And if you're not ready to say yes, then I'm proposing *you propose* someday. If you ever want that."

"If I ever want that." I cup her beautiful face in both hands and pour exactly how much I want that into a long, deep kiss that leaves her breathless and me harder than steel. "You have no idea how much I want that."

"Wait, was that a yes?" she asks, holding up the box after I scoop her up and deposit her on the couch, then leave her sitting there, alone.

I'm back in front of her within seconds, down on one knee with my wrapped gift in one hand. "Call me old-fashioned, but I'd rather hear the 'yes' from your pretty lips."

Emerald eyes shining, she rips the paper from the little box, gasping when she lifts the black velvet lid. "You got me a ring? Oh, Cal... it's so beautiful."

I lift the orange sapphire and diamond ring from its box, then take her left hand in mine. "I was going to give you this as a Christmas gift because I need to see my ring on your finger, even if it's not the one I want to slide it on. But I'd like you to wear it on your left hand, as my wife. I love you, Honey, now and forever. Will you marry me?"

"Yes," she whispers, as tears roll down her cheeks. She squeals as soon as the ring is where it belongs, then launches her beautiful, perfect elf self at me, pushing me onto my back and blanketing me with her soft warmth. "When can we get married?"

"Whenever you want, sweetheart." I press my lips to her hair and wrap my arms around her. "As soon or as far down the road as you want."

"I'd like it to be soon," she says, pushing up from my chest, then crawling over to the Christmas tree to retrieve another present. "This one is for me, but also for you."

Sitting up, I reach into the gift bag and pull out a folded fabric item, then shake it open. It's a Honey-sized apron.

White, with a small gingerbread man in a pink-and-blue heart, in the area below the waist straps.

"Does this mean—" I swallow hard as I meet her shining eyes. "Are you pregnant?"

More tears fall as she nods. "Are you happy?"

"The happiest man in the world," I say, pulling her onto my lap and settling my palm over her abdomen. "How did this happen?"

Giggling, she makes the hand symbol for sex. "I guess it's time we talked about the birds and the bees." She laughs louder when I tickle her until she's wiggling on the hard ridge of my cock. "Okay, okay," she says, catching her breath when I relent. "I forgot to take my pill a few times—again—so I went to the doctor to ask about getting an IUD instead. He said we should do a pregnancy test first, and it was positive."

Not going to lie, part of me hoped she'd get pregnant those other times she forgot to take her pill regularly. But she was always relieved when her period came, so I never suggested we try. "Are you happy? Because I support you and love you, always, no matter what you decide."

"I'm so happy, Cal." Her arms wrap around me, and she nestles in, her head tucked against my chest. "I love you and our life so much. Everything is perfect."

"It sure is." And it's going to be that way for the rest of our lives.

*she said yes
and so did he*

Thank you for reading Gingerbread Man! I hope you
enjoyed Cal & Honey's sweet and steamy love story.
If you have a few minutes to leave a review at your favorite
book retailer, on BookBub, or Goodreads,
I would be so grateful. xo

Join my mailing list and stay up to date on new releases,
bonus content, sales, freebies, contests, and more.
www.karladoyle.com/newsletter

also by karla doyle

Wedded Miss

Dad Bod Wingman (Hope Harbor)

Heart Beats (Hope Harbor)

Last Call Casanova (Hope Harbor)

Fleshing It Out (Hope Harbor)

The Deal With Love (Hope Harbor)

Doggy Style (Hope Harbor)

Resorting to Love (linked to Hope Harbor)

White Lie Christmas (linked to Hope Harbor)

King of Her Dreams (Hope Harbor)

Heart of Texas (linked to Hope Harbor)

Her Pipe Dream (Hope Harbor)

Puck That

Unexpected Addition

Now You See Me (Screaming Woods)

Snake Believe (Screaming Woods)

Once Upon A Beast (Hemlock Woods)

The Beast Within (Hemlock Woods)

Mated to the Minotaur

Shifting Gears (Under the Hood)

Dating the Doubter

Gingerbread Man (Man of the Month: Candy Cane Key)

Just in Queso

Rumpled (Dark & Twisted Fairytales)

Room Twenty: Blind Submission (Club Sin)

12 Days (Hope Harbor)

Gift Wrapped

Cup of Sugar (Close to Home—Book 1)

Icing on the Cake (Close to Home—Book 2)

Sweet as Candy (Close to Home—Book 3)

Body of Work (Very Personal Training—Book 1)

Worth the Wait (Very Personal Training—Book 2)

Game Plan

More Than Words

Crossing the Line

Visit Karla's website for the most up-to-date list.

www.karladoyle.com

about the author

A small-town girl with some big-city experience, Karla resides in Southwestern Ontario with her husband and two young-adult children. She studied fashion design in college and spent 20+ years working in that industry before succumbing to the writing muse. When she's not writing the sexy stories that swirl around in her head, you can find her playing online Scrabble, or cuddled up with a book and her adorable pets.

Karla loves hearing from readers! Connect with her online, or send her an email: karla@karladoyle.com.

Join Karla's mailing list to stay up to date on all her news. www.karladoyle.com/newsletter

- facebook.com/KarlaDoyleAuthor
- tiktok.com/@karladoyleauthor
- bookbub.com/authors/karla-doyle
- goodreads.com/karlad
- youtube.com/@KarlaDoyleAuthor